A PEBBLE FROM ROME

A Pebble from Rome

R.T. PLUMB

DUCKWORTH

First published in 1977 by
Gerald Duckworth & Co. Ltd.
The Old Piano Factory
43 Gloucester Crescent, London NW1

© 1977 by R.T. Plumb

ISBN 0 7156 1244 1

Typeset by Computacomp (UK) Ltd., Fort William
and printed by
Unwin Brothers Limited, Old Woking

TO MY PARENTS
With love and gratitude

1

There were venetian blinds, I remember, in Uncle Conway's study, and when he was agitated he'd bang them shut and open. One Sunday morning I could hear them banging away, so I nudged curiously along the passage. It was hot, with church bells floating outside and, clackety clack, the blinds banging away. Aunt Wells had been trying to dust Uncle's desk. I think they'd quarrelled over a travel brochure for a German holiday. Uncle Conway was often in Germany, though chiefly on business. "Clean, efficient," he was roaring at Aunt. "That's Germany. Clean towns, clean streets, clean doorsteps." I remember Aunt's hands, folded behind her back; their quick clenching. "Clean fräulein, too?" Crash! went the blinds. "Damn it, yes," Uncle bellowed. "Clean fräulein, too!"

This was the year of boyhood I remember best of all. There were other similar years, in that decade of the nineteen thirties, but this was special. Not just the weather, though there wasn't a day that didn't fry us. A pity Germany wasn't fried too, I used to think. Germany meant Adolf Hitler and I didn't like that yelping voice. I liked Mussolini. He had staring eyes which I liked to think resembled mine.

But the thing about those days wasn't politics but our domestic situation.

We lived in two houses.

The first house was by the town square, tall and calm as the giant trees that gave it shade. The other house was just outside town, bleaker, a white, lonely building. I remember all the journeying to and fro, the endless packing, leaving and arriving—for a trip of four miles only! Just Aunt Wells and I, never Uncle. "Gordon," Aunt would say, patting my head in a way I hated (after all, I was about ten!), "Gordon, moving day." Moving day! Blimey, I'd think, proud of almost swearing. Blimey! Moving day again! With our luggage Aunt and I would wait on the pavement outside. "Why not wait inside?" Uncle would rave, mopping his brow. "The damn taxi man will carry your bags. Why stand outside and roast?" This also puzzled me, as did the fact that Uncle would have driven us in his car. I didn't, then, understand martyrdom. But Aunt did. "No, Conway, I shall carry my own bags. Oh no you don't! Not for anything would I have you carry them! You need your strength." Yet at the white house Aunt would let the taxi man lift her bags. "You didn't let him lift them before," I challenged once. "Get busy," Aunt would order. "I can see weeds over there. Roll up your sleeves!"

One thing about Aunt Wells. She never told me that eating crusts would make my hair curl, or muscles grow. "Weeds," she used to tell me, "make a man. Bending, pulling, bending, pulling, all those tendons going up and down. That's why God implanted weeds, to make men tall." At times Aunt would join me in the garden and pick a bunch of daffodils. I remember how she picked them, long hands trembling, blue-veined wrists reflecting cold cream and dew. "He'll remember when he gets these," she'd say. "Remember what, Aunt?" "That the day he proposed he gave me daffodils. Bought from a corner grocer's. Oh yes, in those days he walked to meet me. No car. Your Uncle was a comparatively poor man then, Gordon." "What is he now then, Aunt?" "Comfortably off, Gordon. Rich enough to buy me a thousand daffodils," and Aunt looked sad, though why I didn't know, nor did I wonder, then, how Uncle had become so rich. I'd watch while Sam, our gardener at both houses, rolled, rump protruding, daffodils in hand, up the lane for a bus to town. What Uncle did with the daffodils when they arrived I never knew. I never remember Aunt reading a note of thanks, and Sam, when questioned on his return—not with words but by a look—only growled and rubbed his bottom.

At times I did resent never staying behind with Uncle at town house. Blimey, I would think. Why can't I stay with Uncle? We could slurp soup together without fear of reprimand, and maybe he'd let me smoke. And I needn't pray at night, or if I did pray, I could pray on dirty knees.

After a while Aunt would repack our bags and send for a taxi. Once, since I was particularly enjoying myself at the white house, I asked why we were returning. "Sam says everywhere's dusty," Aunt replied, sadly. "Mrs Hampton doesn't dust at all without me around." "Is that because Uncle is always pinching her bottom, and upsetting her?" "Oh quiet, boy, and open the door. I want the taxi driver to fetch our bags." At the town house, as usual, Aunt carried the bags all the way from under the giant trees right up to the tawny old porch. She must have hoped that Uncle would be watching. Did he watch us? Maybe through the dusty study blinds? Did he, angry, irritated, flick them open, shut, as we tiredly advanced? Every time we returned Aunt had the same tale. "Dust! Dust everywhere! What price your Germany now! They wouldn't have you!" Uncle would push out his short, thick arm in salute. "Rum tum, rum tum, rumpety tum, tumpety rum!" Boy-like, I'd copy. "Rum tum, rum tum, rumpety tum, tumpety rum!" Uncle would laugh, biff my shoulders. "Damn it, we'll make a man of you yet! A musical man. A marching musical man!"

"Uncle Conway, next time Aunt goes to the white house may I stay with you?"

"God, boy, impossible! I swear all day, most horribly!"

I remember looking at Uncle's fancy waistcoat, the light blue checks frail as Aunt's veins. "You—you don't really, do you, Uncle?" But Uncle had already forgotten what he'd said. Ebulliently, pushing out that podgy arm, "Rum tum, rum tum, rumpety tum, tumpety rum!"

Nor was Sam much help. "A-swearing," Sam would growl. "I'll give him a-swearing, the Mister Big!" "But does he, Sam? Does he swear all day?" "That broom tree's a-dying," Sam would complain, wiping his long earthy nose, and hobbling suddenly away. "I told your Aunt, but she won't open her peepers to it. That broom tree's a-dying."

I suppose town house was dying too, in a way. It was so old and replete. As Uncle Conway himself used to say, "Fuller in the belly than white house." Uncle made it fuller by collecting antiques. One oddment was a sword reputedly worn by Cromwell. Aunt would cringe from the mellow relic, in her eye a slow, whimpering tear. "I think Cromwell was a vile, unjust man." Yet, as the white house testified, Aunt was the puritan. Austere rooms, plain tall furniture, no more than one picture to a wall, sideboards without wine or soda siphon, rugs instead of wall-to-wall carpeting, and the front door and windows, even in colder weather, often open. The town house, by contrast, a warren of stale air. Doors always shut, keys turning. "Privacy," Aunt would say, across the table to Uncle. "For a good cry, and heaven knows I've cause with you around, one must have privacy!" And, listening outside Uncle's locked study—for locked it often was—"Rum tum, rum tum," I'd hear him volley, "rumpety rumpety tum!"

One hot day I entered Uncle's study. The slats were open and Sunday dust lay undisturbed. Aunt was at church and Uncle out walking.

I opened a drawer in Uncle's desk. There was a picture inside of Aunt. It was an old sepia picture, and she looked even thinner. But there was, about her, a certain charm, a kind of quaint, respectable coquetry. She was, in fact, almost dimpling at both cheek and inner elbow.

I turned the picture over. On the back, I remember, were four fading words. "To Conway, with love."

It all seemed, even to me, very far away from the perplexing, hectic business of moving houses and carrying luggage, and picking daffodils for Sam to deliver, and pushing out one's hand in daft salutes, and locking oneself inside a room to cry.

2

I once asked Uncle Conway about death. "As we grow older, boy, we grow resigned to it."

Whether Uncle Conway was resigned to it, I didn't ask. He must have been about fifty, Aunt Wells a few years younger. His waistcoats, fancy or otherwise, were always tight, and, after exertion, he puffed in faint dry whistles. His rump, seen from behind, seemed tidily roly-poly, and, at times, that, too, often gave off faint dry whistles. Of my parents, who had died without growing resigned or even very old, I remembered little. "Demolished in a train disaster," Uncle had declared. "Ah well, wagon wheels, wagon wheels!" Aunt Wells trod more gently, creating, with myriad weavings of those long thin hands, autumnal images of drifting mist and lazy bonfire smoke. "They floated from us, Gordon, floated off to greater things." A breeze of leaves, a rustling into heaven—was that really how death appeared to dear Aunt Wells, or was she only being ever mindful of my green and tender youth? In so many ways a martyr, was her favourite vision that of Uncle watching impotently while, suitcases in hand, she floated resignedly from him and life to a white and chilly heaven? Sam, when I asked if *he* were resigned—and Sam was pretty old—spat, ferociously, at the rockery. "They says, Mr Gordon, to live forever hit a ladybird with spittle!" "Who's they, Sam?" Sam had looked up at the turquoise clouds. "See that big 'un. A real wet brute. I told your aunt that it was a-going to rain."

Summers, summers, summers, so many of them, with very little memory of wet brutes a-raining, though no doubt they did.

One summer in particular. Was I ten, eight or nine that summer, that year?

The special year.

The year of the pebble.

At school I swopped cigarette picture cards daily. A little girl with straw-type hair and blue eyes briefly took my heart. I found, under a tree, a small white tin button showing a black train and marked NUR. And a boy with sandy hair and big pearly grinning teeth was greatly envied because his father took him to the speedway.

"Uncle Conway," I said one evening. "Will you take me to the speedway tomorrow night?"

The dining room of the town house had french windows opening on to the lawn. The garden outside, despite Sam's sinewy energies, was crowded as the house. At dusk, although I only rarely stayed up long enough to see it happen, Aunt and Uncle changed, becoming, within themselves, as crowded and dusky as the garden. Aunt, rather desperately, wore thinner clothes and a bright arm bangle and talked too quickly. "The shops were full today. I felt quite nervous. Too many people around can make one nervous." "Wells, you surprise me.

11

How about that church of yours? Usually full, isn't it?" "Yes, but—" "Do you, then, sit and shiver in your pew? Praying for an empty church? Woman, wake up!" "I don't like crowds," Aunt said, stubbornly. Looking dark as the unilluminated flower beds beyond the french windows, "And I do, damn it. Love 'em, love 'em," Uncle choked.

Uncle Conway had spent the day, alone, in his study. Looking through the big worn keyhole I'd watched him examining his round rosy face in a mirror. Now, in the fullness of evening, came explanation. "Think I may grow a moustache. What do you think, my dear?"

"Why, Conway! Didn't you grow one once before, as a young man? I think I rather liked it."

"Fluff, a young man's moustache," growled Uncle. "Be different now, though, wouldn't it?"

Aunt Wells looked carefully at her wine. She rarely drank, and only grudgingly when she did.

"I think, Conway, that what they call an eyebrow-moustache might be acceptable."

"Not the kind of moustache I was contemplating," Uncle said.

Testily I bumped my glass of milk. "Uncle, will you take me to the speedway tomorrow night?"

Absently Uncle seized my milk and tucked it away behind the wine bottle. "Take a few days to grow properly," he said to Aunt. "Vexing sight, a growing moustache. Man really needs to be a hermit."

A breeze rustled the garden. Quickly Aunt Wells rose, clamped the windows and drew the curtains, as always, most exactly.

"We'll move, Gordon and I, to the white house. On Tuesday. For it's not going to be a moustache I'll approve of, is it? Oh I know you, Conway. You intend a moustache like Herr Hitler's!"

"Damn it, woman, a moustache isn't anything. A mere badge. No more."

"A badge, Conway, is never mere. It's everything."

"Wells, don't be so damn daft."

"White house, Tuesday," Aunt repeated. She was trembling, twisting the bangle up and down her thin freckled arm.

"All right, all right, who cares?" Uncle thundered. "Clear off when you like!"

"The speedway, Uncle," I said. "The speedway."

Now that an unpleasant bit of business had been successfully despatched Uncle looked suddenly jollier, though he did refrain from giving his usual exuberant salute. "What was that, boy, what was that?"

"The speedway, Uncle, the speedway!"

"Damn it, boy, why not?" Uncle Conway said. "Oil, petrol, machines roaring, martial music, what pursuit could be more manly?"

"I want my milk back," I said. But it was Aunt Wells who gave it me.

"Milk and wine bottles should never touch," she said, "or be together."

"Tally ho, the speedway!" Uncle cried, defiantly. "Tally ho, the speedway!"

Beautifully scented in a dress of blue, in through the door of town house she came, a floating young lady with the barest, most wonderful white arms I'd ever seen. Although, mumbling, I'd said that both Aunt Wells and Uncle Conway were not at home.

She touched me, on a hank of uncombed hair, with a cool light painted finger.

"You'll be Gordon, Conway's nephew. Right, pet?"

"Aunt's gone to the matinee," I said, quickly. "And Uncle to buy cigarettes. Who—who are you?"

"Betty, that's who I am, pet. Betty Hallet."

Mrs Hampton, the cleaning lady, only came mornings. It was Sam's half-day, and suddenly I felt insecure.

"And you, Gordon. Not at school?"

"I've had a tooth out," I said, grimacing. "One near the back, on this side. I'm ill."

Betty smiled, exhibiting teeth as white, if less soft, than her arms.

I swallowed. "May—may I help you?"

The phrase Aunt Wells had taught me over and over, one hand on mine, one curving the air. "It is what the world expects of boys, Gordon, that they be of use, that they be bright and willing, courteous to ladies, tipping their caps, and

13

showing, to each new day, a staunch heart and two honest, well-washed hands (not, Gordon, hands washed in well water, necessarily). And, of course, an honest well-washed tongue. "A tongue that says," and here, as if listening for heavenly music, Aunt had paused ecstatically, "that says, May I help you, fellow pilgrim, may I help you on your weary way?"

The young lady, though, looked neither weary nor in need of help for, ignoring my offer, she trotted by me to the nearest door. "Shall I wait in here? So many lovely things in your hall I feel quite nervous. Wouldn't do for me to break something, would it, pet?"

The room was small and gloomy, curtains drawn like hot dark grain against the sun. It was also teeming with cushions, some striped and formal, some hard and round and pleated. There were also older, bigger ones, plum-coloured and patchy, much softer these—except for a few odd mysterious inner bumps. It was a room with generally older furniture, a room for meditation or headache-recovery or lazing on a couch. Both Aunt and Uncle used it, especially Aunt. "An awkward room to furnish," Aunt had said once, musingly, to a visiting clergyman, a tiny man with poppingly grave eyes. "I couldn't decide whether damson-coloured cushions, or plum-coloured, would be the more restful." She'd sighed, rubbing her arms while the clergyman listened raptly. "Why do such trivial things seem so important? After all, it's not that long since the Kaiser, and a world war. And the loss," in a voice itself suddenly damson-dark with personal melancholy, "of so many fine young men."

"Well," said the young lady, cheerfully seating herself on the dim couch, "so Conway's gone for cigarettes?"

"Craven A. The packet with the black cat on it."

"Mew, mew," said my visitor, laughing. Opening her handbag she took out a compact.

"I'd like some light, pet. Hold the curtains open."

I thought of Aunt Wells. "The sun will fade the furniture."

"Me, too, so keep them shut. No, don't switch on the light. I'm quite happy."

She sat there, in that room of cushions and gloom, and she looked like the girls at school, only bigger and prettier—jolly, like them, but in a firmer, kinder way. Like Aunt Wells she wore an arm bangle (one so pale and creamy it was almost

14

invisible); but more becomingly, it stayed perfectly in place on the round pale flesh. From the very beginning I loved that pretty arm, and envied the beautiful creamy bangle.

"Lemonade?" I asked. "Would you like some lemonade? It's green stuff in a bottle, and Aunt Wells made it herself."

"Thank you, Gordon. Sounds fine, but I'd rather smoke. May I?"

"Uncle Conway gives me the picture cards from the packets."

"Then you may have mine," Betty said. "Here we are."

It was a cushion, not the card, that was to blame. It lay, dustily humped, on the carpet, a discard from that morning when Uncle Conway, irate, had pillaged the couch for a button off his waistcoat. "Irreplaceable, my buttons. As rare and original as Vatican soldiers. Where the devil is it?" "Guarding the Pope, perhaps," Aunt Wells had flashed, with that queer humour of hers. Anyway, crossing for the cigarette card, over the cushion I fell!

Clutching helpfully at my plunging body, "Whoops!" said Betty, gaily. "Whoops, boy. Whoa, there!"

Once, idly, I'd plucked clean two of Aunt Wells' pincushions. Without the pins they'd been plump and squeezable. Did Betty, under that blue dress, wear pincushions? Without the pins? It felt wonderfully like it as she held me tightly to her breasts.

Blue eyes dancing as she tugged the lobe of my ear, "Clumsy fellow," she taunted. I lay, in fear and rapture while, against my cheek, was the loveliness of arm and bangle.

Out in the hall the doorbell pealed. A fitful, tinny, wrangling peal—rather, I used to think, like Uncle Conway himself. Not that Uncle would have thought so. "Lamentably inefficient, that bell," he kept telling us. "Waning fast." "It was obviously new with the house, and so belongs with it." And Aunt Wells, as if that were ample excuse for any deficiency, would dust, with nostalgic care, the cold metal bun. At such moments Uncle, plainly nettled, fizzed alarmingly. "Ring that doorbell, ring that doorbell, ring that doorbell!" Not a command but a commentary, a singing outburst of obscure, disdainful anger. I can hear him now, cheeks darkening, waxed eyebrows blinking, small mouth jabbing, "Ring that doorbell, ring that doorbell, ring that doorbell!"

15

There was an alternative, a tawny old knocker. This Uncle used as often, and as robustly, as possible. Aunt, however, felt that the noise of a knocker was too public. "Damn it, Wells, the knocker's old as the bell. And reliable. Use it, woman, I beg you. Or never, never forget your key!" "No, Conway. Apart from the noise, it's a bit like an evil spirit. Fancy making a knocker in the form of an old man's head and beard." "Banging the whiskers, Wells, beats tolling the bell any day." "Bells," Aunt usually replied, thinking again, perhaps, of the late war, "can never be tolled too often. Or rung too frequently."

As the last tinny peal died in the hall, Betty rolled me gently aside. Calmly tidying pretty brown hair, "It's probably mother," she said.

The lady in our porch made me feel queer. In a mysterious way she looked like Betty; yet she was older and plumper and not pretty at all. Her cheeks were thick, her eyelashes too richly black, and a beauty spot nestled under curly, hard-looking hair. "Mother's always worn a spot on her brow," Betty told me, later. "She says it's common on the cheek." But the worst thing about the new lady caller was her sudden, fierce, damp handshake. "Hallo, son. Call me Auntie. All the kids do. Auntie Alex!"

Talking over me, her friendly fingers rummaging my scalp, "Conway's out, mother," Betty said.

"Out, is he?" The older lady's pallid thumb twitched impatiently against her shiny handbag. "Oh, write him a note. He'll be round tonight."

"We're going to the speedway tonight," I said, anxiously. "Red Pope's riding. The Aussie speed ace."

"Aussie speed ace, eh? Blimey," Auntie Alex said. Then, ignoring me, "Mark it urgent," she said, handing to Betty a flaking yellow pencil.

Wetting a thick eyebrow, "Men need reminding," she added, gaily, "They're that scatter-brained. Like my late Noel, rest him. Must tell you about my hubby one day, son. A poet, Noel was. One of nature's poets more than your book kind. Always the right word for the right occasion. Should, by rights, have gone in the Great War like those other poets. Ah, I'll never forget that springtime picnic up the valley, will you, Betty? One of the last outings before my Noel deceased. We

16

saw that lamb being born, and other lambs suckling, and your daddy—that's my Noel, son—said it was just like watching woolly poppies sucking at the sun. That was his very phrase, woolly poppies sucking at the sun." Auntie Alex paused for a huge, gratified breath. "Phrases like that don't come easy, not they. Oh, but a clever man was Noel. Just like your Uncle Conway."

"Uncle Conway can't come tonight," I said, "because he's coming with me."

"Sorry, pet," said Betty, propping the paper against the porch wall and writing with some difficulty. "Conway's needed, isn't he, mother?"

"Needed! I'll say!"

For a while, watching Betty's graceful blinding arms, I couldn't speak.

"Gone quiet, has our little man," said Auntie Alex. "What's he thinking, I wonder? One day, son," trying to pat my head and, instead, hitting the porch, "one day Conway must bring you to tea. Betty'd look after you, wouldn't you, Betty? And we'd brew the lad a kipper, and put on lots of butter, wouldn't we? Oh lordy," she said, belatedly, "oh lordy, my hand! Your porch could do with filing, son."

"He can't come tonight. He can't!" I spluttered.

I might as well not have spoken. Finger on plump chin, Betty's mother watched the folding of the note. Then, thumb replacing finger, "That's right, mark it urgent," she said.

Minutes later, each lady walking a little differently yet queerly the same, off they went, not quite brushing each other, under the giant trees.

What time of evening the big cool white stadium clock was telling, I cannot now remember. It was, though, the last lap of a heat. He came, broadside on, sliding royally. It should have been a straight bolt home, a ramming, snarling finish, a final purling aside of roaring rainy cinder. Instead an abrupt evil jump, a lurching, helmeted head foremost, to the track. I saw the puffing, white-coated men, arms up, chests out, running bravely. Then the stretcher. An ambulance. An announcement, rough-voiced and echoing. "Sorry, folks. Instant, fatal concussion. Just one of those things. Nothing to be done." And then, in that same rough, homely voice, "Two

17

minutes of silence, ladies and gentlemen, in honour of a great rider. If you please, two minutes of silence."

Two dragging fidgety minutes marked out on the white clock. Then, again, that booming voice.

"Red Pope just rode his last heat, in this world anyway. And that's where you and I are, ladies and gentlemen, in this world. We wish Red Pope the best in heaven. We're sure he'll triumph on those heavenly cinders. But for us," how mournful that booming voice, " it's little old earth and this stadium. Ladies and gentlemen, we're paying Red our greatest compliment. The sport he loved goes on. Your knights of the cinders, ladies and gentlemen, riding again, for your good pleasure!" And, as the booming died, a rude, barking explosion of bikes across the warm evening.

"Let's go," Uncle Conway said. Until the silence and standing he'd been sitting on the grassy bank, on a folded macintosh. "Let's go," he repeated, lifting the mac, looking red and unhappy under his bowler hat.

Draping his mac over his arm, Uncle Conway began walking. He had a fat walk, rolling slightly at every stride. I wanted to kick him.

"Uncle Conway, don't leave. Not yet. It—it isn't going to rain. And I want to see the racing!"

"Don't aggravate, boy," as I lagged stubbornly. "You know I pledged your aunt not to keep you out late."

The café, of modest size and throttled by tin advertisement plates, was at the end of a row of dull little shops. Uncle stopped the car. "Just a cup of coffee," he said. "And a milk for you. Do us good, eh, boy?"

"Rotten old milk!" I grumbled.

Inside the café I sat, unwillingly, at a dowdy silver table.

"Right then, we'll order coffee and a milk."

It didn't sound like Uncle. Usually, when beverages were mentioned, he made one of his daft, jocular speeches, the kind of speech that made Aunt Wells gaze resignedly down at her folded arms. Was she counting her freckles, I used to wonder? The daft speech itself (this particular one, anyway), as formal and inevitable by now as Uncle's bowler hats, was a kind of adding affair. "One sugar, two coffee, three milk, four water," Uncle would declare. "The four glad components. Could anything be more agreeably, or reasonably, marshalled?"

18

Similar paeans were also made regularly in honour of beer, tea and cocoa and, indeed, most drinks. No wonder, though she tried to hide it, Aunt was bored.

"Why," I asked, returning to the attack, "did we have to leave? Why?"

"I promised your aunt, Gordon. Your aunt's a good woman."

I remember my surprise. Aunt was a good woman, of course, but hearing Uncle say it made the thought both definite and new.

A young tired girl came for our order. As she did so I noticed, under our table on an empty chair, a forlorn and crumpled copy of the evening paper. On the sports page, to which it had been folded by greasy fingers, was a badly grained close-up of Red Pope. "RACING LOCALLY TONIGHT," said thick wording. Also pictured was our local track. "Spruce, ready for the fray," ran the caption. Looking back, now, across the years, and remembering that café, that night, dear, guileful old track, I cannot help but think, how bland you must have looked next morning, broom tidy, sunlit and uncaring. Once more spruce, ready for another fray! The eternal making tidy, and forgetting. For the little boy at that table, though, was it truly real? Even on the night? Could a man worshipped and talked about, a hero on one's favourite cigarette card, exit quite so quickly? As that little boy I knew that it had happened, I'd seen it happen, but my belief was only light. Heroes, one's own heroes, didn't really die. And perhaps they never do. Until we, too, die and join them (to use an Aunt Wells phrase) in the restful shades of heaven.

"Cigarettes," Uncle told the girl. "Twenty Craven A."

The girl brought them with the coffee and milk. Twenty Gold Flake. Uncle Conway didn't seem to notice. Though now less red of face, he was clearly still troubled. "No reason why your Aunt Wells should rush off to the white house," he muttered, restively. "At least, not yet. Why, I might not even grow that moustache."

Had conscience, pricked by an evening of sudden death (no evidence, in Uncle's demeanour that night, of growing resigned to death) leapt briefly awake? After all, he may well have thought, life was as short for Wells as for anyone else, and a moustache, daily on view, no small matter.

19

"You want to grow a German moustache," I said, darkly, pushing away my milk, "and Aunt Wells doesn't like German moustaches."

"Gordon, don't be cheeky. And drink up. We're going home."

Back in the car, still angry at missing the racing, I sat with clenched hands and slanting cap.

"The drink was horrid, Uncle. I feel sick."

"Rubbish. I know a sick boy when I see one. Your colour's fine."

I switched attack. "Shall I tell Aunt Wells that you're not growing a moustache?"

"You'll say nothing. Haven't decided yet. May grow a big one," Uncle said, defiantly.

"A real sprouter, big as an airship?"

"Airships," Uncle said, sounding, briefly, quaint as Aunt Wells, "usually crashed. Wouldn't want any moustache of mine to come crashing down."

"It would float down," I said, "just like a feather." And then, thinking of something I'd read in which a feather had been a symbol of cowardice, and wishing to annoy Uncle further, "A white feather," I added.

After that we journeyed in a fierce vibrant hostility that only ended, with our separation, in the hall of town house.

"Off to bed, boy," Uncle rapped. "At once. Though, damn it, admire your spirit. Almost like mine, at times."

Left alone in the crammed familiar hall while Uncle Conway loped in search of Aunt Wells, and by now a little less angry, I looked around. How dusk made everything smaller. Even the doors looked smaller. Impulsively, on tiptoe, I opened one. The dark little room with its throng of cushions was now really dark. Without turning on the light I crept over, knelt, and sniffed noisily and hungrily at the long, quiescent couch. Not, perhaps, the most powerful of aromas, but there was a scent still, the one that Betty had left. It reminded, did that sweetly impregnated fabric of the couch, not only of Betty but of another time when an aunt, staying one night only, had slept in my bed (because, she said, she must have a bedroom facing south). The next night I'd returned to unchanged sheets and the scent, high-spirited and foolish, had kept me happily, uncomplainingly awake long after the first morning wind blowing from the town square, and long long after the last dark crash of bolts from the ageing hall below.

3

Why, I wonder, did Uncle Conway prefer venetian blinds for the window of his study? Every other window in our town house boasted curtains, usually dark curtains—their heavy velvet bottoms eternally in need of cleaning. Perhaps, though, for Uncle Conway, blinds were a matter of efficiency. Perhaps, in the Germany he so loudly and often admired, venetian blinds, along with scrubbed doorsteps, were commonplace. I do know, however, that Aunt Wells felt very differently. For her slats were the most terrible of all dust gatherers. "I shan't dust them, I shan't bother," she would say, from time to time, losing patience and nearly crying. "Not your job anyway," Uncle Conway would rave. "Leave dusting to Mrs H." Adding, more gently, "In any case dusting all those slats will help keep your arms thin. I like thin arms." But did he? Or, if he had admired thin arms, did he any longer? Once I saw him stroke, lingeringly, the bare arm of a Grecian lady carrying an urn on her head, a lady made of china and an ornament in the hall, and her arm was fat. So, was he, for once, just being kind? And the blinds, what else did they mean to Uncle? Did their clacking act as therapy? Did he like the lean brisk lines of hard material? And why, for Aunt Wells, curtains? To lift blinds the tug of a cord, to draw curtains a more athletic motion, in Aunt's case, happily, a gracious floating motion. The difference between efficiency and the sensual? But was, I ask myself now, Aunt Wells sensual? The thought occurs that so much lies buried in each good quiet lady that might, if fully aroused, have lived delightfully. If only, for example, Uncle's imagination had been less political and more romantic. If only, in the comfort of their bedroom as night fell, he'd declared, "One kiss, two undress, three caress, four pash-un!" I'm sure that Aunt Wells might have whispered warmly back, "Oh, Conway. The four glad components. Could anything be more agreeably, or reasonably, marshalled?"

But perhaps that did happen, and kept on happening until Aunt was bored.

Perhaps.

Aunt Wells had her own kind of efficiency, nevertheless. It flowered, chiefly, at the white house. And it flowered, especially, in dealings with tradespeople. I remember, on one fine hot day, Aunt donning a very tall white hat, the most regal and frightening of all her summer headgear, and our journeying together into town by bus from the white house. Our destination, it appeared, was a very select music store just off the square. I remember our entering through a heavy glass door, with me puffing and holding the door wide and Aunt just sailing in, hat only barely clear of being knocked askew. The shop carpet, freshly swept and an aristocratic shade of magenta, was a never-ending affair along which we travelled (Aunt, at any rate) with the most careless, most majestic of airs. Not once did Aunt look to right or left, north or south. Pianos and sheet music, radios and music stands—not that there was too much of any one thing, and certainly not a price ticket in view—were clearly beneath her dignity and interest. So, too, were junior salesmen, blinking and gaping young fellows capering nervously backwards on black, shiny shoes. Yet, although Aunt Wells moved with commanding grace, it was that incredible white hat that really moved, really commanded. Every eye that flashed her way flashed to hat level, not, I insist, because it was in any way an outlandish hat, burdened with fruit or other freakish detail (it was, in fact, superbly plain) but simply because, apart from being tall, it had a wonderful purity of colour. "White," Aunt Wells once said, I remember, "is never lovelier, or more impressive, than when it's really white. Not dusty white, or spotted white, or faded white, or grey white, but white white."

A senior salesman, domed head bent in ivory respect, advanced and bowed. "Good morning, madam." Then, with a coy little pleasantry in my direction, "And good morning to you, sir!"

"Am I right," Aunt Wells asked, in a voice immaculate and dazzling as her hat, "in thinking your shop the best of its kind? The best music store in our town?"

If not original, Aunt's method was at least effective. The salesman not only began to beam and twitch but made a fatherly effort to hold my shoulder.

"Bubble gum!" I muttered, twisting disagreeably aside.

"Gordon!"

"I think, madam," said the salesman, quickly, "that we may honestly claim to be the premier store in both town and county."

"Not a small county, either," Aunt observed.

"Quite, madam. There are one or two other music stores—in neighbouring towns, as well as here—that are, dare I say it, not immune from ... notoriety!"

There must have been a joke for Aunt smiled, sketchily.

"Prompt deliveries, then?"

"Our deliveries, may I say, are prompter than deliveries anywhere else in the—" hesitating, for a fearful moment, on the brink of absurdity and exaggeration "—in the county."

"And any arrangements—apart, that is, from the sale and despatch of goods—promptly honoured?"

"Naturally, madam. Efficiency, as you may agree, is the only true civility."

I remember Aunt's smile, full and warming now, and my own sudden alarm.

"Don't curtsy to him, Aunt Wells" I wanted to say. "To curtsy is daft and sissy!"

It was, of course, no more than a feeling that she gave me. I never saw it happen, and, unless royalty had called at our town or country house, it never could have happened. "The only permissible curtsy," Aunt would no doubt have said, if she had read my mind, "is performed inside oneself. Besides, Gordon, there's my hat to consider. A hat such as this has a rare and delicate balance, a balance not, at any cost, to be disturbed!"

Arrangement concluded—Aunt Wells had a piano in need of attention, and the store had undertaken to send a tuner—we began the return trip to the heavy glass door.

"It's been a pleasure, madam," our salesman said, with a final beam and bow from which, quite obviously, he excluded me.

"Pleasure, Gordon," Aunt said, tapping me lightly on the ear as we victoriously glided the magenta carpet, a junior salesman dodging at our heels, "in terms of the daily round means oiling the lamp."

"Lamp, Aunt Wells? What lamp?"

"The social lamp that each day brings," nodding, gravely, as the youth, jigging past, triumphantly held open the door.

Dipping into my frugal store of knowledge, "But don't lamps stink, Aunt Wells? Oil ones, anyway."

Aunt Wells herself never smelt, even after hefting suitcases on a summer's day, or dusting round after Mrs Hampton, or pulling weeds with Sam. Not so with Uncle Conway. Even when just sitting with his legs up and waistcoat and collar open, he often had a roaring, biting scent. Yet from the way he talked he was fresh and sweet, and anxious to remain so. Advice he also gave Aunt Wells.

"Too hot a day to sweat. Honestly, Wells, you have no idea of protocol. Sam will execute the weeds."

"Sam's having a day off."

"Ah, yes. A day in, what's the place—Weston Mare? Just imagine the old boy paddling, rheumy ankles in the mud, and briny, upturned bum like a ghastly, tide-borne mushroom!"

And when Aunt, tightlipped at what she thought a disloyal crudity, persisted in donning pale-blue gloves and dabbing graciously away, in some ailing flower bed, with a trowel the handle of which was a pale, matching blue, "Rum tum," Uncle would begin to taunt from the comfort of his chair, his voice carrying through the open windows, "tum rum, rumpety tum, tumpety rum!"

Nagged and drummed at by the silly lively meaningless words, Aunt would eventually retreat, in her eye a shining tear.

"No, Gordon, I am not crying! I have a speck of dust!"

There were ways, though, quite apart from the despised weeding, in which Uncle did exercise, unfortunately ways no more commendable to Aunt Wells than the chanting by Uncle of doggerel had been. One such exercise was by performing, when annoyed, with all possible vim and enthusiasm, a rowdy capriole—marching in one place without advancing—on the drawing-room carpet.

"Up the army," he would thunder, as he capered with knees up, bearing down hard on a favourite patch of carpet, usually

24

a fading yellow rose, "up the army!"

Anything military had only to be hinted at for Aunt to disapprove. Lines, thin-webbed and sad, would rush about her mouth.

"Oh, Conway, must you?"

Halting his capriole, Uncle would look, briefly, a trifle ashamed.

"Woman, woman. Can I help it if you lost your ... beloved, at Ypres? The Great War is over. We must build against Bolshevism. As Germany is doing."

"Germany!" Aunt almost shuddered.

"Yes, Germany. Germany, Germany, Germany!" And, excited again, Uncle Conway's feet would rise and fall.

"Poor rose," Aunt Wells would say, taunting back in her own, quieter way, "poor yellow rose. How terrible, being stamped on!"

I remember to this day, the vast angry throbbings through Uncle's podgy body.

"Stamp? I never stamp. I march!"

Then, on seeing me, "I want a bath," he'd fume. "Want to feel clean again. Go and run the tap, boy."

"Which tap, Uncle Conway?"

"The perishing bath tap, of course. Really, lad!"

"And I," Aunt Wells had said, trying a last jibe, "am off to drink a glass of cold clear water. Inner cleanliness is quite as vital—more so, perhaps, than any outer scrubbings!"

Scrubbed to a fine hot blue, the sky over white house, that memorable yet peaceful (since Uncle Conway rarely appeared at white house and only stayed briefly if he did, weeding time usually was peaceful) day of Mr Edgar's arrival. We didn't know him then as Mr Edgar, or as anything else; he was just a pale little man with dark hair, deep dark eyes and a rather large, faintly sweating, pear-shaped nose. Wrestling a bicycle slightly too big along the gravel, and with his dark, slightly humped suit, not to mention a hard dark hat grasped awkwardly over the bicycle bell, he made me think irreverently of a blackbird arduously pushing bread about! Up he trudged, to our open front door. With a word to Sam, Aunt took off her gardening apron, rolled down her sleeves and bustled forward, though worriedly, for a button at her white silk cuff was dangling by a thread. Flapping vaguely at the thread, as if it were a naughty cobweb, "Good morning," she said, breathlessly. "Can I help you?"

The little man leant his bike against the house, apparently trying, at the same time, to don, and doff, his hat. Unfortunately the hat hit, and rang, the bell, while the front wheel slewed ravenously, biffing his legs. Back he stumbled, grabbing wildly and ending up, obviously bewildered, with Aunt Wells' cuff button and trail of white thread! The hat, meanwhile, rolled and wobbled until finally and dustily crushed—by Sam's clumsy left boot! "Like a big beetle, that un," Sam said, picking it up, and turning it critically over. "No more a-breathing than what a beetle would be, neither!"

"Sam, straighten and dust the hat and return it immediately," Aunt said.

The little man hardly listened. "Oh dear," he murmured, waving button and thread vaguely and apologetically towards Aunt's bosom, "I seem to have—"

"You have a button from my cuff," Aunt said, impatiently and firmly, and regarding, with a mild lift of eyebrow, the cheerfully askew bicycle. "From my cuff!"

"So I have, to be sure. From your cuff." And the little man looked wretched.

"Now," Aunt said, taking button and thread from the little man, and the hat from Sam, "now, if you'll take your hat and prop your bicycle again, and kindly explain—"

"Edgar, Mr George Edgar. I—I understand from Princeton's, the music shop, that—"

"Ah, you've come to tune the piano!"

Now Aunt was suddenly benign. So much so that, as we entered the house, "Before you start would you care for a coffee, Mr Edgar? It is eleven o'clock."

Mr Edgar fumbled at a high pocket, trying, it seemed, to produce a watch in corroboration; but something, somewhere, caught, and instead an old dark handkerchief came floundering out.

"Oh dear! But yes, most kind. A coffee would be just right."

"Are you a country or a town dweller, Mr Edgar?" Aunt Wells asked, pleasantly.

The little man, as he trotted behind her, seemed to gather courage, the slightly bent shoulders of the dark suit lifting confidentially, hiding the tall white collar that cut into jagged greasy neck hair. "Town, actually. But I travel. Only yesterday I saw a rabbit, two partridges, and a raven. Quite a treat, I do assure you. A rabbit, two partridges, and a raven."

Briskly and comfortably, "Well, now come and see a cup of coffee," Aunt said.

We entered the kitchen, a large breezy place swept equally by keen white paint and fresh warm air from wide open windows. Sitting down, at Aunt's invitation, at the green and black chintz-covered table Mr Edgar bent, awkwardly, to remove his bicycle clips. Out, from the high pocket, peeping like a lacklustre half-moon, emerged part of a watch. Grabbing upwards, clip in hand, Mr Edgar tinkered a moment, and then, triumphantly, withdrew his wilful timepiece and its attached chain. "Ah,"he said, his colour rosy now. "Faulty link, caught in the lining. Well I never. Should have realised."

"We can't all be engineers, Mr Edgar," Aunt Wells said, smiling.

"No, to be sure not. We can't all be practical." Tucking away the watch and clasping his hands, Mr Edgar, his dark eyes full of a kind, dreamy humility, gazed out through the nearest window. "A lovely day. Quite a treat. If only it will last." And, "Well done," he added, presently, as Aunt poured his coffee and produced a plate of biscuits as perfectly arranged as the hours on a clock, "well done!"

"You've only taken one bicycle clip off," I said.

"Oh dear. So I have." As Mr Edgar bent a second time, "You've got a hole in your sock, haven't you?" I said.

"Gordon!"

"So I have," said Mr Edgar, wincing. "My fault, though, not the wife's. She's in hospital. Not well at all."

"How terrible for you. I am truly sorry," Aunt Wells said.

Poor Mr Edgar, quite flustered even at sympathy; while Aunt Wells, moving smoothly around, looked utterly at ease.

Clasping her unbuttoned cuff, Aunt sat down and began talking companionably of favourite songs and hymns.

"Naturally, for sacred music, I prefer an organ to a piano; but then, so does everyone."

"To be sure, everyone," said Mr Edgar.

Looking suddenly a trifle misty, Aunt said, "When I was younger I loved the tunes of the day. I used to love the Great War songs. Now, of course, they seem too sad."

"Ah yes, the Great War songs. Not that I ever served. A little too young."

"Aunt Wells lost her beloved in the Great War," I said. "That's what Uncle Conway keeps saying, anyway."

"Gordon, how dare you! I am afraid," Aunt said, looking pink and discomfited for the first time that morning, and holding, as she offered the sugar basin, her cuff even tighter, "that the boy's tongue is quite unpredictable. But it is true that, at Ypres, the young man I was fond of, and hoped to marry, died."

"Ah, Ypres," Mr Edgar said, mournfully.

There was a lull while both Aunt and Mr Edgar solemnly drank, Mr Edgar keeping his eyes not only delicately removed from Aunt's eyes, but full of a vague appropriate sorrow.

"The rabbit yesterday," he said at last. "A lovely little chap. I wish my wife could have seen it. She loves bunny rabbits."

"Does she love partridges and ravens, too?" I butted in.

Aunt Wells glared, but Mr Edgar only smiled and said, languidly, "Well done, well done."

I was captivated. If I kicked his ankle or hurled his bicycle clips through the window, or tugged the chintz, spilling coffee and scattering biscuits, was that what he'd say? Just, "Well done, well done." Would he say, "Well done, well done," if Aunt took thread and needle and mended her cuff? Or if Sam entered and said, "Your bike's been stole!" Or if I stabbed him to death with the big gleaming kitchen knife? Mr Edgar's world, I thought, must be a very happy place, with nothing ever badly done. Yet, "Badly done, badly done," I reflected as, lifting his cup, the piano tuner took a sloppy, voluptuous gulp.

"Sam!" Aunt Wells said, suddenly rising. "Isn't that Sam calling?"

It was. Sam, in the company of a gentleman I'd not seen before, was standing just outside the open front door.

As Aunt and I gustily approached along the passage (Mr Edgar remaining politely in the kitchen), "She's a-coming now, sir, she's a-coming now!" Sam bawled unnecessarily, cupping, in earthy hands, his fierce mouth.

"Thank you, Sam," Aunt said, and looked at the stranger.

A stocky little man in dark clothes, he kept anxiously stroking dark rumpled hair. Behind him, on the gravel, a taxi waited in the sun.

28

"Edgar, Mr Jack Edgar," he said, glancing worriedly at the nearby bicycle. "My brother is here?"

"Yes, he's here," Aunt confirmed, obviously puzzled.

Blinking, the little man peered past her.

"Awful news. George's wife … just half an hour ago. In hospital. I—I have to tell him."

"Please, come in," Aunt said. "You may have one of the front rooms," and, looking upset, she led the way to a big creamy lounge. A ship with orange and tangerine sails, the colours echoed and ebbing in the surrounding water, was afloat in the room's only picture and a big green vase stood coolly in a shining, dust-free corner. Twisting his hair and tugging his nose—the new Mr Edgar looked unseeingly about.

"It was sudden, very sudden. We all thought … well, that she'd recover. Poor George. Awful. Such a devoted pair. Like turtle-doves, you might say. Not a day without cooing."

"I am so terribly sorry," Aunt said, blinking a little herself.

"I used to tell them, you ought to keep turtle-doves. Just the thing for a loving pair like you."

"Bunnies and partridges and ravens," I muttered, scornfully, "that's what *he* likes. Not doves!"

Aunt turned, savagely.

I went through to the kitchen. Mr Edgar, his cup empty, was hovering over the table, waiting, patiently flexing pale fingers in clawing, make-believe piano runs.

"Well done," I said, and he looked quickly round, blushing, a faint pink on the pear-shaped nose.

A moment later I felt Aunt's hands whipping me aside. Her eyes, I saw with wonder, were still damp.

"Your brother, Mr Edgar," she said, gently. "He's in the front, waiting to see you."

I was outside in the heat, strapping on roller-skates and gazing at the taxi driver (who, queerly, wouldn't look at me!) when the brothers reappeared.

Together, dark bowed suit following dark bowed suit, they entered the taxi.

As the taxi began to move I seized a door handle, clinging, rolling forward. Mr Edgar, very pale now on each side of his pear-shaped nose, seemed to be crying. As I thrust against the window his dark wet eyes vanished under pale lids. His brother, apple nose scarlet, waved a fist. It was, I thought, all very disappointing! There might, at least, from inside the taxi, have been a, "Well done," however muffled or grudging, to acknowledge my daring.

Angry myself by now, I put out my tongue, flourishing it frantically before—defeated by the taxi's acceleration—tumbling in the dust.

"Gordon, take off those skates and come inside. At once! I wish to talk to you."

I stood under the picture of the sailing ship while Aunt Wells crossed to a window and took several deep whiffs of hazy air. "In the midst of life, Gordon, in the midst of life."

"Yes, Aunt."

As if disliking my tone she turned, sharply. "A nice little man. Remember that, Gordon. As Mrs Hampton would say, 'Nice men don't grow on trees.' "

"Perhaps on pear trees they do," I said, thinking of that singular nose.

Obviously baffled, Aunt looked angry again. Nevertheless, making a noble effort at control, she clasped her loose cuff and looked steadily out through the big open window.

"You must be aware, Gordon, that your Uncle Conway is greatly annoyed with you."

The vase, in the corner, looked big enough to absorb my whole arm, if ever, that is, I tried to plunge it in. Perhaps one day I would, though if there were a rat inside … I quivered. How terrible! A rat, furry, teeth glimmering, tail dancing, crouching in the gloom at the bottom of the tall green vase!

"Apparently you failed to give him a message. Though not my affair, for it concerns a public house and I dislike anything to do with public houses," Aunt Wells paused, fidgeting with her cuff, "it is, clearly, my affair insofar as you failed in your duty."

Perhaps, before plunging in my arm, I thought, I'd poke in the vase with a stick!

"However, we're at the white house now. So you may, I think, redeem yourself by helping Sam."

"Can I look in all the vases, instead? For rats?"

"Don't be stupid, Gordon. You will help Sam by weeding." Exasperatedly Aunt let her sleeve fly open, massaged ruefully her thin, freckled arm. "First, though, you may fetch my work basket. A neat woman anoints the day, and makes it shine!"

Later, in my big bare bedroom above the kitchen, I took

from my trousers pocket a by now grubby piece of paper, the one that, vilely no doubt, I had failed to pass to Uncle Conway.

With some bewilderment, and not for the first time, I gazed at the laboriously written message.

"Urgent. Wanted at the York Arms—a good man to do his duty. Betty."

Closing my eyes I saw again the young lady in the graceful blue dress, her round arms white and beautiful in the shade of town house porch.

4

"It's just impossible," Aunt said. "Mr Micawber here, Mrs Pecksniff there, Bill Sykes next to Jane Austen, Miss Fanny Squeers upstairs, the whole Dickens set quite disrupted!"

We were back at town house. At six-fifteen on a molten brooding evening Uncle Conway turned off the radio in his study and came prancing to where Aunt Wells and I were attempting a sorting of one of the many big dark bookcases. I remember well that Uncle's face was also molten, and had been all day long. "Here am I," he'd kept complaining, "trying to write a book on modern Germany under Herr Hitler. And does my wife help, or encourage, me? Not she. All she does is pull a face and talk about a new baking tin, and about how many loaves we eat a week, and whether or not some old dress will suit Mrs H. Damn it, it's insufferable!"

And now, as we crouched at the bookcase, Uncle complained yet again.

"Damn the BBC! British Bolsheviks Corporation! Herr Hitler's latest oration given only fifteen seconds of news time."

Aunt Wells, looking with despair at the loaded shelves, reminded me suddenly of a gentle horse tasting, with cautious hooves, the tide of a foaming beach, before deciding, reluctantly, that it was all too much. Rising, and backing away a little as she brushed a hot tired brow, "Oh, Gordon, if only we could take this bookcase, and all the other bookcases, to white house, and get them into shape. Your Uncle's fault. If only he understood order!"

Uncle Conway, dipping into the nearest chair, at once flung out short, dark-trousered legs, a challenging, emphatic space between each gleaming shoe.

"Order is, as well you know, my one firm commitment, my one firm guiding star. Politically speaking, anyway."

As if suddenly prodded, Aunt returned to the books, and, with a thin line of worry all down the middle of her face, grabbed, dusted, and jostled them around. "Why," she asked, in a tone of all-right-let's-row, "were you so rude to Mr Agate when he called? Our new Member of Parliament deserved, I think, at least some courtesy."

"Rubbish," Uncle snapped. "Chap knows we've got money. He'll always be on our doorstep."

"He's a gentleman," Aunt Wells said, quietly, as if that settled all possible argument.

Uncle began writhing in his chair. His legs drew in, his shoes clicked blackly together.

"And Herr Hitler isn't a gentleman, I suppose? Mr Agate, pah! No fire. Storm, Wells, storm. That's what Agate lacks!"

"Oh, I understand exactly what he lacks. Quite apart from any question of thunder and lightning, he doesn't wear one of those dreadful, military-type armbands so popular in Germany!"

Up, bristling, waistcoat buttons a taut flashing line of order and aggression, leapt Uncle Conway. "Yes, armbands, exactly! I believe in armbands!"

For a while no one moved. It seemed, queerly, that some awful declaration had been made, a declaration so awful and belligerent that even the untidy old bookcase was stirred awake. Perhaps even Mr Micawber, drowsing deep in the pages of David Copperfield, and on the verge of some terrible nightmare of penury and the debtors' prison, moved, grunted, and came thankfully awake, though not, surely, to dwell on so absurd a topic as armbands! In fact, despite the anger in the air, the bookcase smiled! for just then, tweaking capriciously the dark evening, out had come the sun, throwing tiny bracelets of light on walls and furniture and books, so that the titles—the brighter ones anyway—gleamed with relish at this latest, incredible, human confrontation. Before, as the sun went in again, darkening critically to frowns!

"Armbands!" Aunt scoffed. "Men who need to wear armbands lack the ability for normal self-expression."

"Rot!"

"Men, Conway, who need to wear armbands lack the ability for normal self-expression."

"Oh, God," Uncle exploded, stamping the carpet in hot damp fury. "Oh for escape, for a German pine-needle forest, and a flaxen-haired Teutonic beauty. I can see her now, lying across tree roots, all unpinned and ready."

Aunt Wells sliced home a book. She had, I think, forgotten my presence.

"Ready for what, Conway? At times I, too, feel ready. But when anything happens it's not exactly what I felt ready for. That I do know!"

Ah, sad.

It's so simple, Aunt Wells. You were frustrated. It wasn't that Uncle Conway wasn't lusty. Of course he was. But your need, felt only instinctively I think, was for a full and lingering sensual love—the drawing of curtains as opposed to the snapping of blinds?—and Uncle Conway, bless him, was explosive. Not for him the detours and smoulderings which your senses, unlucky, barely acknowledged senses, must have craved. Remember that evening (yes, I was lurking again, this time outside some friendly half-open door!) when you discomfited him by saying, "It's hot, unbearably. I'm taking a bath. After which I shall go to bed, probably unclothed!" It was as if you'd asked for something, something special; for do you remember how, turning, he strode to the window, peering uneasily out, and you smiled unhappily, and said rather vaguely and listlessly, "Even Queen Victoria removed her clothes. At certain times." You didn't mean anything, it was, absolutely, a meaningless remark, made, no doubt, because you'd embarrassed yourself quite as much as Conway. Oh not so much by your words—a bath, then to bed unclothed!—as by that deeper need trembling in your voice. But oh, how he reacted! Round, rocking a brass lamp-standard. Uncle spun, remember? Up, in frantic, defensive flurries, cuffs like great white tickets, his waving arms. "Queen Victoria took her clothes off! Queen Victoria took her clothes off! Queen Victoria took her clothes off, la, la, la!" It was splendid, one of his best, very best, retreats: upturned face cherry red, double chin in grey plump flight, tummy forward while all the rest leant back. "Queen Victoria took her clothes off," Uncle Conway sang, voice shiny-edged, fierce and lifting, "Queen Victoria took her clothes off, what a shocking shocking do! La, la, la!" Poor Uncle, he would, almost certainly, have liked to have pleased you after your bath, but he, too, must have felt—instinctively, also?—that a definite incompatibility did exist, that he couldn't, by nature, still your trembling, give that kind of loving, quenching, and sublime perfection that can, by some, be given.

Ah, sad, that I do know.

Our breakfast table, on the morning after the row over armbands, was strangely calm and lovely, with primrose sprigs of sunlight all across the fine old tablecloth—how they waited, those dapper sprigs, to blink and fly at each stolid lift of thick white crockery before, with not a crackle, prettily resettling. I know we all, that morning, watched the soothing flickerings, Uncle chewing toast, his eyes dipped and careful, Aunt equally careful and rigid, especially in the exact, tight-wristed way she poured tea (there had, after all, been a quarrel). But what finally broke the ice was, of all things, the wall calendar, an ornate affair showing, above the monthly dates, a fine reproduction of some impressionist painting. As so often while she ate her porridge—even in hot weather Aunt took porridge—she looked continually at this picture as if finding, perhaps, that the clear light colours brought light and composure to her inner being. So while her spoon, never overfull, rose and fell, she gazed richly and silently until, lowering her eyes a fraction, she suddenly noticed a particular date. Spoon wavering, porridge jumping like a tiny, startled curl of fleece, "Why, Conway, look at the date," she blurted out, and Uncle, startled as the porridge, whipped round, responding, after a moment, half-ashamedly, "Why, yes, the date. So it is. Well I never."

After which, in the middle of the hot steaming morning, Uncle put on his best suit and got out the car, Aunt put on a rather watery-blue dress and rather romantic straw hat (not grand and white but a deep shimmering blue) and, both looking by now at any rate cautiously happy, off they drove.

Aunt's last words, I remember, were: "Be good."

"There's salad and cold rice pudding for Gordon's lunch," Aunt had told Mrs Hampton, before driving off, and, eyeing me without much love in her big cloudy eyes, "I'll set it out for the lad," Mrs Hampton had faithfully promised. The pudding, along with all the boring lettuce from the salad, went down the lavatory the moment that Mrs Hampton, after first treating herself to flowers from the garden, left for home. Which left only Sam, abandonedly trimming hedges and shedding rump wind as he hobbled up and down the cluttered paths.

So that there was no one to stop me when, an hour or so later, I sneaked out into the baking, post-lunch Saturday afternoon.

The York Arms, that afternoon, looked as it always did, full of a comfortable bow-window cosiness down below, higher up rather more plain and stringent due to the flat, slightly leaning, upper windows. Everything was glinting: windows, the grey crooked front steps, the faintly askew red-grey roof, the fading, once charming red paintwork. A hostelry not far from our town house, the York Arms was on a corner, its exposed side facing onto a road that led, tree-lined and straight as an arrow, to Aunt Wells' church. Once, returning later than usual from morning service with Aunt, I had seen Uncle Conway emerging through a side door of the public house into a tiny yard. A memorable Uncle Conway, cheeks on fire, walking with a bantam strut, and already fumbling at his trousers. "Oh dear," Aunt had muttered, seizing my shoulder and beginning a quick, earnest walk. Uncle Conway, very erectly, and apparently not noticing us, had entered a small brick tree-sheltered urinal. On the bricks, boldly chalked, the kind of words one knew to be rude and which had made me, also, want to hurry on. It had seemed, at that moment, that Uncle Conway was no longer a part of our lives. A prisoner of chalk and brick and smell, how could he be? But, "Your Uncle was too late for church," Aunt Wells had said, loyally but unconvincingly (when had I last seen Uncle in church?), Sunday demeanour a trifle crumpled as she'd hurried on. Looking back, now, how sorry I feel for that thin, white-gloved hand on my shoulder, for the swift proud feet on the glimmering pavement. How very, very sorry.

Moving forward I gazed, probingly, at the completely slumbering pub. The space in front, rising obliquely from the pavement, held only an empty weary paper bag. All looked quiet and lonely—even the two wide cellar gratings looked forlorn and deserted in the bright yellow sunshine.

Rounding the corner I stopped by the little yard. Here, also, all was quiet. The rude chalked words, as if at a wipe from the tree sweeping low and green over the walls of the urinal, had merged into one great blotch. The pub side door, propped ajar by something resembling a black flat-iron, showed the dimness of a hall, and a dark-brown, dusty flight of stairs. Two old dustbins, grey lids aslant, huddled to one side of the bent doorstep. A rather dirty crust of discarded bread, caught between two crumbling yard bricks, blinked in the strong amber light before, pecked by a sudden sparrow, leaping into the cold shadow of the nearer bin. This, I thought, scratching tousled hair as I stared and stared, was—in a way that I didn't understand—Uncle's world. This was where that undelivered note, still in my pocket, had summoned him, describing him, mysteriously, as a good man who was needed. Needed for what, I wondered? And *was* Uncle good? Aunt Wells was good. I didn't feel sure about Uncle!

"Why, hallo Gordon. What a surprise! Returning the compliment and paying us a visit, are you, pet?"

This time she was yellow as the day, in a sleeveless primrose dress that gave her arms an even smoother, paler, lovelier look than I'd remembered. (Impossible, isn't it, describing beauty, or the effect of colour? I still, even today, so many rueful years later, like yellow best of all. There still isn't anything in the world, I most firmly believe, to beat a pretty girl in a yellow summer dress: particularly if the day is hot, the summer new, and the dress gently clinging, arms, throat and shoulders bare, and the girl as pretty as Betty was, those years ago. For on such a day, in such a dress, the skin is made marvellously pure and pale, a perfect mirror for buttercups, and a perfection never to be forgotten as life goes on and on, and winters lengthen, and ageing eyes cloud over and have to peer and blink—even at yellow summer dresses, and the wonderful girls inside them!)

"You must come on in," said wonderful Betty Hallet, cheerfully, "and have a lemonade. Isn't that what you offered me, young man—a lemonade?"

We mounted the bent step, Betty just ahead of me, although her hand moved warmly to touch, and guide, my shoulder. As we did so, and before the cool dark hall suddenly gripped me, I glanced almost triumphantly at the two sullen, dozing bins; for how curiously different they seemed, much less forbidding now that I had the right to march past them and into the house!

The narrow hall was as dusty as it had looked from outside, with dark leathery wallpaper and, from along the skirting board, the raw, chilly smell of unfinished painting. But it wasn't the pot of paint, left untidily in view, that I noticed most, or the paintbrush wrapped in newspaper, but, further along against the banisters, a bicycle that reminded me, briefly, of little Mr Edgar's bicycle at the white house. At the time of our leaving for town house it still hadn't been collected, and a poor woe-begone thing it had looked, like its owner. This bike in the York Arms, though, was newer, with a gleaming bell and low, racing-style handlebars. In the middle of the machine a bar of pale pretty blue that Mr Edgar, I felt sure, would not have liked. Much too gay for the rather solemn, wistful piano tuner who so adored dun-coloured bunnies and black ravens.

"Now, pet, you can go to my room," Betty said. "Upstairs, third door along. I'll bring you a lemonade."

And off, smiling, into some dark mysterious room where brass fittings, like golden exclamation marks, gleamed exultantly.

The landing, which I reached eagerly, and with an even greater sense of triumph, was broad and bare except for the thin, continuing stair carpet, its drained brown colours drab as November after the brilliant sunshine. There were indeed, I saw, three doors before the landing turned, the first of which was closed. Since the second door was partly open I paused, took a deep breath, and looked quickly, boldly in.

It was like looking into a thick purple cloud. Everything was purple, especially the bed in the centre; there was so much purple that there seemed no room at all for any other colour. Admittedly there were varying shades, like the fat mauve nightdress case on the bed, but they were pinpricks in the teeming royal vastness. My first quick look was followed by a second one, longer and amazed, and not just because of the purple; for, sitting on the far side of the bed, before a small, purple-aproned dressing table, was a lady I remembered only too well—Betty's mother, Mrs Hallet, or, as she herself had put it, Auntie Alex. But not, alas, the fully clothed Auntie Alex I remembered, but a half-nude Auntie, whose rich breasts seemed almost crushingly to fill the moderately sized looking glass. I think, apart from shock, I felt a sense of wonder, for to me they were breasts of incredible interest, each shaped like a big creamy whip-cream walnut, topped by a podgy light brown nut. My fascination, for such sights were new to me, leapt and flared as she moved to lift a jar, the whole sweet creamy structure beautifully ashake. When she saw me—my eyes, reflected in the mirror, must have looked like treacle pools—she screamed, dropped the jar, grabbed up the purple, white-flowered dressing-table runner, and, while a dozen pots and combs and brushes banged and rolled and fell, screamed and screamed and screamed again.

Why, instead of running off, I had to dive forward to arrest a scudding jar of face cream I never afterwards understood. But just then it seemed the helpful, proper course of action that even Aunt Wells might have approved. Unfortunately, as I hit the floor, the screams heightened and, in zealous panic, under the bed I crawled, still chasing the rolling jar, its green label mocking and smiling as it wobbled from view. Under the bed was an almost purple gloom, and something else. A chamber pot against which my head struck, ringingly, causing, inside the thick china, the sudden alarming swish of disturbed liquid. Repelled, out from under the bed I shot, to be engulfed by the shrillest scream of all that madcap afternoon.

"Betty! Betty!" Auntie Alex howled, somewhere above me. "Betty, for God's sake where are you?"

Out, at last, I rushed. Smash! went the door of the purple bedroom behind me, while, on the stairs, the sound of flying feet.

Trembling, mouth dry, I hurried inside the third room, standing palpitating just beyond the door.

Footsteps along the landing. A door opening.

"Betty, there was a boy. Spying!"

"Mother, really. It was only—"

"A boy, I tell you. At first I thought it was some horrid leering dwarf. He—he saw—wait, he may have smashed my—"

"It was Gordon, mother, only Gordon. You remember, Conway's nephew."

The next few words were blurred, then, clearly, "He saw my tit hills, Betty. My God, what would Conway say?"

"Conway, mother, need never know. Do calm down. And for goodness sake do something about emptying that chamber pot! I'm ashamed of you!"

Betty's room was smaller than her mother's, and very pink. Tiny pink objects filled the room in dibs and dabs, the back of a hand-mirror, a door-knob, a rose on the wall-paper, a comb, the rippled, flying cloak of a crock courtier. The slightly tilting ceiling was clean and white but heavily veined. A brilliant black-and-white rug lay glaring upwards. From the window, towards which I moved uneasily, a view of the pub sign, and beyond that the wide road, and after that the lattice-windowed houses with their neat front lawns and hedges. It was a view, and a reality, very hard to grasp. Was I really in a public house, seeing the world from the York Arms? What Aunt Wells would say, I dared not think.

"Well, now," said Betty, entering, closing the door behind her, and offering, with soft cool fingers, the lemonade. "Here you are, and no thanks to you it's not spilt. I'm afraid you scared mother half to death!"

Briefly, closing my eyes, I saw again the full, bare chest of Auntie Alex beguilingly ashake, nuts and all.

Sitting down at the dressing table Betty picked up the pink comb. "Over here, pet. I want to talk to you."

Shyly, my heart in my eyes, and my eyes on Betty, over I went.

It was beautiful.

She combed her hair. She stroked her throat. She leant nearer the glass, rubbing dainty ears. She rubbed her shoulder, pink-edged where the sun had burnt it. The arm below that shoulder, snowy, still unspoilt by sun, had two pretty marks, from vaccination and from wearing a bangle. I wished, suddenly, that I could touch those marks. I wished too I dare reach and caress the whole slender length of that lovely arm.

"Well, Gordon, why didn't you give that note of mine to your Uncle Conway?"

Startled, my eyes flew in panic to the pink-cloaked courtier.

His round crock eyes were big and staring, reminding me, suddenly, of both chocolate drops and the round, staring eyes of Mussolini.

"Well, Gordon?"

"Signor Mussolini," I stammered. "He—he rules Italy."

"And I rule this bedroom," Betty said. "Now, answer me."

"It—it was the speedway. Uncle promised to take me and I—I wanted to see Red Pope ride."

With a sigh, Betty turned back to the looking glass. "Oh, Gordon, you bad bad boy."

Hopelessly embarrassed, I fixed my gaze on a large ruby coloured ring lying in a corner of the dressing table tray.

"You do know your Uncle plays darts? Here at the York Arms? Well, he was wanted that night. For a match against another pub. One of the gentlemen who had agreed to play was taken ill, so we wanted your Uncle. Now do you understand? Your Uncle is a good player, Gordon."

Defiantly and indignantly, thinking of Red Pope, "Good enough to have his picture on a cigarette card?" I asked.

"Of course not, pet. But remember, you let us down."

I thought I would burst. Displeasure from Betty! I felt a kind of pain, unknown before.

To a suddenly blurred, pinky room, "Darts is a sissy sissy game!" I exploded. "Not like boxing, or—or speedway. You can get killed in speedway!"

"Betty! Betty! Where are you, Betty?" came a rising, husky wail from the next room.

With a final pat to gleaming hair, Betty rose, brushed by me to the window and, opening it, leant gracefully to her left.

"What is it, mother?"

"Has that boy gone? I'd like a massage."

Back inside came Betty. "Afraid you'll have to go now, Gordon."

There was a reason why, suddenly, I didn't mind leaving. My face was hot, my hands burnt. I lifted, trembling, the tumbler of lemonade.

"And best keep your visit secret. Agreed, pet?"

"All right."

At the top of the stairs she gave me a final, cheerful pat. "See you again some time. And be a good boy. I know that you can be."

A few stairs down I halted, listening. From the purple bedroom, popping on the dark musty air like frenziedly opened bottles, came cool fleshy slappings and pattings and curt sundry thwackings. And not just the slappings and thwackings of inexpert but happy massage, but harmony too, for, sounding like a beserk foxtrot, "Ooh ooh, ooh be joo ooh, boo boo ooh joo be ooh," I heard Betty crooning. Then, blending in, though less tunefully, her voice rather deeper, the uniquely foggy, ample sound of Auntie Alex, "Ooh ooh, ooh be joo ooh, boo boo, ooh joo be ooh!"

I had reached the giant trees along the drive to our town house, that daft sublime duet still jigging and curling in my head, before, abruptly and guiltily remembering, I brought from my pocket the large ruby-coloured ring, impulsively, quiveringly seized—while Betty leant from her window—from a corner of the dressing table tray. Thief! I thought, glancing, startled, at the noble frowning trees above me—like Aunt Wells multiplied, standing sternly in row, they looked. And why? Why my theft? To upset Betty as she'd upset me? Or because (oh yes, this mattered) it was something of hers? Whatever the reason, there it was, rich and lovely in my hand. A ring of ruby. Betty's ring.

Ooh ooh, ooh be joo ooh, I thought mindlessly, turning it over and over, ooh ooh, ooh be joo ooh.

5

The other day I buried Uncle Conway. Oh not really the other day, in fact a good few years ago now. But a post World War Two burial anyway, which, in terms of one's own ageing, does seem only the other day. We had trouble, later, with the headstone. The vicar wouldn't allow marble: quite unacceptable, so he pontificated, looking embarrassed. Yet the churchyard already flaunted several fine big marble tombs, though admittedly none of recent vintage. "Unacceptable now," the vicar repeated, offering us a plate of black grapes and a glass of wine, "quite quite unacceptable." Watching him conjure from nowhere a green grape which he gulpingly devoured, why, we asked? Embarrassment ebbing as the wine went down, our vicar explained. Apparently the whole thing was a hangover from the thirties, when Mussolini's troops marched, without invitation, into Ethiopia (then Abyssinia). The reaction, from the church, some boycott of Italian marble! All very worthy and understandable. So that was why, in the end, Uncle Conway settled to eternal rest without the grandeur of that particular kind of headstone. Standing one day at the graveside, hat in hand under the mournful trees, decaying wreaths piled to my right, brave new graves like giant oblong footmarks to my left, I thought how ironical it was that Uncle, admirer of the old Fascist regimes, should be denied Italian marble, and all because of that Abyssinian adventure which, at the time, he must have stoutly defended, though not, of course, as enthusiastically as he would have defended an adventure by Adolf.

"Ah, my boy, the church likes kicking sinners when they're down," Uncle would no doubt have said. "A stone hut where wind may not be passed except from the preacher's mouth, that's your church! Quite futile, damn it! Empty in every way, with vicars kicking like donkeys when anyone suggests just that!"

Oh, Uncle. You should, by rights, have been buried under a pub. Or cremated on a November bonfire under a swastika-emblazoned banner.

November. Yes, it was November that day, chill and autumnal, under the trees, at the graveside. Naturally my thoughts returned to summer, that summer of the pebble, the memorable summer of long ago.

Well, you have to try to keep warm, standing at a graveside in November.

It was frying-pan hot. Town house, as I peered through a bush, looked dead, windows and doors all shut.

I should not, of course, have been lurking in that bush at all. Normally, when Aunt and I trundled off to white house and the country on one of our frequent exiles, that was that. We never saw, or visited, Uncle Conway until conciliation time. Coming from school I never made the error of returning to the wrong house, nor, I imagine, did Aunt Wells after her shopping jaunts. Always we knew exactly where we belonged!

Only Sam, creaking from garden to garden, rump protestingly high, ignored protocol. "The needs of plants is paramount," he'd tell Aunt. "Beg pardon, but gaffer don't a-water nothing!" What Sam really thought I often wonder. Did he understand? Were Aunt and Uncle open books, their rifts clear, easy reading? Or did he think them just daft quaint gentry?

Gentry! How Aunt Wells loved that word!

"So and so is gentry through and through," she would say. "A gentleman farmer to his fingerprints, bless him. Conway, are you listening?"

"Gentleman farmers, pah!" Uncle would growl. "Left-over knights from olden days, more like. Tolerable only in pixy land."

"This is pixy land, Conway. Great Britain is pixy land."

"And Germany, I suppose, is the wicked giant. Woman, you make me ..."

How, at a sudden taut lifting of Aunt's lean head Uncle would abruptly quail into quiet! Not always, though. And never for long.

It was hot, then, the day of my furtive, guilty approach to Uncle Conway, currently alone and aloof at the town house. Though a half day I should have been at school, yelling for our cricket team! But cricket bored me. Much more interesting, I thought, to call on Uncle. What did he do, all by himself, day after day? His business? What business? Those trips to Germany, what were they for? Aunt Wells never explained, properly anyway. "There are books to be written," she would say, vaguely, with a sad, forlorn blink of at least one clear eye. Books to be written! What exactly did she mean? Cowboy books, did Aunt Wells mean that Uncle meant to write cowboy books? "No, Gordon," Aunt had told me, casting a pleading look to heaven, "I do not mean that your Uncle writes, or means to write, cowboy books. Or books about Red Indians. Really, I shall have to talk to you some time. About books, and real books!"

Books and real books! Wasn't that just like Aunt Wells? As for Uncle, he rarely touched a book, even real books like *Oliver Twist* or *Pilgrim's Progress*.

Or was I wrong? Was he, even now, as I lurked in the bush, reading Dickens?

Parting twigs, and gazing out at town house, I thought again

43

how dead it looked. I could almost sniff the mustiness, the dark rich blending of each room, each passage. On the first quiet picture-laden landing frail sunbeams would be arrayed like medallions; sunbeams, too, on the tall calm walls of the narrow upstairs lavatory. Beside the pan, stiff and cool in a white-pure basin, my old friend the brush ('Every lavatory,' as Aunt worthily put it, 'needs its pet hedgehog!') would be languishing and waiting. Everything, like the brush, long-living, comfortable and well-matched. Even the landing pictures, seen as clearly in my mind as the leaves before my eyes, reflecting only town house a dozen dusty echoing times; moulderingly framed daubs of darkly packed rooms in dark houses with the only brightness an occasional cloak or long white smoking pipe, the only grace an occasional pale-necked lady. My favourite painting—seen with longing, as I felt a sudden, natural urge!—the tall gaunt painting opposite the lavatory door of a bull about to charge. To sit, door open, self-imprisoned on the lavatory under the bull's knobbly eye, was, in itself, a tiny adventure! But although, from behind the bush, I could see the inside of the house I knew so well, in another sense I couldn't. A house forbidden, if only tacitly, wasn't surely quite the same? The curtains, half drawn, told nothing. The study blinds were down. Was Uncle in his study? Dozing away the afternoon, waistcoat unlatched, tummy quivering to each plump snore? Or downstairs, in the hall, stroking the bare arm of the china Grecian lady? Was he writing, doing crosswords? Might I catch a glimpse through a window of Uncle smoking or, listening, hear the sound of wireless or thud of brass-band music on the gramophone? Suppose I knocked, or rang the doorbell? "Cricket ended early," I could say, "and I thought I'd see how you were, Uncle Conway." And give him my best, most polite grimace!

As it happened, the side door of town house (the butcher, baker, candlestick-maker door, as Aunt Wells styled it) was unlocked. In I crept.

A very thin corridor, sunless. To the right, its walls a drab, patchy green, a room with a row of obsolete service bells, bells that, in my time at any rate, never had jangled and now never would.

"The unemployed!" Uncle always joked, voice ample with relish, as if, in that idle, rusting row he found the perfect sermon. "Just like soldiers. Orderly. In line. And that's the answer, damn it! Take the unemployed and make 'em soldiers, every man jack!"

On the left, giving a glimpse of knife, bread board, and yellow butter dish, the jar-festooned kitchen, while, at corridor's end, the heart of town house, the dark cramming encroachment of hall and rooms, stairs and pictures, the captivity of the evergreen plant, bowed like Job, the antiques, all bright and cheeky like Joseph in his coat of colours. And suddenly, as I hovered on tiptoe, the voice of Uncle Conway— like a whiplash splash of extra colour—coming from upstairs! Not, I quickly realised, the usual voice of Uncle Conway, though why I wasn't sure.

Up the stairs and along the landing, heart in mouth, to the open door of Uncle's study, a wickerwork basket of pale sunbeams on the landing wall flying, at my passing, tremulously apart.

Again, Uncle's voice.

"Piffle, Mr Quedgely, piffle!"

There was a tiny, rattling sound which made me think of films, with cowboys throwing dice. Was Uncle gambling, then? With a stetson on his round head?

Breathlessly, I looked into the study.

Uncle Conway was behind his desk. Not sitting but standing. And not so much standing as pacing, with little flaunting curls of impatient posterior, up and down. In one hand he brandished, like a baton, his old blue fountain pen, the other hand was clenched. On the desk, pinched to a mad, tormented pyramid, lay a newspaper.

Suddenly, turning, Uncle bent, testily rattling the pen and glaring at the paper.

"Germany exists. Agreed, Mr Quedgely? On that even you and I may surely agree?"

Eyes bulging, I gazed about the study. Whoever and wherever Mr Quedgely was, he was remarkably silent. And invisible.

"Now, it follows then, in view of the existence of Germany, that there has to be a German policy, both foreign and domestic. Are we still agreed, Mr Quedgely?"

If Quedgely disagreed, he didn't say so.

"Now, any responsible policy"—rattle rattle, on the desk,

with the fountain pen—"must answer German needs. If it doesn't, it isn't a German policy. Agreed, Mr Quedgely? The test of Herr Hitler, then"—rattle rattle—"will lie not in what we think of him—damn muddled rot!—but in how he meets those needs: the needs, dare I say it, of his own people! National security, the right to build. Calm, orderly economic growth. An army to keep Bolshevism at bay! These are modern German needs—British needs, too, Quedgely, if chaps like you could but understand!"

There wasn't, I finally realised, after squinting ferociously everywhere, even along the study ceiling, any Mr Quedgely. Uncle, shamefully, was talking to himself!

"No idea how Herr Hitler will solve all his problems," Uncle Conway said, "or what his policy may become. But there could, clearly"—voice, like a suddenly enlarged razor blade, lifting and flashing—"be an expansion of influence, a whitening, metaphorically speaking, of doorsteps over Europe. Is that, then, what we must fear? A whitening of European doorsteps?" A tiny, incredulous pause. "I say not, Mr Quedgely, I say not!"

And snap! went the fountain pen, breaking on the desk.

Was Uncle Conway mad?

Even at the time I didn't think so.

I, too, when alone, had talked to myself.

And what better, more justifiable soliloquy, than one enacted behind one's own desk, gesturing, banging, laying down the law? Putting, as Aunt Wells would say—though in a very different context, usually when recounting a sermon heard that Sunday, or recalling fragments of a day spent, in her youth, with straw-hatted, oar-toting, smiling clergymen at a lakeside conference for Sunday School teachers—the sore and weeping world to rights. Perhaps, also, Uncle was rehearsing, sowing future declamation for club or pub. But essentially—or so it seems in retrospect—it was a lonely, narcissistic game he played, hand spread, pleading, pen stabbing, fist pumping with sudden change of mood through layers of humbly twirling dust motes: in fact the great statesman being superbly, fulminatingly great.

Poor Mr Quedgely. He didn't have a chance!

Suddenly Uncle saw me. His eyes popped. His voice, in the shady, fruity air, leapt cuttingly.

46

"Gordon, stupid boy! Why aren't you at school, for heaven's sake? Or at the white house? I—I was practising a speech."

Ignoring this, and glancing sternly about, "Who's Mr Quedgely, Uncle Conway?" I asked.

"Mr Quedgely?"

Slowly, quiet now as a suddenly punctured rabbit, Uncle seated himself behind the desk. Opening, with quivering fingers, a drawer, he took out an aspirin bottle.

"Who's Mr Quedgely, Uncle Conway?"

"Quedgely? Oh, oh yes. A writer of stupid letters." Trying hard not to look red and discomfited, the way adults always do look when caught out playing games, Uncle Conway jerked his thumb at the crumpled newspaper on the desk. "You see, Gordon, only damn stupid people ever seem to write to papers. Or maybe it's just that the damn stupid letters are the ones that get printed! And this man Quedgely, whoever he may be, has written the most monstrous, stupid letter I've ever read. Completely and utterly unsympathetic to—to Germany and her problems." Opening the aspirin bottle Uncle shook out and swallowed, hastily, two of the round white tablets. "One for you, Gordon? No? Just as well."

It was then, incredibly enough, with the unappetizing aspirin bottle waving briefly under my nose before its quick withdrawal by a confused Uncle Conway, that, blinking, I saw, or thought I saw, Mr Quedgely. Quite suddenly, there he was, alive and languishing in the shades of Uncle Conway's study— a sad, morose little highwayman, waiting, on a chilly November night for a long overdue coach which he meant to rob! A heavily moustached little highwayman, as tired by the weight of his pistol as by waiting in fog! And, later, the same shivering little man (the coach never did arrive) at a nearby inn, with the ample bosom of the friendly landlady stretching out over his bed as she administered—yes, I actually remembered the name—Dr Limplow's Rich White Pills! The whole rheumaticky little tale, highwayman and all, an illustrated advertisement in an old Edwardian magazine owned by Aunt Wells! It was Uncle's aspirins that had brought—so vividly it was almost a vision—that old advert back to mind, and linked the little highwayman with the name of Quedgely. For surely, I thought, still blinking into space,

47

that was how anyone named Quedgely *would* look—worn out, frustrated, and half toppled by huge sad moustaches!

"Mr Quedgely wears moustaches, doesn't he?" I said, confidently, to Uncle. "Not a moustache like Hitler's, but bigger. With dew drops at each end."

"Herr Hitler, Gordon, Herr Hitler. And what in damnation are you talking about? How do I know what Quedgely looks like!"

"He's a highwayman, isn't he?" I said. "Or he would be, if there were still highwaymen." I paused, thoughtfully, thinking now of Herr Hitler's moustache. "Is Hitler a highwayman too, Uncle Conway?"

"Herr Hitler, Gordon. Herr!"

"You never say Herr Mussolini," I protested, "so why can't I say Hitler?"

"Signor Mussolini, Gordon, Signor Mussolini!"

"But you never say that. You just say Mussolini."

All around the ears Uncle Conway's rumpled, thinning hair was sticking out. He looked, I thought, increasingly wild. Startled, too, as if I'd genuinely surprised him.

"Why," I continued, unrelentingly, "do you just say Mussolini, Uncle Conway?"

"A matter of temperament, boy. Yes, that would be it, a matter of national temperament. Of being British." And, throwing back his head, Uncle Conway gulped another aspirin.

"Yes," I said, "but why don't you say Signor Mussolini?"

After a while, eyes almost desperately prayerful, Uncle Conway tottered round the desk.

"Your good aunt, Gordon," he said, presently, "would explain it this way. There are people one naturally thinks of as 'Mr'. There are others ..."

"I like Mussolini," I flared, unimpressed. "Hitler's got a daft moustache. It's dafter than Mr Quedgely's moustache!"

Uncle's mouth, clearly at a loss, opened, wavered silently and grotesquely, and then shut.

"In a scrap I bet Signor Mussolini would win! He's bigger than Hitler!"

Uncle Conway took a deep agonized breath. From that rusty breathing, and the watery, off-white width of his eyes, I knew that patience was ending. "That, Gordon, is doubtful," Uncle said, striving only too obviously for calm. "There are rumours … that Mussolini wears special, built-up shoes! However, I have nothing against Mussolini, or Italy, nothing at all. He has, I believe, done a fine job of government. Yes, indeed. Even the Italian trains, they say, now run on time. So I affirm," and Uncle's chest puffed out—one felt he needed the desk to bang at—"the competence of any man who can bring about that. We may say, I think, that despite the climate, and the church— two powerful and demoralising factors of Italian life—that there are certain clean hard commendable policy lines emanating forth. Yes, indeed, clean hard policy lines." Uncle, speaking now with deliberation, puffed out his chest a little further—it was, briefly, as if he'd forgotten me and had returned to lecturing the provocative, letter writing, invisible Mr Quedgely! "Not a bad epitaph," Uncle mused, breaking suddenly from his main flow, and looking wistful, "if it could be said, on one's tomb, that one had made the trains run on time. By Jove, no. Wouldn't mind something like that on my own marble, when, that is, I kick the bucket!"

Uncle kick the bucket! Young as I was, I suppose I knew that one day Uncle would do exactly that; but part of me at any rate found the notion of his dying quite fantastic. One had only to look at him, red-faced, breathing fierily away, smelling faintly of his last not-so-far-away drink, to know that Uncle Conway was much too real to die.

"You won't ever kick the bucket, Uncle Conway," I said, stoutly, "not ever!"

Uncle Conway looked at me, surprised, as well he might be.

"You may be right, Gordon," he said, smiling suddenly with a rare, pleased warmth. "All the same, if one did—die that is—be nice having something like that on one's marble!"

"Marble, Uncle Conway?"

"All the best tombs, of the best people," Uncle said, complacently, "are of finest Italian marble."

Uncle Conway's car, halted before the white house (after careful thought he had decided to return me personally) was something to be exclaimed over! There should at the least have been celebratory flags and blazing cannon! Instead there was Sam—a Sam who turned away, frowning scornfully and sniffing hard up his long tanned nose—to his job amidst the flowerbeds. Not, for him, pleasure at the sight of Uncle, or Uncle's car. "Cars," Sam had been heard to say, "especially a-coloured ones, fumes the air, and buggers up the bees!" And Uncle's car, though a respectable black with, here and there, one or two distinguished streaks of silver, was doubtless no better in Sam's eyes than any other car. "What I'd like," Uncle gritted, watching Sam bend over, "would be to put him in a bacon machine and slice off his rump. Slowly and carefully slice his buttocks. The man's a secret Bolshevik, I'm sure of it! He'd have my heart and guts out if he could, not to mention all my money!"

"Have you a lot of money, Uncle Conway?"

"Enough to exist on, anyway. Now, out you get. And next time you play truant don't come pestering me!"

As usual the front door was open. In we marched, Uncle muttering something about a quick word with Aunt Wells.

"And then I'm off, Gordon. Back to town house and a bit of peace. Hallo, what's that?"

We both, at the same time, heard the strange noise—and, strange it was, a soft forsaken bubbling occasionally broken, or enlivened by harsh, bellows-type huffings.

"God alive," said Uncle, loudly, glaring, with some bewilderment, at a nearby closed door, "it's coming from in there!"

"Yes," I said, listening, "it is!"

Taking one of his deep, rusty breaths, Uncle grasped the door-knob, trying, it seemed, to pierce the woodwork with his writhing eyes.

"Go on, Uncle," I urged. "Open up!"

After a trenchant pause, Uncle did just that. With considerable clumsiness, the knob sliding and bucking in his damp palm, he shoved open the door and stepped one pace inside.

"God alive!" he said again. "My sainted fish and chips!"

It was the big creamy lounge adorned by the orange tinted painting of the old-time sailing ship, and with the big green vase in an immaculate corner; and they were sitting decorously on two austere, spindle-legged chairs in the room's middle: Aunt Wells and little Mr George Edgar, Aunt Wells sitting erectly and gravely, Mr Edgar squatting and forlorn as a

50

dark-eyed toad, unshaven cheeks wet with big peeling unashamed tears.

"God alive!" Uncle said, for the third time, stepping back.

A slim hand sweeping up and down the length of her other, slightly thinner arm, out Aunt Wells swished, closing the door hurriedly and firmly on the sad wet scene within.

"And what, may I ask, are you doing here?"

"That ... man," Uncle said. "Who ...?"

"He came to collect his bicycle," Aunt Wells said, tartly. "His bicycle, that's all."

"But ... he's crying," Uncle said, looking with amazement and horror at the closed door. "A grown man, damn it, crying!"

"He's a piano tuner," I said, contemptuously, "and—and he's got a dead wife!"

"Into the kitchen, Gordon," Aunt said. "There's some milk and cake. No, not later, at once!"

"But ... can't I speak to Mr Edgar?" I wanted, suddenly, a close-up of all those shining tears.

"Kitchen, Gordon!"

Presently, from the kitchen, I heard Uncle's departing car. His last words, thundering down the passage, had not been comforting for Aunt or her little visitor. "At least make him work, make him tune the piano. Man's probably a damn Bolshevik, weeping crocodile tears for the sympathy of his betters!" Perhaps Mr Edgar overheard, for a little later, spindle-legged as Aunt's chairs, the notes of tentative piano-plucking filled the air. Unforgettable that plucking, its lop-sidedness settling, gradually, into a sad and fumbling familiar tune. The piano room, across the passage from the drawing-room, and holding a glass case of Aunt's best china, was rarely used by me, but I could imagine the little man, dark slightly baggy jacket neatly folded on a nearby chair, tall white collar fully exposed, prodding soberly away, his small tidy behind dutifully riveted to the stool, his pear-shaped nose—faintly red from the mopping up of tears—twitching nervily at every stark and plaintive note. Poor sad Mr Edgar, plonking and pining, tired as fading summer grass, frail, and robust, as a breeze. Yet such a silly little man, I thought, unrepentantly. Surely only Aunt Wells, with her fund of sympathy and patience, not to mention, as she herself put it, her 'good constitutional tummy', could stomach such an abject creature!

"Goodbye, and thank you," I heard her saying, some time after the last plonk had vibrated away into the hot endless afternoon. "And do, please, trust to time for recovery."

"Time's rosy stitch, sewing up our sorrows. Ah, to be sure," said Mr Edgar.

When, presently, Aunt appeared in the kitchen, her eyes were glistening.

"Now you're crying," I accused. "What is it?"

"Nothing, Gordon, nothing. Only, perhaps, that sometimes we must feel for others."

"Feel for others, Aunt Wells?"

"For the sorrow of others, Gordon. For great loss, in time, comes to each and every one of us."

6

It was easy enough to understand why Aunt Wells hated Germany. She had lost her sweetheart, or 'beloved', in one of the bleak and muddy battles of the Great War, and it was both natural and inevitable that she should hate (so far as her Christian nature would allow) the very name of Germany. "My original sweetheart," she would tell close friends, with that slight misting of her normally clear eyes, "perished ignobly in blood and filth, a German helmet—put there to hide his wound—across his poor British face, and not only that but dressed in a soldier's rough uniform, its quality as offensive to a man of sensibility as any cruel bullet or bayonet!" I often wonder, now, how jealous, if jealous at all, Uncle (who could wear the coarsest of underwear with equanimity) was of that 'original sweetheart', that 'man of sensibility'. Did such eulogising prick and sour him, and make him wilfully enthusiastic over Germany, and other matters painful to Aunt? Indeed, how account at all for an enthusiasm which could only result in strain and squabbling?

The answer, though at the time I didn't appreciate it, was given me by Aunt herself, one Saturday morning, in a little room on the top floor of town house. It was a room of dust, junk and memories. Old black Bibles and brown old books were everywhere, a discarded fire bellows, its formerly golden glory now badly tarnished, lay poking, as if for warmth, into an old velvet bonnet, playing cards (from Uncle's side of the family) half-tipped into an old blue chamberpot, the pot itself half-full of necklaces and brooches, mostly broken brooches that clawed nastily like gilt beetles, while, as in so many similar rooms in other houses, the room's dark corners bulged with unhung ancestry, monochrome pictures of elderly whiskered worthies and prudent high-collared dames—ancestors Aunt's side of the family.

"These pictures would be better at white house," I remember Aunt musing, as she gazed, reverently, at some great grandmother with a beaky nose and eyes all but faded to extinction. "Too prim and abstemious, my relatives, for Conway. Yet good, hardy working folk of the lower merchant class, all of them."

"Has Uncle got relatives, who looked like that?" I asked, pointing at a smugly bearded jug-eared man.

"I don't know, Gordon. Your Uncle's family were chiefly poor, leaving little in the way of pictures and heirlooms."

"Poor, Aunt Wells?"

"Yes, child. At least, except for one!"

That one (I learnt years later) was Redvers. Redvers, after first ripening, with rampant seed, the bodies of several English ladies—the ladies, as a result, unhappily brimful of child, and all at the same time!—had sailed blithely off to Holland and married a wealthy childless lady, and it was her money, every lovely blessed guilder of it, that came eventually to Conway. Quite a bounty it must have seemed. But not to Aunt Wells, for in an old thirties diary of hers I recently found this observation: 'The tragedy of that money! Political extremism! Is there anything worse?' Which does, perhaps, explain. Uncle, suddenly rich, had developed a right-wing fetish, which had led to idolatry of Germany, not from spite of Aunt, or her former sweetheart, but from a conviction that only Fascism could defend the rights of money and property. A common enough belief of the time, and apparently Uncle's. No doubt, though, the ghost of Aunt's beloved did play some small part—that and Aunt's own extreme loathing for things Teutonic.

I wish, however, Aunt had mentioned Redvers and his ladies on that morning in the junk room! It might have been worth the telling to see her blush, not so much with disapproval as with delicacy and warmth. For Aunt was warm, with a great and varied delicacy of feeling. I sensed it even then.

Although she believed in heaven, to where, presumably, her soul would one day floatingly repair, Aunt did not, sensibly enough, hanker for a premature take off. Life, despite Germany and Uncle's politics, was as sweet to her as most. "Life is never so bad that death can be agreeable," was, in fact, one of her favourite sayings, a saying usually bravely uttered during a bad headache, or a bout of genteel diarrhoea, or on a morning when apparently securely bottled fruit was found to have gone mouldy. It was a saying, free from politics, that even Uncle Conway could accept, though not without his usual hearty bellicosity. Once, flushed, I remember, from his Sunday trip to the York Arms, "Certainly there's nothing agreeable about death," he told us, grandly, with a matching Olympian jab at wilting treacle pudding, "and that's partly because there's nothing agreeable about heaven, either. Harps, are there? Fine. But are they in rows, dozens and dozens of rows, far as the eye can see, and is every harpist dressed the same? Because if not," pause for breath and another lofty jab, "then heaven's a damn and damnable disgrace!"

"What," Aunt Wells asked, "is the point of having, in heaven, rows of harpists all dressed the same?"

'There's beauty in order, Wells. Imagine a thousand harpists, a thousand arms, lifting, falling, lifting, falling, all at the same time."

Was Uncle thinking admiringly of Hitler addressing row upon row of faithful adherents? Was he thinking of a thousand outflung arms saluting as one?

"Rum tum, rum tum, rumpety tum, tumpety rum!" I said, inconsequentially (through a mouthful of pudding) from the far end of the table.

For once, Uncle decided to note my intervention.

"Why aren't you in the Scouts? Wells, Gordon should be in the Scouts!"

"Gordon," Aunt Wells said, "will never, as long as I live, join anything even remotely military."

"He'll have to eventually. When we fight Bolshevism."

"Gordon will never join anything even remotely military."

"A sensible, practical alliance with the realist powers. The only way," Uncle said.

"Mr Agate doesn't believe so. He has the gravest reservations about Germany."

"Agate! Agate! That pale-blue Parliamentary puppy, wagging his fluffy new tail. Why we elected him I can't think!" A piece of pudding, as Uncle waved his fork, spun across into Aunt's decorously high Sunday neckline, vanishing out of sight and leaving, like a golden worm-cast, a compact trail of treacle on her fine skin. This, though, except for a guilty blink, Uncle superbly ignored, instead stabbing, fork almost parallel with the table, into the tatters of his pudding. "No, Wells, my dear, there's only one question. Which do you prefer? The shoe-polish powers, black and brown and gleaming, neat and tidy, or the other kind?"

"The other kind," Aunt retorted, squinting and shuddering as she mopped up syrup and hunted the vanished piece of pudding. "Anything rather than the brownshirts or blackshirts, or whatever those dreadful Germans and Italians call themselves!"

"If only," Uncle raged, "you'd take a German holiday with me, see for yourself!"

"Gordon," Aunt Wells said, "you cannot separate treacle from the rest of the pudding. Kindly do not try!"

"As for Agate, our new so called MP," Uncle raged afresh, cupping his small bursting mouth and furiously working to and fro his light-tan-and-gold, treacle-pudding-flecked tongue, "just wait till his next call here. Reservations about Germany, has he? I'll give him reservations, squarely on the meat of his new timid pale-blue Parliamentary pants!"

"You'll do no such thing," Aunt said, angrily. "You'll behave yourself." But Uncle, looking suddenly contented as well as malicious, said no more, merely resuming, with crafty noddings and blinkings, his grand attack upon the dwindling and, by now, chilly treacle pudding.

In the quietest corner of our town house garden, rather like a big broken snail shell, with varying patchy shades of brown and a look of brittle rusticity, was the summerhouse: a summerhouse splashed by flowers, for all the tallest, brightest flowers bloomed about it. The veranda looked glued together, as warm and anyhow as a conglomeration of sticks and old leaves. The veranda chairs, glimpsed between the flowers, looked ill-assorted, and were. There was a big, comfortable three-legged cane chair, partly resting on an old tall tool box, and with a black, hole-riddled umbrella, unfurled, strapped to the rear chair rim, where Uncle Conway, wearing his summer straw—its wide black band zealously renewed each year—his shoes only just brushing the boards, liked to sit and nap. There was a plain little chair for me, and a straightback, once handsome survivor of a former dining-room set, and now dappled and peeling from too much sun, for Aunt Wells. There was also, behind the chairs—and this really made it a summerhouse—a tiny room. This room, full of companionable insects and made of rough warm wood, was where Aunt's old umbrellas all eventually came to rest, piled in one of the corners to rot and wither and make, whenever a gale blew through, their last grey and black and dark-blue rustlings. Sam, kept busy elsewhere, did little to tidy or preserve the place, although he had, peculiarly enough, given it its one strange, baleful ornament, a big fanciful crouching rat cast in cheap and glaring china. "A-won it at the fair," was all he'd said, dumping it regretfully beside the brollies, and adding, lamely, "The missus can't abide it!" Aside from the rat, dulling over as it crouched and waited, and a few old watering cans and big rogue broken-handled spades, the summerhouse was empty. Oh, there was a light bulb, but not in the roof. It lay in a corner like a cracked and ghastly giant eye.

Down along the crazy-paving path towards this summerhouse came Aunt Wells. It was the afternoon of the day of the treacle pudding, and Aunt looked barely recovered. She had changed her dress, and looked—despite the golden fluffy ripples at throat and wrists of the new, prettier dress—ominously severe. Looking carefully at me, she sat down on her straightback. Her thin graceful hands came suddenly, coldly together in her lap.

"Now that we are alone, Gordon, I wish to say how sorry I am that I was unable to accompany you to church this morning."

"Doesn't matter, Aunt Wells. You were busy."

Aunt arranged across her hair a handkerchief, a long blue corner hanging down between her eyes and along her nose like a fine new flag draped against a cathedral interior.

"Indeed I was busy. Amongst other things, tidying your room." Aunt lifted her slender fingers. "And I found this."

She was holding a ring. A ruby ring!

Huddled in the quilted depth of Uncle's chair, betrayed by my own daft carelessness, what could I say or do except silently and miserably swing my feet?

"We have a long hot afternoon ahead of us," Aunt Wells said. "By the end of it, I want the truth."

Writhing in my mind I tried desperately to summon demons from the room behind me, to make the crouching rat come creeping across the boards between Aunt's feet. If only it could eat her, Aunt Wells and her pretty dress vanishing in one vast gulp! Dropping, on her way into the rat's mouth, only the ring.

"I am waiting, Gordon, with ample disquiet. Shall I call your Uncle?"

"The York Arms," I spluttered. "I—I got it from the York Arms!"

The handkerchief, jerking, dropped at last. Aunt did not even stoop to pick it up. It lay unheeded in the sunshine and dust of the veranda boards.

"The York Arms?"

"Y-yes."

"The public house?"

"One of the ladies there knows me," I said, looking despairingly up into the old black cullender of an umbrella above me. "I was passing, and the lady gave me lemonade."

Aunt's eyes, too, looked black, the way they looked on Sunday lunch times as we passed the York Arms and she thought of Uncle inside drinking.

"And?"

"I—I saw the ring on the floor and picked it up. I—I forgot to give it back."

It was the best I could do. Not very good, but the best I could do. Throat dry and heart hammering, I waited.

Stooping at last to pick up the handkerchief, her arm stiff as a pole, "This ... lady," Aunt said, carefully. "Not—not a German?"

I was astonished. "No, Aunt Wells!"

Aunt, if only fractionally, relaxed. Pulling the handkerchief up and down between her hands, she gave me several long considering looks.

Better, I thought, say no more. Judgment, with Aunt Wells, always followed long considering looks.

"Very well, Gordon. I accept your explanation."

My heart leapt; though prematurely, for Aunt was looking strangely bleak.

"But I cannot, Gordon, spare the rod. The ring must be returned. And you must return it!"

I looked at her, incredulously. Aunt Wells was sitting so straightly that her straightback chair seemed curved.

"Oh don't worry, Gordon. I hate the idea of your having any contact at all with a public house. It is my punishment, too, that you should have to go. However," and Aunt's eyes raked me firmly over, "young as you are, you are old enough to be a man!"

"But men smoke cigarettes," I said, hopefully, "and I don't! And—and can't Uncle Conway take the ring back? Couldn't—couldn't he say he found it? And what of Sunday school? I can't miss Sunday school!"

Liberating the handkerchief, Aunt let it drop precisely into her lap. A tiny gesture, and a final one.

"All right, Aunt," I said, wretchedly. "I—I'll return it!"

"Excellent, Gordon. And after you have discharged your task—with a full and polite apology—you will find me waiting for you in the park. It is," she added, looking upwards, and speaking as if determined to find at least some good not only in the azure afternoon sky but in the day as a whole, "fine weather for sitting out. And that, Gordon, is what I shall be doing in the park. Sitting out, and waiting for you!"

It was exactly as before, the afternoon glinting and quiet, the old dustbins huddled to one side of the bent step, the tree sweeping over the urinal like a dark-green brush. The side door open, and that same look of dowdy dark-brown calm within.

Quaking, I mounted the step and took a closer peep. The bike with bar of blue still leant in the passage; the stairs climbed dustily. Only the skirting board, now fully painted, was different, and although the reek of paint had gone the new colour, silvery as snail tracks, looked glisteningly pure.

What now, I wondered? Should I rap on the door, or strike the bannisters, or just call out? How could Aunt Wells have inflicted such agony on me?

"I shall wait here," Aunt Wells had said, in the park. Her bench, under a tree, had been scrutinised for dirt, wet paint and bird splashings, the branches immediately overhead examined for prankish squirrels. Sternly she had crossed her ankles and looked thinly away at the boats on the lake. It had seemed, as I stood miserably by, that she would never again relent. "You will return as promptly as possible," she had said, suddenly. "And remember, please," leaning forward, the ruffles at her throat shuffling together like golden playing card backs, "that I am not far away. If there is trouble, fetch me. Or better, bring the person in question here, to see me!" A pause, and then, softly, "Remember also, Gordon, that I trust you." A typical act of faith? Perhaps. Uncle Conway, despite his thunderous and eternal praise of fraülein—"Big blonde beauts, flaxen-haired yum yums!"—Aunt Wells tried to trust. To trust me was at least easier!

In the hall she might have doubted. For, suddenly weakening, I turned to leave.

As I did, between the jamb and partly opened door of a small room on my right, a door ending almost where the stairs began, I thought I caught a movement. Thinking it might be a rat—a real one this time, for an abrupt, stealthy rustling could be heard—I looked timidly in.

It was a rather derelict, purposeless room, with broken chairs, two furry old dart boards on the faded carpet—grey carpet, with bits of ghostly, trampled red—and, pushed away under a cheap mournful sideboard, two empty crates and a lonely, empty beer bottle. There was also a piano, old and tawny, in places its wood almost black. Leafing, with pale fingers, through a heap of sheet music on the dusty top, was Betty!

"H-hallo!"

Even I was startled by my own weird painful squeak!

Betty, really taken by surprise, turned quickly about with

arms and papers raised as if to ward off mice.

"Oh! Oh gosh! It's you, pet."

I said nothing.

Recovering her breath, and laughing a little, Betty, after giving the stool of the piano—old and creaking and topped by balding plush—a gay, relieved whirl, sat firmly down on it and waved me inside the room. "Now you're here, young squeaker, let's see how fond you are of music!"

Again, I said nothing.

Imperturbably Betty swivelled round. Notes, chunky and bright, filled the drab little room.

"Don't really play from music," she murmured. "Just by ear."

Then, as suddenly finishing, up she jumped.

"Well, will I do? Is my playing good enough? Tell you what, let's dance!"

Around we romped, hot awkward hands in Betty's hands, Betty's voice trailing melody.

"Please," I gasped. "I—I've come about the ring!"

The dancing stopped.

"The ring?" Betty said, staring. "Oh, my ruby ring! I see."

"I—I picked it up off the tray," I said, frantically, "and—and forgot to put it back!"

"I see. And where is it now?"

"Here. Just the same. Not even a tiny scratch!"

Hopping, now, with eagerness as well as dread, I gave Betty the ruby-coloured ring.

"Sit down a tick," she invited. "Yes, fine. On the piano stool."

Miserably aloof on the stool, I watched my knees.

"I wondered, we all wondered, where it went. Somehow we never thought of you."

"Sorry," I muttered.

"Well, I'm glad to see it back. You see, pet, Jack bought it for me. Jack Brightside, my gentleman friend. He travels for the jokes mail-order house in Cathedral Lane."

"Jokes house?"

"Oh you know, pet. Cushions that squeak in a naughty way. Dirty Fido doggy jokes! Beetles that aren't, and ink blots that are only tin. That's Jack's bike in the hall, by the way."

"It was there when I came before. Can't he ride it?"

She laughed. "Jack's away at present, and his landlady doesn't like bikes cluttering things up."

"I like *motor* bikes!"

"So does Jack, only he can't afford one."

"He bought the ring."

"Well, yes. I guess he must have saved for that."

"Perhaps he got it from Woolworths. Things don't cost much there. Only threepence or sixpence."

"Well, maybe it didn't cost all that much. But it's pretty, isn't it? And it must have attracted you. Well, you kept it, didn't you?"

Blushing I stared at her hand, now bearing the ring. Often, in the sanctuary of my bedroom, with the trees outside rustling warmly, and the sounds of town house—Aunt Wells whisking eggs, Uncle Conway slamming his study door, Mrs Hampton and Sam quarrelling—vaguely heard and reassuring, I'd tried on the ring. And always, strongly and beguilingly recalled, her strange lovely nearness, her beautiful arms. For the ring, red ring, had lived with her. On that dressing table tray. Amidst powder and hairpins. Her powder. Her pins.

It had brought, had that little magical ring, something of the wonder of her bedroom to my bedroom.

"Was it a present? A birthday present?" I asked, for something to say.

"Wrong, Gordon. This came at Christmas. My birthday's on the first of next month."

"How old are you?"

She laughed again. "That isn't gallant, pet. If I said twenty-two you'd think me an old, old lady, so I won't say it! Instead I'll let you light my cigarette. Just like Jack does!"

Bare arm languorously outstretched, she took from the piano top behind me—oh the sweet whiff of her as she leant across—matches and cigarettes, and gave me the match box. I gulped into her blouse. It was cream-coloured with crotchet dottings of red and green. Tit ·hills, I thought suddenly, remembering Auntie Alex—did Betty have tit hills that looked the same as her mother's? Whip-cream mounds with nuts!

My body flamed. My eyes misted. Matches tumbled.

Clucking tenderly, Betty bent for the box. "Really, duck. What are you thinking of?"

Giving me back the matches, she put a cigarette between soft vivid lips.

"Now, strike," she ordered. "No, not like that! Strike with the match moving away from you."

Strike!

She leant forward, fierce nails, like the red talon tips of Aunt Wells's favourite cactus, around my knee.

Strike!

Even now, decades later, that word still recalls Betty, and that moment in the little room just off the hall of the York Arms.

"There. I knew you could do it!"

Smoke, dusty yet beautiful—was it not her very breath?—blew around me. My eyes watered. I coughed.

Quite suddenly, I reached out and touched her arm.

It was smooth and cool, like one of the benign old marble mantelpieces at white house. Only not like one of the benign old marble mantelpieces at white house!

My finger moved down, and then quickly away.

"Smooth, isn't it?" Betty said.

She was smiling a trifle sadly, as if, for the first time, she understood something.

"I—I ought to go now," I said, strangely shamed, feeling the piano stool on fire beneath me, yet happy too. "Aunt—Aunt Wells is waiting for me in the park!"

In the park Aunt Wells was sitting on the same bench. Her head, turned towards the lake, made me think of heads on pennies—regal, and not to be disturbed! I had the feeling there ought to be a door on which to knock, so private did she look. Was she, I wonder, thinking of me? Or of Uncle Conway?

"I—I'm back, Aunt Wells!"

She turned then, looking steadfastly at me. "Ah, Gordon. You returned the ring?"

"Yes, Aunt Wells."

She leant and put her arms about me. After a moment, I pulled away.

"I'm proud of you, Gordon. You've courage."

I nodded, head partly turned, the shine of the nearby water half in, half out of, the corner of my eye.

"And courage, Gordon, is what our Christian faith requires. It isn't easy."

"No, Aunt Wells."

She turned, looking once again towards the lake. The sun, fully in her eyes, was like a sudden melting of much that lay within.

"Do you know, Gordon, I feel quite outrageous. Happy. And I think that you're the reason. In fact, I'm certain. So," she reached, lifting with a warm thin finger my startled chin, "just to celebrate we'll go boating! Yes, and you may even try to row a little! After all, Gordon, I don't really think there'll be broken harp-strings in heaven over just one gentle naughty little Sabbath escapade, do you?"

7

Although it was Saturday Mrs Hampton usually arrived to dust politely here and there, and, less politely, make the beds. No one in all my life, and this I swear even today, ever made beds quite like Mrs Hampton. Beds, to her, were like pepper pots or salt cellars with the holes bunged up. It was almost hurtful to see her madly shaking pillows, madly shaking sheets, leaning down to pound or bruise a counterpane, or smash white-fisted at a bolster, rudely puffing and groaning while, with her other meaty, porridge-coloured arm, wrestling on a clean cover. Despite laughter lines that spoke of inner kindness, Mrs Hampton's face at such times was quite wild, great lips apart, big tongue lolling steamily out, broad pink cheeks mildewy with damp, and fine bleached hair.

It was a Saturday of Saturdays, with the sky over town house looking like the porcelain blue of one of Uncle's finest pieces. From a summerhouse still cool and quiet from night chill and the vanished dawn, I took the lonely china rat, carefully dusted it over with Aunt's whitest, cleanest kitchen towel, and then, gleefully and artfully, dumped the sinister crouching ornament inside my unmade bed.

Waiting downstairs, as the minutes of that sunlit morning ticked away, was like waiting for eternity.

First, I knew, Mrs Hampton would dust her way upstairs, nibbling and winkling (with her angry red duster) at whatever caught her fancy, the frame of a picture, the breast of a vase, the knob of a banister rail. Even an occasional flap, mild but clearly censorial, at one of the many shadows that filled each and every painting! "That there blessed moon needs cleaning," she always said of one particularly gloomy effort. "Why, if I'd courted Hampton under a moon like that I'd have gone to my wedding night heavier than a Welsh dresser. It's in the dark that evil happens, that I do know!" Then, the stairs navigated, the inevitable prelude to the raking, shaking, and baking of beds, a trip to the lavatory, in itself a somewhat desperate affair! Once, moving on quiet fleet feet, I'd glimpsed her sitting there, huge arms outstretched, hands flat against the narrow walls, homely face lathered in shame at the richest, loudest tinkling ever heard. "Are you all right, Mrs H?" I'd asked, rooted. "Run, quick, and get me a peppermint," the good soul had gasped. "Quickly, now!"

What presence of mind! A peppermint! Off I'd scampered, and by the time I'd returned Mrs Hampton was in a bedroom, pommeling as if her heart, and dignity, would break.

And so, begrudging the lost sunlit minutes that filled the garden, touching summerhouse and the tall flowers and the dewy lawn with all the promise of a hot and endless day, I waited in the hall.

Would dusting, tinkling, never end? Would she never find the rat?

"Wheeeeeeeeeeeeeeeeeeee! Ahhhhhhhhhhhhhhhhhh! Wheeeeeeeeeeeeahhhhhhhhhhhhhhhhhhhh!"

It was the most curious, most sobbing of wails.

I heard Aunt Wells, in the kitchen, dropping a saucepan; Uncle Conway bursting from the library.

And I saw, weeping and lurching down the stairs, hands and forearms jerking together in a crazy image of prayer, Mrs H!

"In the boy's bed, under the sheet! A rat, a rat, a terrible sleeping rat!"

"Sleeping? How do you know that? Might—might it not be dead?" Uncle Conway asked, looking uneasily upwards.

"Conway, do something!" Aunt cried, cradling Mrs Hampton as if she were gold.

Without further ado Uncle opened the door and called to Sam. Sam, only recently arrived, came unwillingly, boots dragging, the fingers of each earthy hand poised for a disdainful snap, eyebrows bunched in shaggy reproach.

"Frit, eh," he said, nearly spitting, and looking especially hard at Uncle. "A-frit of a little rat?"

Uncle turned pale. Only his blue, criss-cross veins kept their colour.

"Rats, damn it, aren't my province. Get upstairs and do something!"

"Please, Sam," Aunt said. "Mrs Hampton's very upset."

"I ain't a-taking my boots off," Sam said, glaring at the stairs.

"I quite agree," Aunt said, bravely. "I know how long it takes you to put them on, and how painful your rheumatism is. Besides, they don't look muddy to me."

"I ain't a-taking my boots off. Not if they was muddy," Sam amended.

"Damn Bolshevik!" Uncle muttered.

Suspiciously, one hand on hip, one clutching his rump, Sam half-turned.

"A-frit of a little rat! Don't that beat the band?"

"Oh it wasn't little, horrible crouching thing! All I can say is thank the lord my carrying days are over, else poor Hampton might have had a shock!"

"There, there," Aunt said, patting Mrs Hampton's shoulder, "there, there."

"What are carrying days?" I asked.

"I'm a-going up," Sam proclaimed, rough nails biting into the polished hand-rail. "I'm a-going up, boots and all!"

The hall, as Sam vanished, fell silent. Uneasy now, I held my breath.

Presently, holding the china rat out of sight, presumably against the warmth of his rump, down the stairs lurched Sam.

"What news?" Aunt asked, quickly and calmly. "Did you find it?"

Uncle took a backwards step. "If you've got it in your hand, say so, damn it! Couldn't you just throw the thing through the bedroom window and break its neck?"

"Oh, I'm off home!" Mrs Hampton, also retreating, began to sob again.

"Wait, missus, wait."

Slowly, with obvious relish, Sam brought the china rat into view.

Mrs Hampton was the first to recover.

"Why, that old junk from the summerhouse!" she said, angrily.

"A-won it at the fair, I did. This was hand a-picked from nigh on a hundred ornaments. Dogs, cats, I even remembers a big green fish."

"Scandalous!" said Mrs Hampton.

"Oh, take the damn thing out," snapped Uncle Conway.

Temper, pale as the artichokes he pulled cantankerously up each late autumn, drained Sam's cheeks. A gift, that china rat, if only for the summerhouse. A gift to his betters, and held in contempt!

"That's me thanks, then. Damn thing, eh? Time he went a-packing then, I'd judge!"

And out, tossed through the open front door, sailed the china rat, hitting, in the chest, a dapper little man who happened, with the greatest of ill fortune, to be exactly half-way up the middle of the drive.

"Mr Agate," Aunt Wells gasped, fluttering. "Why, it's dear Mr Agate!"

Whether Mr Agate was hurt, or even surprised, was impossible to tell.

Twisting in the dust the ferrule of a dark grey umbrella, he came briskly on towards the porch.

"A terribly bad moment for a social call. A terribly bad moment. Am I right?"

"Oh no, no you're not right! Please do come in!" Aunt Wells's early-morning apron had, by now, wriggled as completely from view as had Sam and Mrs Hampton.

"Just popped from the club. Can't stay for long as I have appointments with constituents. But I did," said Mr Agate, suddenly turning to Uncle, "wish to thank your good lady, who, with other good ladies, so bountifully helped at our recent fête."

"Please do come in," Aunt Wells repeated. "I insist, at the

very least, upon brushing your suit. Our gardener, I fear, lost his temper."

Mr Agate grinned. "Even in Parliament missiles aren't unknown. We, too, have our, er, domestic altercations."

Inside, with Aunt Wells hovering anxiously over him (Mrs H had been ordered to prepare coffee) Mr Agate sat neatly down, still holding, between immaculate knees, the dark-grey umbrella. Uncle Conway, breathing hard, his chest puffed up and out like the lectern at our church, stood a little way off. Aunt would, I think, have preferred his exclusion, so obviously was he writhing with contentious vexation, but how to accomplish this must have been beyond her. My own presence, cuddling low with bulging eyes in a big cushiony chair, went largely unnoticed.

"The coffee won't be long," Aunt said. "You will, of course, take a biscuit?"

"Of course. Of course. I always take the biscuit, especially from a charming lady!"

Although much more elegant and bland, and, perhaps, superficially merry, Mr Agate reminded me somehow of Mr Edgar, and not only in stature. His nose wasn't pear-shaped but thin, leaning slightly to one side under pat black eyebrows; but there was in his manner that same touch of the unctuous, that same resolute deference towards Aunt Wells. Everything she did and said clearly had his approbation. No bicycle clips on the perfect trousers, but a perpetual gentlemanly plucking, with dainty groomed finger, at the shining crease that somehow, in a strange way, played court to Aunt's notion that here, indeed, was a gentleman.

"Now you're there," Uncle said, pointing vaguely south east, no doubt with London and Parliament in mind, "what do you make of it? Not what Cromwell would have wanted or tolerated, eh?"

"Ah, coffee," Mr Agate said, as in Mrs Hampton sidled. "And most welcome, too!"

Uncle Conway, standing near my chair, waved away his cup. His breath, floating down, made me wonder if, earlier, in the library, he'd been both browsing and drinking. The library, strangely enough, had only one bookcase—the rest being all over the place—but that one bookcase often faintly smelt the way Uncle smelt after returning from the York Arms. How I wish, now, that I'd been more of a bookworm! There might well have been many a delightful little bottle, or flask, tucked away behind the teeming leathery volumes, adding piquancy and adventure to staid memoirs, collections of sermons (each page thick and clammy) and mouldering, yellow-spotted, unread verse.

"Well, Agate, when is the government waking up? Damn it, I voted for action, for the marshalling of power. I want Britain like a falcon—high, strong, cruel!"

"Cruel?" murmured Mr Agate, looking deep into his coffee.

Stepping forward, Uncle Conway upturned a pink, urgent thumb.

"At home I want the ordered society. An end to discord. Bigger army. Vigilante police."

The umbrella, as if rigid with disapproval, did not move between Mr Agate's knees.

"Well, Agate?"

"Conway," said Aunt Wells, "I—"

"Wells, get the man a brandy. Not that he deserves it. Playing merry hell with our vote!"

Aunt Wells turned wan. Not just because of Uncle's rudeness, but also because the only brandy officially in the house was kept for medication. And no one was ill!

"I am," said Mr Agate, no longer merry, "quite content with this delicious coffee!"

"Tell you a secret, Agate," Uncle said. "The world's full of chaps like you. Good dishonest chaps who drink morning coffee, decline brandy, and think they're somehow superior! But the world's not a tea party for sissies! The world's real, Agate, real and tough. No room in it for paper tigers. All paper tigers can do, with or without brandy, is sire other paper tigers!" Uncle paused, both thumbs stabbing in the direction of Mr Agate's frozen knees. "Know what I think? Know what my solution for Britain is? In a nut-shell, stiffen the racial backbone! And not even with brandy. Oh dear no! With fraülein, Agate, fraülein!"

"Conway, please!"

But Uncle, his voice suddenly as round and confidential as his tummy, only bent closer to the MP.

"Import a few hundred fraülein. Only the best. Virile

wenches from the Rhineland. The best blood, the fullest breasts, the most strapping thighs! The result, babies that are babies, not filleted coffee-swilling milksops! A touch of Prussian blue, of the old military iron, that's what British babies need!"

Aunt Wells looked as if she couldn't speak, and never would again.

It was, not surprisingly perhaps, Mr Agate who first rallied.

"A lively man, your husband," he said, smiling bravely at Aunt. "Must use all that in a speech. The House likes humour."

"A touch of the goosestep!" Uncle roared, leaping suddenly forward and all but saluting. "A touch of the goosestep!"

It was a terrible moment. Uncle had really lost his temper. Even I trembled.

Mr Agate, gazing down at his creases, appeared also to be gazing from under those neat brows at Aunt Wells, as if awaiting, deferentially, her intervention.

"Conway … occasionally visits Germany," Aunt faltered, too spent for even anger. "He—he's writing a book about Germany."

"Ah, indeed. Most interesting. I shall await its publication with impatience. However, the theory just propounded is, I think, hardly original and, worse, hardly practical. Politics, as one speedily learns in the House, is essentially the art of the possible."

"Dung!" Uncle Conway raged. "Dung, vomit and all waste matter!"

The umbrella, at long last, slid an appalled inch forward.

"Sir! Please!"

But Uncle couldn't, or wouldn't, stop.

"The House! The House! What a bloody daft expression. Makes me think of rooms and lamp standards and—and wall-paper. The gutless kind of wall-paper, with pink roses and a sissy pink border!"

"Thank you, Conway," Aunt Wells said. Abruptly she was tall again. Tall, and in command.

"If you don't mind, I'll look after Mr Agate."

Into the quiet that followed I threw my first remark.

"Hitler paints houses, doesn't he? Does he stick on wall-paper as well? Wall-paper with roses?"

"Herr Hitler," Uncle muttered, a trifle less ferociously, "was formerly an artist. Not a damned house-painter, as the ignorant suppose, but a palette-and-easel man!"

I looked at Mr Agate. "I like Mussolini. Do you?" Mr Agate positively looked through his trousers. "Well—"

"Gordon," I said. "My name's Gordon."

"And you will leave the room this instant, Gordon." Aunt's eyes were like needles.

"Alas, and so must I leave. Appointments, as I said. But I must thank you again, both for the excellent coffee and for your recent help."

"Dear Mr Agate," Aunt said, weakly. "So good of you to call. What would we do without you? Without the right man in?"

"Quite," said Mr Agate, twirling his umbrella just once, and ignoring Uncle as he headed for the door. "I think we may fairly claim to be the party of—"

The smooth voice faded as Aunt swept him away. He might have been another apron, so efficiently did he vanish.

Suddenly, lifting the poker, Uncle chucked it in the grate.

"Smug devil. Never lost his temper. Never lost his temper!"

Back came Aunt. The lashes about her eyes darker than I'd ever known them.

"Conway, it was unforgivable! A gentleman like Mr Agate—"

"Gentleman, pah! I've said it before, damn fellow smells money here. Only reason he calls!"

Aunt Wells began to cry. "I'm off to the white house. I cannot bear another minute of this."

As Uncle flung through the door and into the drive I scampered after. The trees along the drive looked like shadowy dignified bankers only partially blocking a profligate sunshine as I asked, breathlessly, "Uncle Conway, where are you going?"

"Off for a drink, boy. What else?"

"Please, take me with you then. I—I want to see you play."

Uncle Conway halted. His face turned dark as Aunt's lashes. "Play? Play what?"

"Darts, Uncle Conway. Darts, of course."

But with a testy sweep of his arm, Uncle had already moved away. "Off and help your aunt. By now, if I know her, she'll be packing."

70

She was. Peeping in I saw a small suitcase on a chair and Aunt sitting on both chair and suitcase, trying, with her noble behind, to close the always difficult lid.

"Gordon," she called, as I moved away. "See if Sam, or Mrs Hampton, have cleared the drive."

"Cleared the drive, Aunt?"

"Of that wretched china rat. Those pieces could be dangerous."

Someone had cleared the drive. When I looked in the dustbin there inside were all the sad, cheap, shattered pieces.

Suddenly I felt near to tears, for instead of playing a joke on Mrs Hampton I could have put the china rat into one of Aunt's old shoe boxes and, on the first day of next month, have given him to Betty—as a birthday present!

A birthday present for Betty. What a chance I'd missed!

8

Looking back to that long hot summer of the pebble I remember Dapperings as just about the most shady of all the big stores in our town. There were, in that old-fashioned emporium, so many cool dark corners, so many counters made dark and cool, in drapery anyway, by heaps of material cold to the touch, so many high stools on cold dark legs. Stools sometimes cool, sometimes warm from the previous sitter, but always hard — even for a boy. I remember the darkly dressed gentlemen and pleasant ladies who assisted, and I remember the customers, the men also soberly dressed, the ladies also pleasant. Indeed some of the ladies — before they became, by the grace of marriage, ladies—had themselves probably worked in the great cool store. Dapperings, in fact, was universally well regarded, even beloved, for not only the rich of our town but also the poor, dowdy and busy as brown moths, haunted the dark labyrinths in search of bargains. There were always bargains at Dapperings. Even in Soft Furnishings. I remember, best of all perhaps, Soft Furnishings, a round vaulted department, its air full of clean spinning dust from the thudding reels of curtain and other fabric that perpetually engulfed the counters. I remember, particularly, a scarlet velvet reel, unfolded in drumming bumps, that was like the firing and flaring of cannons, and I remember the smell of its dust as one might remember the aroma of battle, definite and lingering in the nostrils.

I remember, too, in a little annex not far from the vaulted drapery, a row of pattern books on stands, and I remember, on one hot morning when entering, Dapperings had been a wonderful relief from the steady sunshine, as I walked past that row of stands in company with Aunt Wells, and the sudden leaping of my heart in panic, the sudden prickling flush up and down my body. If at that instant I could have run, I would have done!

Standing on tip toe, plump bosom in a bright pink dress brushing and battling with the pages of a giant pattern book, was Auntie Alex! There was no mistaking the pallid thumb darting wetly at some unfortunate pattern, the thick cheeks and heavy make-up, or that strange beauty spot under the curly hair.

Unhappily, recoiling from the book—as if her toes were suddenly too tired to bother any longer—she glanced round and saw me.

From the way she jumped, a little jolt that went throughout her body, I knew that memory had clicked. Auntie Alex had remembered me.

"Ooh be joo de da ooh," I thought, jigging anxiously behind Aunt Wells into Soft Furnishings, "ooh be joo de da ooh!"

It was a desperate, unhappy little song. The last thing I wanted was for Auntie Alex to introduce herself and tell Aunt Wells all about my being in that purple bedroom when she, Auntie Alex, had been half nude. That Auntie herself had wanted the episode kept quiet was quite forgotten. The ping of the chamber pot under the bed, the white of Auntie's nut-tipped breasts, seemed suddenly, threateningly, to fill Dapperings to bursting, along with the bursting of my thundering heart. Could such a terrible thing happen? Auntie telling Aunt about my misdemeanours?

"Madam, may I assist you?" asked a man nearby, smiling at Aunt.

If only Aunt Wells had gone right through Soft Furnishings into some other department, and then out of the store! But no. Aunt, beset by one of those irritating whims all ladies get from time to time, decided to respond. "You may indeed help me," she said. "I'm thinking of new curtains for one of my best rooms."

There would, I knew, be no quick exit from Soft Furnishings. Aunt was a stickler for seeing everything. It would be a case of thud thud thud as reel after reel assaulted the counter.

"How I do love selecting curtain material," Aunt Wells cooed rapturously above my peering, worriedly twisting head. "Feel, Gordon, feel this exquisite material."

Into Soft Furnishings came Auntie Alex. I didn't look directly at her, but saw, from a misty corner of my eye, the bright pink dress and shiny handbag of the enemy.

"Somehow," said Aunt Wells, sounding both majestic and utterly relaxed, "fine material always recalls the Song of Solomon. Why, I'm not sure."

"Fine material, madam," said the gentleman assistant, "has a ... sensuality, isn't that the word? Fine material, if I may put it this way, gratifies the fingers as much as—as fine verse the eye and brain."

He was a ginger-haired, ageing little man with ultra-clean gingery hands. And wearing a huge ultra-clean wrist watch.

Bright-faced, and obviously sprouting inspiration, "The meadows of the plain, madam," he added, displaying a length of splendid golden green.

How Aunt Wells loved him. She beamed, then shook her head. "Too light. Dark blue. Can you show me dark blue?"

Promptly presenting dark blue, "Pillars of midnight majesty, madam," said the little gingery man.

"Very grand," said Aunt, obligingly, running her fingers up and down.

I looked round. Auntie Alex was sitting across the department on a stool by the opposite counter. She was gazing not at me but at Aunt Wells. At the same time she had taken a compact from the shiny handbag and was powdering her nose. Shuddering I looked quickly away. She was the foe all right. Not just because of the bedroom and the bare tit hills, but because—most terrible of all—she resembled Betty! Even now, as I look tolerantly back from a too ripe maturity, it seems wrong, even hideous, that an older woman, looks beginning to sag or fade, should still resemble a pretty daughter. As a boy I felt uneasy, disgusted by this inevitable fact of nature. As a man, ruthlessly forgetting Betty and remembering, for an instant, only Alex, I can admit that she may not have been unattractive. Even those knees, tight against the pink dress, may not have been without a plump and cosy charm. If only, though, she hadn't gazed so intently across!

"Not quite the right shade," Aunt Wells said. "Darker still, perhaps. One must allow for fading."

"Exactly, madam," and yet another reel was happily disrupted.

Clearly the gingery little man adored his work—the flinging and banging, the expert twisting of wrist with which he made each reel into a long and heaving and colourful giant tape worm. But what of his watch, I wondered, trying frantically to forget that Auntie lurked. What of the big radiant watch on the small darting gingery wrist? How could it stand all the knocking and bumping? Or was it thriving on all the exertion?

Again I looked behind me. Auntie Alex, no longer powdering her nose, her gaze full and deep, was still surveying Aunt Wells. And this time, as if sensing at last that something other than curtain material engaged my attention, Aunt Wells also glanced suddenly round. The eyes of the two women briefly locked. Snap! I thought. And it was like my favourite card game, with each lady wearing the same look of rigid surprise.

After that uncertain moment—Aunt had definitely not been ready for Auntie's searching, gobbling look—everybody turned away.

Another reel, post-midnight blue, was being elongated.

"Nobility, madam. Elms at night."

"Gordon," Aunt asked, quietly, "that woman behind us. Do you know her?"

"She—she lives at the York Arms, Aunt Wells."

"Hush," Aunt said, quickly. She always hushed quickly if we were in company and public houses were mentioned.

The counter before us resembled a maze of bright rumpled hills.

"If you will leave me for awhile, to consider."

"With pleasure, madam, with pleasure."

Aunt's fingers trailed absently over the nearest material. "Is she the one to whom you returned the ring?"

"Oh no. Not her!"

Thoughtfully Aunt stroked another colour. "Then who is she?"

"Oh," I said. "I—I think she is the mother of the other lady. The lady I gave the ring to."

"And she is in charge of the public house? This lady behind us, I mean?"

I nodded, vaguely.

"Hmm," Aunt said. Tapping her nose (just once, twice would have been inelegant) she appeared to be thinking. Although at the time I had no notion at all of what Aunt might be thinking she was undoubtedly, I now believe, pondering the advisability of a few words about me and the ring. A few cordial words that would amount to a final apology. Or was there more than that in Aunt's mind? Was there some other, fleeting thing, too vague for thought, merely a feeling, an impression, something indefinable that was yet strangely without comfort. Did summer for Aunt Wells suddenly shiver, not outside or in the cool of Dapperings but in the heart? Ah, who knows and who, now, can say?

I do know that, after her brief cogitation, Aunt turned suddenly and calmly round, half stepping away from me and the counter to cross the department floor.

But the stool at the counter opposite was empty, its worn top forlorn as an old saddle. Auntie Alex had gone.

The local cemetery, even in summer, with sunshine turning the newer tombstones to various shades of milkiness, and the older tombstones to a look of lighter grey or brighter black, was never for me a happy place to be. The epitaphs, however much sun fell on them, and however warm the stark lettering when touched, were mournful to read and think about, and although angels unquestionably had appeal for Aunt Wells the sculptured species in the cemetery, half-flying off the tops or edges of the tombs and headstones, did little to fire and lift my heart. Indeed the only pleasure was the feeling, as one looked about, of being alive and superior, able to wander the straight paths or tread across the neatly growing grass or wrestle, if one had to, with the one and only, ramshackle water tap. This tap, brassy and erratic, had to be passed on the way to Mrs Bert's grave. And Mrs Bert, or rather her grave, was the reason why, on an afternoon hotter than ever, I mooched along the path by the tap holding—as if I hoped they were invisible—a sissy bunch of flowers! "Take these roses," Aunt Wells had said, sadly, "to old Mrs Bert's grave. That we, in our turn, be remembered." The truth was that Aunt Wells thought little of the cemetery and would not for anything have been buried there herself. It was almost as if she felt that no grave could be at peace without a church nearby, that death, or one's last remains, needed the shadows and sounds of a church, either for respectability, or as a reminder of hope. But Mrs Bert had been our daily, preceding Mrs Hampton, and it was not perhaps to be expected that a daily would do other than end up in a public cemetery, least of all godless Mrs Bert who, as Aunt had often regretfully observed, was, though always on her knees, never one to pray. On the one occasion when Aunt had tempted her to church to see our harvest festival I remember, as she'd knelt in the pew, how her bones had creaked almost angrily. Yet I never remembered those bones creaking in the ordinary course of her duties with soap and floor-cloth and bucket.

When I got to Mrs Bert's plot, a grave marked by a plain little stone with just her name, Nellie Bert, and her age and year of death and the age and year of death of her husband, Billy Bert, there wasn't even a tin vase; so I put the roses just as they were in the middle of the grassy hump and turned back.

A lady was standing, vase in hand, by the water tap. She must have been watching me, for as I approached she stepped forward.

"Hallo, son. It's Conway's little nephew, isn't it? Remember your old Auntie Alex?"

And, bending close, she tapped me lightly on one cheek, and then, less lightly, pinched the other cheek. On her breath I caught the same kind of whiff that often graced Uncle Conway's breath after a jaunt to the York Arms.

"Nice to see you again, son. Saw you this morning, didn't I? In Dapperings?"

This time she wasn't in the bright pink dress that I'd seen her in that morning, but was wearing a dress of royal blue with elbow-length sleeves. The white halter collar neckline dipped revealingly as she turned away, wobbling a trifle, and bent to fill the vase.

The tap water was coming out in small wild jets. Obligingly I gave the rusty bend of the connecting pipe a mild kick. Out streamed the water causing Auntie to skip quickly backwards, jigging her white summer shoes out of danger.

"You've got to kick it," I said, sternly.

"Thank you, little man." She put on the ground the by now brimming vase, added flowers, and stood back wiping plump hands and watching me.

"Saw you over at that grave. One of your relatives, I expect. Some old uncle?"

"Old Mrs Bert's grave," I said. "She—she used to clean for us."

"Well, isn't that nice. How many of us would do that?"

"Do—do what?"

"Put flowers on the graves of our old dailies. Takes a lady."

"My Aunt Wells is a lady," I said, stiffly.

"Wish I was. Even my late Noel, bless him, never accused me of that." Auntie Alex, presumably righting some secret undergarment, wriggled a hand inside the halter collar. "I seem all thumbs today," she said, almost giggling. "All thumbs and straps. That's what gin does for you, son. You ask Conway. Now," withdrawing her hand and, after a meaningless lick at her thumb as if it had been plunging about inside a honeypot rather than inside her dress, "now, son, I saw you putting down those roses. That won't do at all. You don't just want to leave roses without a vase and water, do you? Whatever would that good aunt of yours say to that?"

While I shook my head my companion, rising on tiptoe and still faintly wobbling, looked carefully around. "There, that vase over there. Go and fetch it."

"Does—does it belong to us?"

"Empty, isn't it? Waiting to be filled. And call me Auntie Alex, Conway would want that."

Fetching reluctantly the somewhat grubby vase (the equally reprehensible stealing of the ruby ring never entered my mind!) I filled it with water, took it over to Mrs Bert's grave, and crammed in the roses. Auntie, looking pleased, picked up her vase, adjusted her shiny handbag over the other arm and, deliberately, as if about to march off, turned abruptly round. "Now, son, come and see my grave! Where Noel—the late Mr Hallet—now rests in peace."

Gathering confidence as we crossed between the tombstones, "What's that black thing, under your hair?" I asked.

"A beauty spot. Don't you like it?" She laughed, clapping my shoulder and spilling water that only just missed a tripping white shoe. "Not to worry. Conway always says you never really see a woman until-"

"Until what, Auntie Alex?"

"Never mind, son, never mind. Just look at this. My Noel's grave, where he lies deceased!"

"Betty—Betty's father?"

It was a strange, unforgettable moment under the hot sun. The part of the cemetery to which Auntie Alex had led me seemed especially crowded, nearly every grave a big one, tombs and headstones as thickly together as junk in a yard, many, although not new, still white and dazzling, of finest alabaster, and this was the part where cherubs and angels literally glutted the view. The grave to which Auntie pointed was much more modest, though with a good clean bright headstone and a fender-type surround. All the same, I felt a quiver of horror. It seemed queer and unreal, Betty's father under the hot white chippings!

"That's it, son. Betty's father." And, to my dismay, Auntie Alex actually shed a tear. A big scudding romping tear that, dropping from the side of her nose, ran off her chin and into the cavernous depths of the halter collar neckline. Whenever now, these long years later, I ponder what sort of lady Auntie was, I remember that tear. Not that I saw her then as a being brimming and prodigal with warm wet feeling. Instead, I thought her almost sinister. A vase thief. Someone who'd glared at my Aunt Wells.

"All's well that ends well, so they say. But what if it ends in the grave, eh, son?"

"What killed him?" I asked. "Was he a speedway rider?" but Auntie, suddenly and awkwardly kneeling, had apparently found, among the chippings, the green of an errant weed.

"That was your aunt I saw you with this morning? The nicely dressed lady?"

"Yes."

"And a nice person she looked, too. Thin though. A breeze might blow her away, sort of thing."

"What—what did kill him, then?"

"Needs building up a bit, I'd say. A bit too thin and straight. Ah, I'll never forget how my late hubby felt about things like that. Ladies shouldn't be straight, he used to say. Straight is how we travel from point A to point B, as the crow flies. If a crow can fly up a lady there's something wrong with that lady, he used to say. Because, of course, a crow can only travel in a straight line! Ah, funny was Noel. Clever, too, just like your uncle."

Each of us, seemingly, on different tramlines of thought, we gazed down at the late Noel's grave as if that, at any rate, was something we had in common.

Auntie Alex, sniffing a bit and still kneeling, began to thoughtfully smooth, palm uppermost, a section of the chippings.

"Son, mind if I say something? As my late Noel would have said, knowing me as he did, 'Alex, you're going to lecture!' "

"Lecture?" Uncomfortably I looked down into her curly scented hair.

"Yes, son. It's something we won't need to mention again, so we'll get it out of the way. I'm thinking of that time in my bedroom, that time when you caught me half-undressed. You do remember, don't you, son?"

Face burning I stared at the grave while Auntie, rocking a little, continued to smooth the chippings.

"It's simply this, son. I was put out at the time, quite upset—that I'll admit—but not any longer. And I don't want you to feel put out or upset any longer. It was something that happened, and no harm done. The fact was," Auntie paused, delicately coughing, "that you saw my tit hills. The first you ever did see on any grown lady, I'll be bound." She raised her head, looking earnestly at me. "Tit hills, that was my late Noel's phrase, and very poetic and pretty too. Oh lordy, Gordon—you are Gordon, aren't you?—he was a man, was Noel, who loved a bit of beauty, and mine were beautiful, so he said. And that's really what I want to say, son. You've been lucky. It's something that I want you to remember. You've seen the best, and you've been set a standard. Never, ever, settle for less!"

Eyes glued to Noel Hallet's headstone, I nodded jerkily.

Auntie, following my gaze, turned reverently back.

'"You and him, son. You've that in common that I've just mentioned. Both have seen the best, both of you! Remember that, son, remember that."

"Yes," I said, turning hopefully to go. "Yes, I'll remember."

Looking well satisfied, as if delivery of her lecture had been easier than she'd thought, Auntie Alex rose, dusted at her knees, and then, none too gently, grabbed my shoulder. "You know," she said, nodding bleakly at the grave behind us, "though we buried him in summer I wanted a carol at the graveside. The First Noel. Why not? him having that name and being, at that time anyway, my first and only. But no, they wouldn't have it, even Betty wouldn't, tot though she was then." Then, while I shrank inside, and to the accompaniment of another ripe fulsome tear, she began, voice curling and cracking, to hum the famous carol, using as a fat quavering baton her shiny handbag.

"G-goodbye," I spluttered, edging hastily away.

"So long then, son. And if your aunt," she paused, loftily, "should ever need a daily—Being in trade I know so many cleaning ladies. So remember, son, if I can be of help—"

There was, that hot surprising afternoon among the white burning masonry of the cemetery, and with Auntie Alex only just left behind, a forlorn sight ruminating and wobbling and humming amid the tombstones—one more shock.

Near the gates—the cemetery had at least two imposing, golden turning to dowdy golden, exits—I noticed, bending over a new and unmarked grave, a small, familiar-looking, dark-suited man. He was patiently arranging, in a jug that shone as whitely as anything in that cemetery, several yellow roses.

"Mr Edgar!" I chortled, bounding impulsively up. "Well done, Mr Edgar!"

The man turned. Stocky and wan-eyed he just looked stonily at me.

It wasn't, I quickly realised, Mr George Edgar, the piano tuner, but his brother, Jack, the one with the apple and not pear-shaped nose! And, only too obviously, he didn't know, or remember me, at all.

This one, I thought, was the one who'd shaken his fist at me from the taxi on that day at the white house, when the sad tidings of bereavement had arrived for little George, and, what with my mistake and the heat and having to carry sissy flowers all the way to the cemetery and queer old Auntie Alex, I felt suddenly quite incensed.

"Is that where she is?" I asked, rudely, pointing contemptuously at the modest, fresh little grave. "Is that where the dead wife of Well Done is buried?"

9

That evening I couldn't sleep. Despite the partly open window and a door left open, the heat of the cemetery seemed to have followed to my bedroom; shadows were like tombstones on the walls, and the bedclothes against my wet body felt earthy and heavy. It was, to judge from the sounds from town square, still relatively early—our clocks were so familiar I rarely even heard them strike, let alone bothered to count—as well as relatively calm. Only the occasional roar of a bus, the occasional hoot of revellers openly wolfing fish and chips (was there any greater sin than this, in our mild and happy town?) on the corner by the monument, only the rare and cosy purr of a sedately driven car. Nor was there, on this particular evening, a murmur from the trees outside; crouching up in bed one saw them in the dusk like tall exhausted ladies, sitting straight-backed and petrified with waiting on some night-bound station platform. The sounds of town square, the trees waiting for a train, all these were dearly familiar, and it was only after a restless while of roving from side to side of my bed that, gradually, I became aware of a new, strange noise. It wasn't very loud and it was, I thought, someone talking, but somehow not talking normally, or even as a voice on the radio talked. Indeed I might not have heard anything at all but for the wide open door of the bedroom.

But if someone was talking down below, then who? Not Uncle Conway, for Uncle was out. Darts, drinking, politics, no one, least of all Aunt Wells, knew where he was or what he did. Nor had there been any visitor, banging the tawny old knocker or, more discreetly, ringing that cold metal bun of a bell, for I should have heard.

Which left only Aunt Wells.

Yet, if it was Aunt talking, there was something ... different.

Moving to the landing I listened again, carefully, and then, watched only by ebbing picture frames, as usual half-lapped by summer dusk into the dark scenes they encompassed, and by the dead wooden night whorls of the banister, down the stairs, pyjamas flopping, I crept.

Opening the nearest door a cautious inch, I peered inside.

Aunt Wells was sitting, reading aloud, at a table. Frequently, between half-whispered words, there was a long faltering gap as she paused to finger her throat and blink a little. The pages of her book shone gold-edged, while behind her the plum-coloured window curtains had been drawn across to allow the switching on of a fine old brass lamp standard.

"Aunt," I said, suddenly advancing to the table, "why are you reading the Bible?"

It wasn't by any means a stupid question, for although Aunt attended church and received the vicar and extolled charity she hardly ever, to my knowledge, read the Bible. "I am one of the world's Marthas," she was fond of saying, rather wistfully. "By your labour, small though it is, be ye known." Not perhaps that Aunt, in her heart, really considered any of her labours small—she would have been a saint if she had. Probably what she really valued was not the size of the labour but its reticence. "The hidden nettle quietly plucked," she used to say, impishly, to both Sam and Uncle Conway, "eclipses the hedge so noisily clipped!" Or, admonishingly to herself when in a hurry to get busy in the oven, "More worthy the empty milk bottle punctiliously and thoroughly washed ready for collection, than the baking of a hundred cakes for the annual church fête!" Occasionally, returning Aunt's fire with philosophical salvoes of his own, "Bigger the clouds," Uncle Conway would rumble, "greater the storm! Bigger the deed, greater the honour!" It was, I used to think, all most peculiar! As for reading, Aunt did, of course, frequently read, though rarely novels. "Novels, Gordon, are too often nonsense. In the seed bed of our minds there should be little room for highly coloured rubbish procured from novels, remember that." Oh Aunt, I do remember, and I don't believe a word of it, and neither, deep down, did you. You avoided novels, good or bad, because you didn't wish to encourage your own romanticism and sensuality and emotionalism, because the aches and needs you felt were better left—didn't your subconscious tell you?—in a vague half-slumber, left like traditional dozing dogs that only fitfully stretched and shivered. But if rigorous selectivity in reading was for your own good as much as mine, you did, that casual once in a while, weaken and err. You read the Bible, or more exactly, a certain part of it.

"Adam and Eve and Pinch-me," I said, carelessly, looking at the fine black print of the verses, "went down to the river to bathe."

"Gordon, really! I am not reading Genesis!"

"What are you reading, Aunt Wells?"

She hesitated, then, gently blushing, shut the silky pages. "The Song of Solomon, Gordon."

"Why, Aunt Wells?"

Doubtless the conversation with the little salesman in Dapperings had put the Song of Solomon back into Aunt's mind, though unquestionably the real answer lay in her breasts and limbs and in the most innermost throb of her being. (How beautiful are thy feet with shoes, O prince's daughter! the joints of thy thighs are like jewels, the work of the hands of a cunning workman. Thy navel is like a round goblet which wanteth not liquor: thy belly is like an heap of wheat set about with lilies. Thy two breasts are like two young roes that are twins; thy neck is as a tower of ivory. How fair and how pleasant art thou, O love, for delights!).

Abruptly, rising and crossing to the window, Aunt drew apart the curtains. "Turn out the light," she said, as if that were the answer to my question and, on tiptoe, I obeyed. We stood together, quietly, in the gloom, looking at the rich evening sky.

Presently, sighing, "You must go upstairs, Gordon," Aunt said. "You'll catch your death."

"You sounded funny reading," I said. "Were you going to cry?"

Again no proper answer, only a quick tight folding of those thin arms.

83

"You're shivering!" I accused her. "You're the one who's cold!"

"Gordon, upstairs this instant."

"When Uncle Conway comes in will he be cold, and will his breath smell?"

"I said upstairs, Gordon!"

But in the comforting gloom, with the plum curtains at my elbow turned to black, and with the glass of the window like a cool thumb against my hot pressing nose, I saw my chance to say, without embarrassment, what I had wished to say ever since that afternoon.

"Aunt," I said, boldly, "that lady at the York Arms. She can get a cleaning lady for you, any time you like."

It seemed, as I spoke, a healing bridge, a link between two worlds, Betty's and mine. For though I loved Aunt and therefore distrusted the York Arms, I didn't dislike or mistrust Betty. Although at the time I didn't think of it that way, there had to be a bridge.

"What are you talking about?" Aunt said. She hadn't moved.

"That lady we saw. In the shop. She—she was at the cemetery. She can get a cleaning lady for you, any time you like."

Did Aunt, as she watched the night outside, feel again a flicker, some stirring of she knew not what? Or did the stars content and lull her with their peace and goodness, their bright eternal studding of a summer velvet sky?

"A cleaning lady for you any time you like, Aunt Wells."

She turned at last, grasping my shoulder. Through my thin pyjama jacket I felt each separate finger.

Then, suddenly relaxing, "Thank you, Gordon," she said, flicking gently at my ear, "but Mrs Hampton, God willing, is sufficient unto the day." A pause, then, "Of others, and cleaning ladies are not hard to come by, I—I have no need!"

In the dusk, moving quickly, Aunt Wells put away the Bible and followed me to bed.

"Ah yes, ah yes, to be sure I remember you," said Mr Edgar, rolling in pale hands his hard dark hat, and twitching reflectively the tip of his pear-shaped nose; "you were the boy at that big white house, were you not?" And out, while he held the hat with one hand only, from his big dark sagging pocket came a large bedraggled bag of toffees.

Scornfully (was the little man buying off trouble?) I accepted one.

"I live in two houses," I said, tearing contemptuously at the wrapping, "not just the white one!"

"Ah, so do I, so do I," said Mr Edgar.

Then, while I stared, he gently explained. "My second house isn't a real one, like yours. Merely a castle. A castle in Spain."

A castle in Spain! Ironically one of the most popular sayings of the thirties, a decade in which the hot Spanish horizon was smoked and torn by a civil war involving even Englishmen. A castle in Spain, synonym of longing, of one's own special daydream! And little Mr Edgar's castle in Spain? I asked him, then and there as we stood together, and he didn't answer— not that day anyway—but just stood looking sadly at me as I let unwanted toffee paper float irreverently down on to the oblong mound of earth below us. Sighing, and with a despairing fan of his hat, he bent to pick the paper up.

"Lad," he told me, mildly, "this is a cemetery. And a sad, sad place for both of us to be in, to be sure."

Of that I hardly needed telling. Every day during the past week, on my way home from school, I had turned hopefully in through the big golden gates. Every day, on entering, I had looked eagerly towards the grave marked only by faded yellow roses. I'd haunted the cemetery. This is the last time, I'd told myself. If he's not there today—

He was there, hat doffed above the grave. Even the little man's bicycle clips—as if in an extra act of homage—had been removed and hung, beside the bell, on the bicycle handlebar, the bicycle itself leaning dolefully on nearby railings.

In case he was praying, or weeping, I'd waited—for at least five seconds.

"Hallo!" I'd said, marching cheekily up. "Remember me?"

During my sojourns in the cemetery I'd drifted from stone to stone, reading, with growing boredom, each cold stark eulogy. What dreary people these must have been: Fanny, beloved wife of Joe; Edward, beloved husband of Daisy; Mary, beloved daughter of Danny and Dodo—surely only grey, meaningless people like these ever did die? And then I'd remembered Red Pope. He'd died, hadn't he, and all in one ride on one night, died quick as the turn of his bike or the skid of his wheels in the cinders. But it still hadn't been real, the thought of Red buried and gone. No more real, indeed, than the thought of Mr Edgar's wife buried and gone. Unreal, for a start, that Mr Edgar should have had a wife at all. To have a wife, and to be allowed to kiss ladies, surely you had to be strong and handsome and dashing? Not a timid little fellow like Mr Edgar. I could only think that the late Mrs Edgar must have been a timid, pear-nosed little woman with rheumy eyes and with both the colouring and movements of a brown mouse.

"I bet she ate cheese," I said, looking down at the grave with sudden conviction, and speaking with a logic hidden from Mr Edgar. "I bet she nibbled cheese every day!"

Mr Edgar just looked at me.

"Perhaps it killed her," I said. "Perhaps eating all that cheese killed her!"

"Well, now," said Mr Edgar, fidgeting and looking faintly reproachful, "haven't you tea to run home to?"

Suddenly, blushing, I could look only at the ground.

"Is there something?" asked Mr Edgar, clearly puzzled. "Something you wanted to say?"

A few tortured minutes later all was over. I'd done my anguished, halting best. Now it was up to Mr Edgar.

The little man, evidently amazed at what I'd had to say, took his time before replying, and not only figuratively. From his high pocket he produced, thoughtfully, his watch and chain.

"Ah, time, the restless bully! Except," and he glanced, tenderly wry, at the grave, "for those in eternity."

"You mean," anger stiffening my voice, "you haven't got the time?"

"Now, young man, let's get this clear. You want me to call, next week, at a—a public house—"

"The York Arms!"

"Ah yes, to be sure. Not that I know it, mind. My wife and I, we didn't—unless, of course, the occasion was festive—"

"And tune a piano there!"

"I understand." Mournfully, almost tragically, as if the ticking of time were suddenly an affront not only to his wife but to all the other cemetery incumbents, Mr Edgar put away his watch. "And it must be next Tuesday, you say? The first of the month?"

"Yes," I said, blushing.

"Well, that's clear," said Mr Edgar, blinking vaguely and tapping, with the rim of his hat, the swelling pear-end of his nose, "very clear."

He stood awhile, still pondering and tapping. "May I ask, young man. The people at the—the York Arms. They know of this?"

I shook my head.

"So that you, young man," said Mr Edgar, softly, "will pay me for my trouble?"

Pay him? I looked incredulously at the little man, at that mild alert neck imprisoned by the high white collar, at the suddenly alert mild eyes. Pay him! After all, I was only asking him to tune one rotten old piano!

"No?" said Mr Edgar, still quietly. "Well, that's even clearer. Quite a change, I must say, from my usual commissions." Lowering his head the little man gazed plaintively down at the rumpled earth of his wife's grave. "Quite a change, eh, my dear beloved, quite a change."

"I—I could pay a bit!" I exploded desperately. "And then, later on, another bit!"

"Well done," Mr Edgar said, still looking at the grave, "well done. But not, I think, necessary."

He turned, plodding abruptly to the railings. There, at a safe, respectable distance from the grave, he put on first his hat and then, after bending awkwardly, the bicycle clips. Easing a thumb between collar and thick dark hair, "I was given kindness at that big white house of yours," he said, soulfully. "Enough said, eh, young man?"

"No—no money?"

"Not this time." Grasping the handlebars he swung the bike around, flicked me a wan, reassuring smile. "Run on home, lad, and eat your tea. I'll not forget, I pledge."

Elatedly I watched him manoeuvre through the gates, that dark hat, on its way through, somehow brushing the dowdy golden bars and nearly jumping off. Clumsy, silly little man, I thought, as full of scorn as ever. It had been so very easy, after all, asking that favour.

87

Looking down I noticed that fresh roses, red this time, lay on the late Mrs Edgar's grave. The yellow roses brought by the other Mr Edgar now lay on nearby grass, dead and discarded. With them, like a crushed ivory butterfly, lay that discarded piece of toffee paper.

He might, at least, have offered me another toffee from that big bedraggled bag!

10

It was Mr Agate, that polite diligent gentleman so admired by Aunt Wells, who initially prompted the decision. Or was I responsible? Certainly I brought the matter to Uncle Conway's attention while Aunt Wells, most certainly, would not have mentioned it. The fact was that Mr Agate, pluckily risking a fresh encounter with Uncle Conway, called one day to discuss, with Aunt, some new fund-raising endeavour. As Mr Agate, delicately fingering the right-hand corner of his dainty mouth, while twitching his umbrella between sedate knees, himself put it, "Money, that gladsome thing, without which the political phoenix cannot rise!" Aunt, pleased to be rid of Uncle for the occasion, joyfully produced not only her best pale-blue china but also—very wickedly—a cigar from Uncle's cedarwood cigar box!

"Not really a smoking man at all," Mr Agate told her, while I, at Aunt's command, stood nearby poised to strike a match. "It's just that, once in a while, one feels indulgence to be good for the soul. Am I right?"

"How I admire a man who can admit that we have souls," Aunt Wells exulted. "Souls that, at death, flit the body in luminous glory to find a greater freedom."

"Indeed yes," Mr Agate said, gallantly enough, though with a long drenching look at the reassuring reality of his cigar, now affably alight and giving lots of unangelic blue-veined smoke. "Luminous glory. Greater freedom. Very apt."

But it wasn't the topic of soul-shedding or even fund-raising, but a remark casually made at visit's end that was to effect a subtle shattering of our lives that summer.

"Shan't be seeing you and the other good ladies for quite a while," Mr Agate said. "Off to Rome in a few days. Ostensibly a holiday of course, but one hopes to learn."

When, later, I told Uncle Conway, the world turned purple!

"What? Agate going to Rome? I don't believe it. That miserable effete worm going to Rome!"

"Why not?" Aunt Wells asked, adding coldly, "One expects our Members of Parliament to travel."

"Ah yes, but Rome!" Uncle began a fierce diagonal strut across the room while Aunt, biting her pale lip, folded her hands and glanced, as if she hoped for the distraction of spiders or peeling paper or a tiny winking crack in the plaster, into a particularly ornate corner of the ceiling. "Not Agate's meat, not his meat at all!"

"If you mean," said Aunt, addressing the corner of the ceiling, "that he has no admiration for Signor Mussolini—"

"Admiration! He hates the man! When you come to think of it, any worm would hate a lion!"

"Mr Agate," Aunt retorted, "hates no one. Nor is he a worm, and, even if he were, what better or more ennobling task on earth than to provide nourishment for birds."

"Why not say dicky-birds? That's what you mean, isn't it?" Uncle raged. "Dicky-birds! Feathered friends. Dear little tweet-tweets!"

Aunt's eyes, now, seemed as much part of the ceiling as any of its embellishment, so far removed were they from Uncle's glare.

"Well, our little wormy-wormy isn't getting away with it! The quick, prejudiced visit. The gentlemanly return. Public platforms. Ladies' afternoon committees. Agate speaking with all the baa-lamb authority of a wrinkled palpitating belly button! Rome hot and sunny, ladies dear, but otherwise things not quite nice. Thank you, Mrs Jancy, I will have another cup of sweet and lovely English tea. Thank you, Mrs Pike, two lumps will be incomparable! No, Mrs Box-Salmon, Signor Mussolini does not, to my knowledge, drink tea—even without sugar—and, even if he does, you can rest assured, dear lady, that he definitely does not crook his little finger outwards from the tea cup, not the lovely posh way you do, dear, elegant, adorable Mrs Box-Salmon!" At this point, inflated with indignation, Uncle teetered and had to grab a chair. There was, I suddenly realised, an old familiar aroma on his livid breath.

"All right, all right," Uncle continued, dabbing his brow and hooking, for greater security, one foot into the burnished rear of the low-seated chair. "Rome isn't Berlin. As I've said before, old buildings, old churches, too much stone and decay. But they're trying, by God they're trying!"

"What is to be will be," Aunt Wells said. "We can't, in any event, stop Mr Agate's trip."

Unhooking his foot and nearly falling, Uncle gave Aunt Wells a formidable glare. Then, by degrees, the glare softened, as if somewhere behind Uncle's eyes, like an invisible rusty crane, thought was beginning to heave and grind and crank.

"True, Wells, true, but I'll not be beat. No silly birds' breakfast is besting me!" With a flourish of both short arms Uncle looked past Aunt, who was herself still looking at it, to the corner of the ceiling.

"Instead of going to Germany again I'll—I'll go to Rome!"

"The fraülein," Aunt said, bitterly and quickly, "will break their hearts!"

"That's settled then," Uncle declared, sounding suddenly and surprisingly mellow. "Fine, fine. Need facts, for my book, on the Italian wing of the new politics, anyway. There is, I believe, a burgeoning comradeship, a flowering understanding, between Herr Hitler and Signor Mussolini. As for Agate ... Just let the silly devil try lecturing to me. I'll tell him what's what in Rome. I'll have the facts at first hand. All of them!"

Aunt, for the first time, looked away from the ceiling. "You mean it. You really intend going? To Rome?"

"Course I do. Course I do. Damn it, woman, why not? Need the facts."

"You do realise that I cannot accompany you?"

"Course I do. Course I do. Wouldn't do to offend the dear departed beloved by your hobnobbing with Germans and Italians, would it?"

"Gordon," Aunt Wells said. "Why aren't you upstairs reading in your room?"

But my heart, suddenly, was beating faster. Rome, surely, was where Mussolini lived, and where the sun shone even brighter than in our town, and where the old Roman soldiers had tramped, and I thought I remembered, from school, of a man called Nero playing the trumpet while Rome burnt. But Rome, no doubt, had been repaired since then so that Mussolini could live in it without discomfort or getting ash blown into those big round compelling eyes of his.

"Please, Uncle Conway," I said, brightly. "Can I go to Rome with you? I'd like to see Mussolini!"

"Upstairs, Gordon!" Aunt Wells ordered, while, "Signor Mussolini, Gordon, Signor Mussolini!" Uncle grated.

Tears began to gather.

"Please, Aunt. I want to go to Rome!"

Deciding perhaps that my youthful aspiration should not be entirely discouraged, least of all by Aunt Wells, Uncle Conway calmed down. While Aunt's eyes, bleak as the sleek grey buttons of her blouse, turned back to the ceiling Uncle, with a creak of pudgy knees, knelt soberly, though still with very lively breath, beside me.

"Eventful times these, Gordon. Europe girding its political loins. Everywhere tigers, clean-limbed, honest and fearless, waiting to spring. To root out the idle, the unhealthy, the red spots of political decay. Eventful times, boy, eventful times."

"I want to see Signor Mussolini. I'd be ever so good, really Uncle."

"Impossible, Gordon. I've work to do. Besides, too much travel wearies a boy. You have to stay and protect your Aunt."

"She doesn't need protecting," I protested. "She prays for help all the time. And, as well as God, there's Sam!"

"I really think," said Aunt, whose eyes, by now, must have been strained with staring, "that the corner of this ceiling needs attention. I'll have Sam look at it."

"You will not!" fulminated Uncle. "If you do, that Bolshevik will have the roof down about our ears!"

"Better, Conway, that the walls of Jericho should crumble and destroy than that a child should hear counsel within an ungodly temple."

"Bankrupt!" Uncle volleyed, a vein, running down from his hair to above one short eyebrow, beginning an abrupt, mad hop. "Refuge, as usual, in that Jewish collection of wet verse. Who wrote the Bible anyway? Stanley Baldwin? Or do you quote from the Authorised Queen Wells Version? Words anyway, all meaningless words! Democracy exactly! A load of daft pious air! I tell you, boy," glaring hazily at me, "we'll have red-white-and-blue swastikas outside the town hall yet. The only way. Armbands and carbolic acid, the only way to purify our race!"

"How dare you, Conway, appropriate carbolic for your disgusting armoury. The sword yes, but not an antiseptic like carbolic!"

"I want to go to Rome, Aunt Wells. Please please let me go!"

There was a limit to even Aunt Wells' regal fortitude. Suddenly rising, and looking as proud and defiant as if she wore some amazing imaginary antique hat with fruit on its one side and an ostrich-feather plume on the other, "No, Gordon," she said, a freckled hand sternly between her breasts, "the road to Rome is not for you. Not, at any rate, for many many years."

After that there wasn't much else for me to do except grasp a small and mean revenge.

"Uncle Conway," I said, blinking away tears and hurling Aunt a vicious look, "Aunt Wells gave Mr Agate one of your cigars. A big one, from your cedarwood cigar box." Adding, as out flowed further tears of rage and frustration, for why, indeed, should Mr Agate be going where I most passionately wished to go, "And I—I lit the match for him!"

On the day that Uncle Conway left for Rome Aunt Wells and I had an outing together. We travelled by bus to a nearby beauty spot. From the white winding stone steps and earthy inclines to the top of a hill. There, sitting on a bench outside a white painted café—the name of the café, Bluebird, was in a blue as fresh as the sky—we sat listening to a blind man playing old airs on a sunlit accordion. How well now I remember that day, and that hill, and all the other hills rolling greenly away into the vast charitable sky. Shadows skating on the gilt and pale-green grass, fast summer shadows, and the warm air, with the swift skating through it of summer birds, and the slow shadows of trees, and the slow skating of pennies pushed to and fro across the café counter, the small children writhing at the blind man's feet, spilling ice cream on his old but polished boots and nearly spilling his cap of coins, fussy mothers looking soberly into handbags for handkerchiefs to mop up messes and only half hearing the accordion's lament, all, all remembered. It was, after all, the summer of the pebble. A summer to dwell on. An important summer. It was a summer with the asking of questions well worthwhile, now as much as then. Whom, indeed, I ask now, did I really love that summer? Aunt Wells? Yes of course, but it was Betty who filled my mind and gave me secret joy and fear. Betty (tit hills like pincushions) in the dark little room at town house, Betty in her pink bedroom, and Betty at the fusty York Arms piano. My birthday gift to Betty, the tuning of that old piano, both buoyed and scared me. What, if he knew, would Uncle Conway say? And would he tell Aunt Wells?

Not easy that summer, being in love.

Was Aunt Wells in love that summer and, if so, with whom? Not, perhaps, with Uncle Conway.

"Don't bother to communicate," she had told him, over and over, a thin anguished line stretched across her brow. "Not that you ever do. But in any case I just don't want to hear from you!"

"Your wish," Uncle had flared back, arms folded, chin jutting, "is my high command. Ha, ha."

After that Aunt Wells had taken me off to the white house saying icily that she could not bear to view his packing and departure, for, if she did, "I should have to help him, Gordon, I really should. It is at times of arrival and departure that the steadfast wife is needed most. There is an analogy, Gordon, between a dutiful wife and a lamp burning in the night. Both are points of reference, to be utterly relied upon."

"Yes, Aunt Wells."

Uncle's last words, yelled down my ear after several gallant attempts, in his study, to kill two whisky bottles at one session, were typically rousing, already smelling, to my mind, of sunny Italy, the country that, on a map, looked so much like a long hobbling Sam-type gardening boot.

"We march forward through the hot dust, Gordon, we march forward through the hot dust!"

"Hurrah," I'd said, feeling like a Roman soldier on parade, "hurrah!"

A little later on two triumphantly empty bottles had come walloping downstairs.

Aunt Wells, grabbing them up, had held them almost loathingly, as if the glass burnt.

"Oh, Gordon, I hate town house at times like this!"

The blind accordionist stopped, wiped his nose. Another tune began, one I knew. The old sad strain of Danny Boy filled the afternoon air. I heard it freshly then, curling slow and brave across the summer hills. It will never be that way again. It will, instead, like all tunes with a built-in, as well as a particular, nostalgia, be even sharper, even more poignant, for being, along with the hills and sun and Aunt Wells as she then was, only in my mind. Ah, Aunt Wells as she then was, that warm and gentle afternoon. For, presently, when I looked at her beside me on the bench, she was crying, tiny tired glimmerings escaping her tight pale eyelids.

"What is it, Aunt?" I said. "What's wrong?" And then, wise in the ways of our household, "Is—is it the frowlane?"

"Gordon, Gordon," Aunt said, in the tone of one betrayed, and took my hand, squeezing fiercely.

"The music!" I exploded. "It makes you cry!"

"No, not the tune, Gordon, but you!" Aunt Wells drew out a tiny lace-bordered handkerchief of pale, washy blue.

"Me, Aunt?"

"I am," Aunt Wells said, "feeling sentimental. And sad."

"Aunt?" I said, baffled.

Aunt's nose dipped into the hanky, wriggled briefly, and then reappeared, almost shyly, to inhale bravely the hot hill-top air.

"You see, Gordon, I know all about your birthday gift to a—a certain young lady. Anyway," Aunt Wells finished, looking carefully down at her shoes, "I know all about it!"

It was as if a secret haven in my mind had been suddenly, cruelly exposed. So she knew. How my body burnt.

And not only with embarrassment.

"Mr Edgar?" I challenged, wrathfully. "Did he tell? Did he sneak to you? The rotten little twitter!"

Aunt dangled the handkerchief, seeking a fresh corner upon which to dry her eyes.

"No, Gordon, I have not seen Mr Edgar. He has told nothing. But your Uncle ... "

So that was it. Uncle, on a visit to the York Arms, had learnt all.

"Your Uncle, let me say, thinks it amusing. I do not. A public house, however honestly run, is still a public house. Not, Gordon, a suitable object of interest for any boy. And while I'm sure that the young lady is pleasant and friendly, I am also sure that she would consider gifts from a boy ... quite unnecessary."

The blind man began a jigging, jagged tune. Gone, with Danny Boy, the afternoon's contentment.

"Mr Edgar said he wouldn't charge me, Aunt Wells, Mr Edgar said he wouldn't charge me any money!"

"That, Gordon, is most unfortunate. I shall pay. I shall insist on paying. Really, pestering that poor, lonely man ... But what I really find upsetting," Aunt, tucking her handkerchief plaintively away into her handbag blinked unhappily at me in a kind of newly dry, patient slow motion, "what, indeed, I really felt was ... All the times we've had, all the love we've shared, and never, not once, for my birthday, have you ever thought of ... "

"I give you liquorice all sorts," I reminded her, indignantly. "Every birthday I give you liquorice all sorts!"

Aunt Wells stared intently across at a patch on the blind accordionist's trousers. It wouldn't take much, I knew, to bring the floodgates back.

"We'll say no more about it, Gordon. By this time next year you probably won't even want to remember that young lady's birthday. But you will remember mine, as, indeed, you always do. Remember also," Aunt's hand reached for mine along the bench, "that what really counts isn't the money, but the thought. A good creative thought, Gordon, is the most expensive of gifts. Do you understand me?"

I snatched away my hand. "You want something expensive?"

The Bluebird café lettering, looking as if it might at any moment fly off and merge into the sky, drew Aunt's envious eyes.

"No, Gordon, that is not what I mean. I want, simply, a good thought such as—such as you've proved that you can give. Oh I shouldn't be saying this I know. It's just that, at this time ... "

I said nothing. I looked about me, at the hills and shadows and sunlight, and felt suddenly very, very happy. Had Betty found my gift a good, creative thought? It was, at any rate, I decided gleefully, clearly a better gift than a china rat or a box of liquorice all sorts would have been!

95

Suddenly, rising from the bench and opening up her handbag again, Aunt Wells crossed, dropped a coin in the accordionist's cap, and briskly returned. "Here am I, wallowing in self-pity, and that poor man has the most terrible patch on his trousers. Next time we come I'll bring a pair of Conway's discarded flannels. Really, we could all do with cheering up. And I could just leave the trousers in a bag, next to the cap, and say nothing!"

Was that, I wondered, with a newborn sense of infinite superiority, really such a good, creative thought? Suppose the trousers didn't fit? The blind man looked rather bigger than Uncle Conway and I could imagine the trousers splitting under strain, especially if the blind man made a rude noise! But perhaps blind men, to me a race apart, never ever made rude noises and Uncle Conway's trousers, veterans of so many explosive moments, would end their days pressed not only to a blind man's bottom, but in a peace as rich and sanctified as prayer time at our church.

11

During that time of Uncle Conway's absence there was in Aunt Wells a genteel frustration. It was I now believe, looking carefully back, not so much a momentary or temporary frustration as a frustration of life itself or, more accurately, a life's span. It was, for Aunt Wells, a frustration unto death, for any kind of lasting separation, or divorce, from Uncle Conway would have been out of the question, as infidelity, for her, would also have been out of the question. With Uncle at home there was at least a masking conflict; without him emptiness, a frustration complete and tormenting. While she needed, both mentally and physically, and with or without knowing it herself, a particular kind of love, one which Uncle Conway apparently never gave her, she still needed him for whatever kind of joy, or restricted fulfilment, their life together gave. Better a marriage with too little salt in the savouring, Aunt herself might have said, than no outlet, or marriage, for giving

96

any salt to at all. And Aunt herself was always ready to give salt, whether from the packet in the kitchen or in the ready brine of her forbearing tears or in the stern, yet fair and considered, judgment of her words.

Tears apart, Aunt Wells had a particular way of giving vent to her feelings. Left alone, and lonely, there was, despite our living in the heart of summer, still the consuming consolation of spring-cleaning! For, according to Aunt, "A real cleaning always is spring-cleaning, if, that is, the cleaning is done with spring feeling."

"What, Aunt Wells, is spring feeling?"

"The feeling, Gordon, that the cleaning should be thorough. As the Bible, if it had included a book on modern housekeeping, would undoubtedly have said, Be diligent lest the least dust mote be an offence to the seeking eye!"

Well, plausible enough, even if it seemed to me that eyes should not be seeking dust, for mine never did. Why not spring-cleaning at any season of the year, even with snow weighting the bough or swallows emigrating across the chimney tops or the calendar finally turning its page, and back, on May? Not that Aunt would have listened if I had objected to summer spring-cleaning, or if Sam and Mrs Hampton had also objected. Sam and Mrs Hampton were old hands at living through it all. They remembered other times with Uncle away and Aunt's inevitable, frowning yet concerned, "Before Conway returns I must clean his study."

Sam and Mrs Hampton knew, even if I didn't, that, in practice, the cleaning, far from being thorough, was only play, a brave pretence for being where she so seldom was allowed to be, in the venetian-blind-shuttered heart of Conway's empire, his study.

It was the middle of the week. Excused school because of a summer cold I was sniffing in my room above the kitchen when Aunt appeared and said, firmly, "There isn't enough for me to do! White house was never so neat."

She was right. Even the warm breezes through the open front door and along the austere passages seemed miraculously dust-free.

"So let's be off to town," Aunt said, incongruously wearing her newest costume and Sunday-best gloves, "I want to spring-clean!"

Both Sam and Mrs Hampton were there, Sam in the garden

tying bushes with endless, muddled unwindings of bright-green string, Mrs Hampton indoors poking and sliding her duster-covered thumb in the whorls and clefts of a dark old clock.

"I've come to spring-clean a little," Aunt told Sam, guiltily, and Sam, grunting, went placidly on mauling the green string.

"Weather's a treat," was his only comment. "Fit for queens."

"What queens, Sam?"

"Queen bees, lad, a-lusting on the wing!"

Aunt went quickly inside. "I've come to clean a little," she told Mrs Hampton. "Conway's study. Oh I know you keep it dusted, but I thought ... It won't take long, a mere half hour."

"Least his majesty ain't around," said Mrs Hampton, meaningly. "If I was you, though, I'd watch out. Wouldn't do to cut a finger on some broken bottle, would it?"

"Gordon, you will sit on the lawn, read a comic, and let the sun get to your cold. At once, do you hear?"

Wondering at Aunt's sudden irritation, I went outside. The lawn, slashed obliquely by sunlight, was pleasant, but boring.

Behind me, as I sat, the windows of town house brooded from dark and secret sockets while, round at the front, the tall trees along the drive basked in haze, looking like thin spriggy ladies etched against a summer sea.

Presently, the comic finished, I trailed upstairs to find Aunt Wells.

The door of Uncle Conway's study was shut. Opening it I looked inside.

It was the queerest spring-cleaning I ever saw. Even for summer.

Aunt Wells, face pale and pinched with tears, sat behind Uncle's desk. Her hat—one of her summer straws, a large, rather beautiful mauve hat that gave dignity as well as gentleness and shade—was still on her head, and her gloves, thin and proud and dainty, were still on her hands. The slats of the hot blinds were closed and a wan-faced clock atop Uncle's copy of *Mein Kampf*, by A. Hitler, ticked coolly in the shade. A drawer was open. Just above it Aunt was holding, while she gazed at it, that picture of herself, the old sepia one marked, 'To Conway with love.'

She was crying all right. The tears, running fast, made two silvery streams.

How long she'd sat there, just gazing at that picture of herself, who could say? One thing only was certain. She hadn't entered that study to pry. That wasn't Aunt Wells. If a thing forced itself upon her then she took notice, but she never looked for trouble. That I had reason to know only too well. "Now, Gordon," she would admonish, when, from time to time, a youthful fret began. "Remember that wise old saw. Say it now, with me," hands lifting as if about to conduct, and the faintest of twinkles in her eye. "Never trouble trouble till trouble troubles you, it only doubles trouble and troubles others too!"

Anyway, there Aunt was, behind the desk ("The drawer was open, Gordon," she told me, later, "that's why I looked.") Gazing, wet-eyed, at herself when young. As she looked, what thoughts, I wonder, in her troubled mind? Sad and grieving thoughts of youth and love and Conway, of some romantic dream that somehow hadn't happened, or matured? She could, of course, have looked with equal pain at an old picture of Uncle. Except that Uncle, even in his earlier poorer days, always looked hopelessly dandified, as if dressed by the photographic studio into someone quite unreal. As if a suit, rather than a man, stood posing for the world! Worst of all, though, in terms of pain, Aunt might have gazed at a picture of her dear beloved! For if she'd married him, poor Great War victim, would not her life have been happier? Less wealthy, but happier? Strange to think that fingers, chill and grey on a battlefield, pointing at a mudcaked sky and still trembling to the thud of guns, might have made, by their tenderness, her life more pleasurable and rewarding.

And did the tears and remembering, as she pondered that day in his study, reading through a mist her own simple wording, 'To Conway with love', bring Uncle closer? Was there ever any more for Aunt Wells than a futile, questing nostalgia, a hankering back to a time when hope still sprang eternal, a legacy from Holland had yet to arrive, Bolsheviks were only rarely thought of, and marriage still lay ahead. Even the sunshine, largely held at bay by his beloved slats, must have seemed more like a burning, mocking reminder of Rome

99

than the remembered heat of some modest, optimistic seaside honeymoon of bygone years.

I don't know why I did it. Had Aunt's tears lit some deep down jealousy? Did I sense, boylike, an exclusion from her mind?

It was the worst thing I could have done.

Puffing out my chest, thrusting out my right arm, I pranced, Uncle-like, across the study.

"Heil, heil, heil! Spring-clean, spring-clean, spring-clean!"

Aunt Wells, clutching the photograph to her pale-blue costume, just looked. Under the mauve straw her eyes were wet and wild.

"Rum tum tumpety!" I chanted, inexpertly. "Bim, bam, biff!"

And then, standing rigidly by the slats, arm bristling upwards, "We march through the hot dust, heil! We march through the hot dust, heil!"

"Gordon!"

Dropping the picture, Aunt, her face pink, stood quickly up. As she did so the pallid clock, as if trying to salute, teetered on pudgy golden legs before toppling over the edge of the desk.

"Gordon, how dare you, how dare you, stupid child! And now you've made me knock over the clock!"

Aunt Wells must have been upset, for instead of ordering me to pick up the clock she took off her gloves, came round the desk, and picked it up herself. As she did so, holding the bronzed circular wood and bright legs almost tenderly, I had the impression that she was picking up not a clock but a fallen inebriated Uncle Conway, one she could be gentle and ministering to without being answered back or bellowed at. The fancy, strengthened as Aunt stroked one of the two squat legs before setting them squarely back on *Mein Kampf*, made me suddenly switch my mood, laughing harshly in a cloud of saliva spray.

Obviously shocked and bewildered, Aunt retreated behind the desk.

"You are becoming impossible, Gordon. Your Uncle is very fond of that clock. We must both hope it continues to keep satisfactory time."

"He's got other clocks now," I said, anger returning. "There must be, because Uncle says that Mussolini makes the trains tick on time!"

"I think I follow your reasoning, Gordon," Aunt said. Calmer now, relieved that the little clock still ticked, Aunt blew her nose, opened the slats, and came across to grasp my shoulder. "Undoubtedly there are clocks in Rome, and not only in the railway stations. Some, no doubt, are very beautiful."

"Why didn't he take me then? I could have seen the clocks, as well as Mussolini."

"You're at school, Gordon. That, for one thing, made it impracticable."

"He'll see Mussolini," I said with venom. "He'll see Mussolini!"

Aunt's thin left hand rubbed impatiently along my shoulder.

"Really, Gordon. An important man like Signor Mussolini won't be bothering with your uncle, or walking the streets. And Rome is a very big place. So big a boy could get lost."

"Lost? Not with Uncle Conway!"

"Even your uncle could easily get lost in Rome," Aunt Wells said, confidently, blinking in the brighter light and plying her usual, sturdy calm. "So many, many people live there. There's the King, for example, and all his servants. At least," she added, wistfully, thinking, probably, that Mussolini, like Oliver Cromwell, was no king-lover and gave His Majesty a hard time, "I imagine the King lives there, though I couldn't say for sure. But the Pope does. Of that I am sure."

"Pope?" I cried, to aggravate her. "He's dead!"

"Not that unfortunate speedway rider, Gordon. The head of the Roman Catholic church." Turning my shoulders about, Aunt moved me firmly nearer the door. "And now off, young man. I haven't time to waste!"

It was strange but I didn't want to leave. Perhaps, in that cherished study, I felt a little nearer Uncle, and Rome.

Trying to delay and dragging my feet, not easy with Aunt propelling me, "How old were you when that picture on the desk was taken, Aunt Wells?" I asked. "You haven't any lines in your face. Not like now."

Under the mauve hat Aunt's face, too, looked suddenly mauve.

"Downstairs, Gordon, and quickly, before I get angry!"

But I did not, immediately, go downstairs. Turning in the corridor I peeped back. Aunt had sat down again behind the desk and was looking, in turn, at both the little pale-faced clock and the old photograph. The story of the photograph, brief, almost naive, I remember hearing from her own lips later that day. Her face, in the telling, had held some of the hope and sweetness of that fled bright hour when all that mattered in the world was looking pretty and being photographed for Uncle. "I went to a studio, Gordon, the best studio that I knew of. There was, I recall, a yellow sign between two drab shops, and a flight of stairs to climb. And the studio itself seemed full of cardboard, potted plants, and bibles. And so dusty that I coughed. That rose I'm holding the photographer gave me from his own lapel, a striking gentleman with a black beard and cheeks like ivory, so dignified. He told me I was pretty and, when I looked in a mirror, that I was, myself, like a rose in the water of the glass! Oh I expect he told all the ladies things like that, but he was kind, I think, because he made me feel not only happy but at peace. And to make anyone feel at peace, Gordon, is very wonderful indeed. It is the greatest gift that one human being can give another."

And of what was Aunt thinking as she looked at the little clock, still ticking nervily above *Mein Kampf*? Was she thinking of Uncle, and of his oft-expressed liking for those squat golden legs?

"Wish I'd legs that colour," he'd often joked, banging against the desk his own short mottled ones. "If I had, auction them off, that's what I'd do! Give legs for guns. Guns for sanity and order and preservation of all decent people's rights. Then stump the world the greatest armed, bayonet-toting peg-leg of 'em all! You'd see the Bolsheviks scatter! Scatter, with bleeding bums, right·back into their little red fox-holes!"

12

Outside in the garden, after my summary dismissal, I found it hotter than ever. Ignoring Sam, picking his nose over the currant bushes and still enmeshed in green string, I made for the summer-house. There wouldn't be anything there for me to do, but at least I could day-dream and regret the smashing of the china rat, for, if nothing else, that ornamental rodent had been good, if slightly sinister, company. When I did get there, bounding eagerly into the gloomy rear, I realised that if ever a place needed a spring-clean that little room did. There were spiders obviously alive and spiders one had to touch before one knew. Webs linked all the old watering cans and not a few of the old spades. There wasn't any damp, either—everything, down to the last grain of wood and half-detached splinter, was bone dry. At this stage of summer even the old umbrellas relaxing in their dusty corner squalor looked as if rain was something they would not have recognised, let alone opened up to in flapping, dark-winged panic. As for the cracked light bulb on the floor, it lay as if turned to a shell of grey powder by summer hibernation.

Instead of sitting on the veranda on Uncle's cane chair under the brolly, with sun gleaming at each ragged hole, making the umbrella into a canopy of monocles, I decided to stay in the room and sit, cross-legged, in the dust, playing one of my own very special, very peculiar, games.

I was Signor Mussolini, in Rome, squatting on a throne (a throne of gold, even brighter than our town cemetery gates with the sun on them, and one filched, no doubt, from that unlucky Italian king Aunt Wells had spoken of).

The watering cans and spades were my faithful army.

Like the Signor, I had the power of life and death.

Nearby a chubby little brown spider crawled, halted, crawled again.

"Shall we kill him?" I asked the largest spade, a grudging, earth-crusty old fellow.

"Yes!" clanged the spade, as I rapped him.

"And you!" I asked another.

This spade, apparently unsoured by a broken handle and a split down its shaft, said, "No!"

"And you!" I asked a third. "Shall we kill?"

This spade reacted differently. He became gloomier, and it was nothing to do with my imagination.

I spun about. Behind me, peering warmly down across my shoulder, was Betty! Her bare arms—she wore her yellow dress—were by now brown, but only mildly so, as if the lightest dusting of white pepper had been scattered along the smooth skin. Her feet, graced by sandals with lemon-coloured straps, showed small patches of clear white skin. And those painted toe nails, a world removed from the austere unvarnished but trim and clean toe nails of Aunt Wells. (I had seen them often, Aunt Wells's feet, paddling at the seaside, and in mustard baths where, like white leaves deep in a discoloured pool, they had remained stoically unwavering in very hot water.) But, more than anything, it was again Betty's arms, slender and lovely, that took my eye. Looking back over the years I see them still, and still, in memory's sunlight, looking pale and beautiful. In all the years they haven't altered. I suppose they never will.

Smiling she held out a bottle. "I've brought you this," she said. "Best lemonade. OK?"

"OK," I mumbled shyly, rising and grabbing the gift.

"Well, pet," she said, brightly, "what's the game? Something to do with killing, isn't it? Am I in danger?"

"No!" I said, looking for the spider, but the spider was gone. Just as well. I was in a mood to prove my manhood.

Turning to the entrance, Betty stood gazing out. At least half of her, I sensed, had suddenly left me. She seemed uncomfortable, almost troubled.

"Came to pop a little note through the door for you," she said at last, "and leave that lemonade in the porch, but your Aunt saw me coming up the drive and said that you weren't at school."

"She's spring-cleaning," I announced. "We came up from the white house to spring-clean. Although," I added, whispering, "she's not really cleaning, she just sits about and pretends."

Still gazing from the entrance, Betty did not comment.

Needing, badly, something to say, "She didn't always have lines in her face," I said. "Not when she was young. I've seen an old picture of her."

Then, as Betty still did not respond, "She had the picture

taken for Uncle Conway," I told her. "A long long time ago. Before I was born. She wore a rose picked by a man in a black beard, and the man told her she looked like a rose in water. She wrote on the picture and gave it Uncle. He keeps it in a drawer. In his study. He never looks at it, but Aunt looks at it and cries. Would—would you like to see it? I could creep upstairs and get it."

"First time I've spoken to her," Betty said, in a way that meant she hadn't really listened. "She seems ... quite nice. She said I could ask the gardener for some flowers."

Since flowers, to me, were anathema, I tried another tack.

"Uncle Conway's gone away," I said, hoping to impress her. "To Rome."

The faintest shadow moved on Betty's face. Without speaking she stepped outside.

Another shadow, this time of a bird, whipped across the hot veranda. I shivered, for a moment strangely cold.

Without knowing why, I glanced towards the house. Aunt Wells was standing at a window, a quiet, resolute, watching figure. Lonely, too, as if she were quite alone in that big house without even the presence of Mrs Hampton.

"Well, pet," Betty said, quickly, "I still haven't thanked you for your lovely birthday gift. I must thank you and go."

"Is the piano all right?" I asked, excitedly. "Did Mr Edgar tune it properly?"

"He did," Betty said, smiling. "He tuned it very well indeed. Quite a concert grand now. I think we could play Chopin on it."

"I think that Mr Edgar's a sissy," I informed her, regally. "He cried at our house. Not this house but the other. Real tears, like when Aunt Wells or Mrs Hampton have been peeling onions!"

"Oh dear," Betty said. Suddenly she turned, looking down and touching, with a curved velvet finger, my scornful jaw. "But aren't there times when all of us cry? When we all have something to cry about?"

"I bet Red Pope never cried," I said, stubbornly. "Or Mussolini!"

"How do you know? Gosh, I've cried enough," Betty said, moving down the steps. "So has my mother. Wait till you've lost someone very precious to you!"

"Why did you cry?"

"Well, it wasn't really over my father. I was too small. But I have cried over one or two gentlemen!"

As she spoke, a bush nearby began jerking and rolling like a green dragon in labour. A hand suddenly poked from the stalks, then withdrew.

"It's only Sam," I assured her. "He's tying things!"

"I should think he is," Betty said. "Well, goodbye Gordon. Be good."

And with a curious, almost angrily defiant glance towards not Sam, who had startled her, but the house, off she went, yellow dress twirling, along the path and round, past town house, to the drive. Whether or not Aunt Wells saw her leave I do not know, for the windows now looked empty, though as full as ever of their own dark thoughts, and more than that it was impossible to tell.

Every evening during Uncle Conway's absence, Aunt Wells prayed. I do not mean, of course, that this was exceptional; naturally she prayed every day of the year. This was an extra prayer, a prayer that began at about six p.m. and ended five minutes later. Maybe Aunt thought that prayers for Uncle Conway's welfare, made at the beginning of the evening, would carry him safely, firmly, through to bedtime. That the start of Italian evenings might not coincide with the start of English evenings would not have occurred to Aunt or, indeed, to me. As for the prayers themselves, that I should know their content was quite inevitable, for Aunt prayed aloud, ardently, in, of all places, the airy kitchen of the white house. Perhaps to Aunt a kitchen was the most holy room in any house, a place of work and cleanliness where, sitting hands folded at the table, voice bright and strong as the sun streaming outside, one could really pray. "Wherever Conway is, Lord, guide and guard him. Use your strength to give him strength. Make tranquil his mind and thought."

Were such prayers answered? Was Uncle wafted through the dense Italian evenings on cool air-borne cushions of angelic concern and regard—Gabriel himself, armed with icy sword, keeping at bay greedy amorous signorinas? And did the brilliant green-and-black chintz covering of the kitchen table, under Aunt's folded hands, add dazzle, like a jazzy prayer mat, to her pleas? Mind, I do not think, even now, that

Aunt's prayers were pathetic: they weren't—they were pillars of strong fine words—but the mood and comfort of such prayers Aunt could not possibly sustain, not through every hour of every day. Often, passing her in a corridor, I could hear her muttering, "Fraülein indeed!" and then, obviously remembering where Uncle was, "Signorinas indeed!" Following which, after a deal of banging about the kitchen, on would come the cold water tap, so loud and dashing even I was drowned.

Obviously, on and off, Aunt was unbearably tormented. (Never hearing from Uncle at these times, not even a card, must have been additionally harrowing, even if she'd said she didn't wish to hear.) Yet could she really have envied any fraülein, any signorina? She was loyal, she was hopeful, but for what? She would stand in the white house doorway, statuesque, feeling the sun and breeze. She would move thin hands up and down thin freckled arms. She would rest parted fingers on the silk flat breast of her dress as if desiring, with all her being, that romance of life which only love exactly right can ever bring.

Now, remembering her, and remembering that time, I think of that slow sad unfurling in the doorway, and then I think of Uncle Conway, loud and jerky and quick.

And I remember (oh my habit of remembering) a certain evening.

It was at the end of another tirelessly hot day, with dark-grey clouds low over the tall trees and, across the garden, a growing whistle of wind.

I loved the tall trees with summer storm brewing up behind them.

Ladies caught in the open without umbrellas, stirring and whispering in ever brisker unease. Tall lonely figures on a greying coastal promenade. People chatting and fidgeting and indecisive against the background of a sullen sea.

I was alone indoors, waiting for Aunt Wells and Uncle Conway. It was the day when both had commented, mysteriously, upon the date, as stated by the calendar with the impressionist picture, and then driven off together in the middle of the morning, Aunt in deep-blue straw hat and watery blue dress, Uncle in his own best togs and gruffly and strangely gallant: the day when, after lunch, I had gone to the

York Arms and seen, with my own eyes, the unbuttressed glory of Auntie Alex's tit hills, and stolen, wickedly, Betty's ruby ring. It would have been a day to remember if nothing more had happened, but more did happen—happen, at any rate, to Aunt and Uncle.

Before me, unopened in the darkening room, *David Copperfield*, a story commended most earnestly by Aunt on the grounds that it was possibly Mr Dickens's masterpiece, and more practically on the grounds that the financial distress of Mr Micawber was a salutary example for me not to follow. But instead of reading I kept seeing Betty, the pink warm tints of her bedroom, her white arms. I kept seeing the pink comb running through her hair, her reflection in the dressing table glass. Why, oh why, hadn't I reached out, touched her in the glass? It seemed to me now that so doing would have been almost as wonderful as the real thing. I closed my eyes and felt my forehead burn.

I was still sitting there dreaming when I heard the car.

I rose, aware of the gloom, and the grunting car outside, the voices of Aunt Wells and Uncle Conway.

My heart was thundering. I had been to a public house. I had stolen. I was altogether guilty.

The car went on grunting and I knew that Uncle was putting it away. Aunt Wells stayed outside, in the porch, which wasn't usual, and when the front door opened they entered together.

Uncle, hat tilted, tie loose between sun-curled wing collars, looked relaxed and jolly. Aunt Wells, blue dress a trifle crumpled, ankles somehow a trifle tired above white shoes, nevertheless also looked happy. What mattered most was the way she held her hat. She held it contentedly and tightly, as if the shimmering straw still held the sunnier moments of the day, and must not, on that account, be easily relinquished to a dull old hat-peg on the stand.

"Seven o'clock," said Uncle, peering at a clock. "By Jove, earlier than I imagined."

"Yes," said Aunt, sadly I thought.

"Ah well," said Uncle, "we should be pleased. The night is young."

To my surprise, as I stood watching in shadow, Uncle Conway took Aunt's hat and placed it on the stand.

Without removing his own hat, still wildly tilted, he put his arm about her shoulders and turned her towards him.

There was something desperate and private about the way they kissed. Uneasily I stepped back, deeper into shadow.

When they parted it was as if neither knew what next to do.

"Oh dear, my hair!" Aunt said, and Uncle, "Did I bring my cigarettes in? Oh yes, can feel the packet in my pocket."

A silence. A sudden, clumsy movement. Again they kissed.

"The boy," Aunt said, not moving. "I must see where Gordon is."

"Yes," Uncle said, clearing his throat, "yes."

Still neither moved. There was something powerful and strange abroad, that evening in the hall. As if two people were trying to put back the clock of their lives and create something better.

Uncle moved. A lunge to grab Aunt again. And, in lunging, he trod on something.

"Oh," Aunt squealed, "oh my foot! Oh oh oh, my poor poor foot!"

Even in the gloom I could see her face was tight with pain. Elbow just missing the Grecian lady, she leant weakly against the wall.

"Damn it, I hardly felt a thing," Uncle roared, suddenly defiant, "I hardly touched you!"

"Oh you did," and Aunt, helplessly, waggled her foot.

Uncle, looking as helpless, stood glaring down at his shoes.

"Sorry," he said at last, red-faced. "Sorry, damn it."

"Doesn't matter," Aunt said, limping towards a chair and sitting down beside the tall pendulum clock with the dark quaint scratchings on its leonine face. "It just hurt, that's all."

"Never do anything right, do I?" Uncle growled. "Well, I'm off to the kitchen ... see what the boy's left uneaten, if anything."

"Oh yes, do," Aunt said. "Conway, I—" but Uncle had already stumped from the hall, and Aunt, sighing, was left alone to rub her toes.

It was as if town house, with its years of uncomfortable living, had once more taken over.

All the same, there had been that moment of entry, the gladsome clutching of the straw hat, the memory of a very special day.

"Today was our wedding anniversary day," Aunt told me later, as, while summer lightning flashed, she drew my bedroom curtains and bade me drink my cocoa. Her voice, happier than usual, obviously still basked in the warmth of the outing and the occasion. "The day our lives, mine and Conway's, were blended," she added, almost shyly.

13

But if Aunt Wells did not get a postcard that summer, at any rate from Uncle Conway, no doubt immersed in political research and sumptuous living among the signorinas, Betty did—from her mother. On the back side of a very respectable black-and-white card showing a view of sand and sea, ran, in letters choked together like inky blue weeds, the words: 'Blackpool, as ever, full of wind. C as usual. In his black trunks, a real Canute. Leap a frog, that man. Believe me, a nice hotel, thanks to C! Look after yourself, darling. Love to you and all at the Arms, Mother. PS. I paddle every day. C swims, and floats on his back. He has the dearest round tum! My own tum is turning more chocolate every day!'

I saw the postcard, and Betty, quite by accident. Passing the park near the York Arms I saw her sitting under a tree on the same bench that Aunt Wells and I had occupied earlier that summer. She was reading and smoking, the smoke curling up like cotton strands of fiercest, purest blue. In the torrid afternoon light, and even at a distance, her arms looked fresh and beautiful and smooth. Again I knew the longing to touch and stroke them.

Heart thumping, I turned through the gates. As I did so a small child, pushed by another toddler, fell over, rolled down a bank and ended, screaming, by the water's edge.

When I reached the bench, Betty was by the water, comforting the child. But her book was there, and when I picked it up out fell the card.

Minutes later, back loped Betty. "Pet, really!" she murmured, looking annoyed. "That's my bookmark!"

She seized the card, returned it to the book—anywhere it seemed to me—and looked at me with impatience.

"The boy that's always turning up unexpectedly, that's you, isn't it?"

"Sorry," I mumbled, feeling suddenly wretched.

"Is it good?" I added lamely, nodding towards the book, cradled now beneath her warm and lovely arm. "The one I'm reading is about chinamen and tongs."

"Tongs?" said Betty. "Oh, secret societies!"

Aunt Wells usually checked and approved my reading, but this time the approval had come from Uncle Conway shortly before his departure. I suppose, to Uncle, the Yellow Peril was as real as the bars of yellow soap in a great glass jar in town house bathroom, or as real as the grapefruits and lemons that littered fruit dish after fruit dish on gloomy sideboard after gloomy sideboard. Aunt's latest reading recommendation, on the other hand, had been *Little Women* because, in Aunt's words, "all women, and boys too, should be as the little women are, good patient industrious and loyal, though it can't be easy to be any of those things and, I think, never will be." Even Sam, once, had tried to guide my reading, easily the least interesting reading I'd ever encountered: a damp, old-fashioned book about trees, with each type of tree fully illustrated.

"Get to know 'em," Sam had said. "Them's the steadiest living creatures in all the world, is trees!"

"But, Sam, trees don't move at all."

"That's what I said. Steady. Not like kangaroos and such," and Sam had looked across the lawn at Uncle Conway, jousting, at that moment, into a deckchair.

"Of course they do move a bit," I'd said, thinking of the trees along the drive. "When the wind blows."

Sam could perhaps have added that trees also gave shade and wood and beauty.

However, as Uncle Conway in the deckchair was now lighting a cigarette, "Trees don't smoke," Sam had said. "Too much sense to a-draw smoke in they lungs. Not like the Mister Big!"

"Do you like trees?" I asked Betty.

"Why surely. Don't you, pet? So tall and noble, or just pretty. Of course I do."

When we resumed living in town house, I decided, I'd find that book of Sam's and read it properly. Then I could talk to Betty about all the trees, the tall noble ones, and the pretty.

"We're at the white house now," I said. "But I'm calling at the other house. To see Sam."

"Sam? Oh, I know. That quaint old man."

As if reminded of something, she looked at her watch. "Gosh, time's getting on. Won't you be late for tea, or miss your bus?"

We left the park walking briskly, Betty's book still tucked hard beneath her arm. She kept looking at the tiny glittering wrist watch.

"I'd like," she said, "to play you a tune or two some time. On our newly tuned piano. But I guess your aunt wouldn't approve."

"Even if I didn't drink anything?"

"Except lemonade, eh, Gordon?"

Everything, that afternoon, was golden and still. The straight tree-lined roads, the hot quiet houses with their cool little porches.

"The piano?" I asked hopefully, as we reached the side yard of the York Arms, but she shook her head.

"Another time, maybe, but only if your aunt agrees."

Why, after she'd gone inside, I ventured as far as that open side door, still isn't clear to me. Perhaps, despite her firm wave of farewell, I thought she might relent, perhaps I just had to linger for another moment, or perhaps I just wanted to feel that nothing, since my last visit, had changed. What could have changed anyway? But something had. I knew it from the instant I glanced inside. The passage, dusty even on the recently painted skirting board, still held the musty stillness of summer, and the stairs still leaned their threadbare, weary way upwards. Somewhere I heard the slamming of a door, then Betty's voice as if greeting someone, and then a distant, ambling voice, quite blurred. There was, I noted vaguely, still a bicycle in the passage, but not, I realised suddenly, the same bicycle as before. Gone the bike with the low handlebars and pretty bar of blue. This was an older machine, quite undistinguished yet strangely familiar.

14

It didn't occur to me—why should it have done?—that instead of being in Rome Uncle Conway was in Blackpool with Betty's mother absorbing, most probably, both winkles and wind, as well as prancing in and out of the tide in black trunks that must, on his short legs, have looked like the wide black water pipes down the side of white house—that he was, in fact, the C of the postcard. The card had been read and dismissed by me as of little interest. Betty's mother I resolutely disliked. To me she was still a weird, slightly frightening caricature of her daughter. "Call me Auntie Alex," she'd said, sounding warm, but deep inside I thought her just plain eerie. In those days anyway, she baffled me.

But if I failed to understand anyone it was, surely, Uncle Conway himself. Even today I really know no more. Did he, as we'd thought, ever go to Germany on business? Or was every trip abroad a bluff, an excuse for a Blackpool, or an Auntie Alex? Did he ever see a fraülein in his life? Certainly old passports, if any there are, remain undiscovered, but I do have odd, small objets d'art reputedly from Germany. It could be that Blackpool, that summer, was an exception. But I don't know, and now, perhaps, it's not important.

Whatever the truth, one thing must forever be certain. Aunt Wells herself would never, willingly, have gone to Blackpool. Such a popular resort could never have appealed. "Blackpool?" I remember her saying, in a voice as genuinely surprised as cactus in rain, to a friend just back. "Oh yes, of course. But wasn't it rather ... rumbustious?" I think she thought that brass bands marched eternally along the promenade, that local lassies resembling Gracie Fields and bursting with jolly song leant from the upper windows of salty, aspidistra-laden boarding houses, and that George Formby and his ukelele played nightly on the sands. Aunt, naturally, had her own performing heroes, drawn not, however, from the world of variety, but from the world of politics.

Mr Stanley Baldwin, for example, and, more modestly, Mr Agate.

Not, unfortunately, that great amateur politician Uncle

Conway, still absent though hardly forgotten. "Conway has his virtues," Aunt used to say, "but they are not, in my opinion, political ones."

Sam, for one, if he'd been asked, would have agreed, but asked he never was. One asked Sam about turning the sod but never about politics. Deep in our beings I think we all believed that Uncle was right, and that Sam was on the a-boil for revolution! We could have been wrong and probably were, but there were strange frightening days when Sam never even lifted his spade, just gripped it and muttered and sniffed and occasionally backheeled, with his boot, stones and worms and clods of earth or clay. "Spade's a-stuck," he told me once when I asked, politely, what was amiss. "Daddy Neptune I'll be bound, a-holding it down with his own bare hands."

"But, Sam," I'd crowed. "Neptune. Isn't he in the sea?"

"Not round here, he's not," Sam had sniffed, adding crossly, "Need beef tea from your Aunt to get that spade a-moving, that I do. Tell her, Mister Gordon, that Samuel's joints need a-beefing!"

Yet, generally, Sam seemed happy enough. Spending, now, most of his time at the white house, he worked with an extra contentment in the country air, although, in his own crotchety words, "Keeping an eye weathered, the weeds in town house yonder will be a-coming back." Not only the weeds but Uncle Conway, and Sam would certainly want to be first with that news!

"Rome!" he would mutter, nostrils twitching, one nostril, much bigger than the other, sprouting hair like a cosy dark damp cauliflower. "What's Mister Big want there? Ain't right, a-sporting on foreign muck heaps. What's Mister Big want there, I say?"

"Research, Sam, material for a book."

Aunt Wells, restrained as ever, floating in pale green above the straight vegetable rows, always corrected Sam with gentle regret. It seemed a pity, especially in a sweet and honourable English garden, that Italy be mentioned at all. Particularly so as Mr Agate was back from his own Roman trip, and far from happy.

"Incredibly hot, Rome just now," he told my aunt, over tea one day. Then, with a playful pat at those deft black eyebrows, "If only they could export heat they'd be the world's most bountiful nation! Am I right?"

I see Aunt now, basking in Mr Agate's apparent regard, pouring tea from a pale blue spout, in that heavenly moment of tranquillity even unaware of Sam, outside the open window on a path, pointedly wiping his corduroyed behind to and fro along the nearer shaft of a sunlit wheelbarrow.

"Still," Mr Agate added, "one is left uneasy. That chap of theirs—Signor Mussolini. Don't like his eyes! Or his dress. Not a gentleman!"

Until that moment I had been silent, waiting hopefully for a biscuit from the rich assortment Aunt had put out on a fancy, silver-handled plate. Now, like Uncle Conway, I began to seethe.

"I do! I like his eyes. I bet he can see further than anybody else since Robin Hood!"

Aunt, who was appropriately wearing the watery blue dress in honour of the pale-blue MP, tapped the silver handle of the biscuit plate, closed her own eyes, and tilted her head at a familiar angle towards either heaven, or the ceiling.

"Gordon, absurd boy, please leave us."

"I really mean," said Agate, recovering, "that I don't like his mettle. His bombast. And," he lowered his voice, looking at me rather than at Aunt, "they even say he keeps a—a mistress or two!"

I really do have sympathy, looking back, with Uncle Conway. What did Mr Agate come calling so frequently for if not to keep on the right side of well-to-do people? And could one believe, if, that is, one were anyone but Aunt Wells, in that implied disapproval of a mistress? Was Mr Agate who was, after all, a Member of Parliament, really shocked, or had he made a shrewd assessment of Aunt Wells's character? Was he, indeed, quite the gentleman she thought? Would he, if Uncle Conway had been present, have even mentioned the word? Almost definitely not, for Uncle Conway would have seized upon it, pounding it into the very walls with a barking, mocking, "Signor Mussolini has a mistress, Signor Mussolini has a mistress, Signor Mussolini has a mistress, la la la!"

"Anyway," Mr Agate said, as Aunt kept a grave face, "I don't like Mussolini's flair for the unfortunate political alignment. I distrust, as you know, our friend Adolf Hitler."

"A-bugger!" I said, copying Sam and disliking Mr Agate even more.

That summer, except when Mr Agate called and pale blue

was thought obligatory, Aunt wore her pale green copiously. The flowing sleeves hid her thin arms, and she seemed to like the loose neckline with its cream-coloured, prettily quilled border. She also wore a wrist watch with a black strap that matched her belt, and she wore her white shoes constantly. Once or twice I even caught her looking wistfully in a mirror, especially after Mr Agate's visit and his remark that Italy was intolerably hot.

"This dress might have done very well in Rome. Yes, very well indeed!"

But Aunt Wells didn't really hanker after Rome, or any other hot, Roman Catholic country. Not so much because of religious prejudice—she was, surprisingly perhaps, only mildly wary of ornate ceremony—but basically because of her belief, stated with the same kind of plopping emphasis as lumps of sugar dropping into tea, that only England, and in particular her kind of England, held the right moral fibre. "I believe," Aunt would declare, as sunshine filled the large pleasant rooms of white house, "in the English gentleman and gentlewoman. And in the homes and lakes and gardens of our green and quiet land."

Yet, as I remember, not everything in England was to Aunt's liking. There had, maybe, to be something near at hand for her to castigate, especially at moments when, despite those calm evening prayers, thoughts of Uncle drinking in the bars of Rome came flooding in.

"I dislike public houses, Gordon. I dislike public houses very much indeed!"

Which was why, no doubt, Aunt Wells invited Betty to the white house.

"Gordon," she told me, in the kitchen one morning, "I met that young lady friend of yours in town yesterday. We were waiting for shop service. Cut price handkerchiefs, but of very good texture." Aunt sounded pleased, as if she hadn't thought a girl like Betty capable of such discernment. "And though it may surprise you, I have invited her to tea. She said something about wishing to play the piano for you some time, and I thought ... well, why not? So there it is. The young lady is coming, and you must look your best!"

Startled and confused, all I could say was, "But, Aunt, I—I like the public-house piano best!"

Since Aunt was trying to please me it could not have been a happy remark. Pausing in the act of pommeling a basin of flour, she raised despairing white-caked arms, looked round at me, and said sternly, "I much preferred to invite Miss Hallet here. Is there something wrong with our piano, because if there is we will cancel the invitation!"

On the great afternoon of Betty's visit, Aunt Wells blew through white house like a pale-green breeze, as usual with company expected checking absolutely everything, from making sure that a tiny mouse hole in a skirting board was suitably masked by the base of a vase to dusting the piano several times over.

"Shouldn't we send for Mr Edgar?" I asked disagreeably. "This piano was tuned before the other one."

"Don't be ridiculous, Gordon. However, you may place a cushion on the stool for the young lady to sit upon."

Betty's arrival—she came by bus—had one blessing. Sam was away at town house. Having Sam as a bewildered glaring spectator would have been too much. It was bad enough, I felt, having to look at and talk to Betty right under Aunt's well-disposed but severely practical and no nonsense eye. How much better if I had been allowed to the York Arms, to sit in either that dusty derelict room beside the stairs, or the magical pink bedroom in which, according to my fevered imagination, Betty slept only on pink pillows, pink sheets and the pinkest of pink mattresses!

"Happily a lovely day, Miss Hallet," Aunt said, wafting briskly forward in greeting. "First you must see the garden. Gordon, escort duty please."

But Aunt Wells did the real tour of duty, pointing out almost everything that could be pointed out, while I, thumbs in pockets, trailed along behind, my eyes, as usual, on Betty's bare and slender arms. It was curious, though. Betty wasn't quite at ease. She kept changing her handbag, a new one with a clasp of shining silvery militancy, from arm to arm. "It's lovely," she kept saying, as she gazed around, "it's all lovely." Or, "What a treat to breathe country air." There didn't seem to be much else that she could think of to say.

Tea consisted of fruit and cream, with various jams, thin buttered white bread, and a mixture of crab and salmon. The fruit was served in Aunt's best fluted glass-ware, the dabs of cream like curled bleached snails among orange half-moons of peaches and streaky pineapple chunks, all awash in a thick cloudy pond of syrup. The table, I remember, was near the window, so that the sun shone perpetually on Betty's arms, more graceful than ever as they moved and stretched and shook things like pepper and salt and vinegar. Salmon and crab were my favourites, but for once taste was dead. I shovelled in food automatically, while through my head, why I don't know, ran one of Uncle's cherished little mealtime ditties (whenever we had salmon), "Heigh ho, salmon o, heigh heigh heigh, salmon o o!" Then, drumming with his fish knife, "Heigh heigh salmon o, vote for the party, o ho ho!"

"Unfortunately my husband is away, in Rome," Aunt said, dabbing delicately at her mouth and looking, with mild dislike, at the way I held my fork. "How he will be faring, if the heat there is worse than our own heat, I cannot imagine. Poor Conway, I do hope he wears his hat and keeps in the shade."

"I believe Rome can be hot," Betty murmured, reaching quickly for more vinegar. "You—you don't travel much yourself?"

Aunt shook her head. "I've never been abroad. My own choice, I suppose. And nowadays, well, so many countries seem so ... unpleasant."

"Is it hot in Blackpool?" I asked suddenly, remembering Auntie Alex and the postcard.

Aunt Wells looked amazed, as if I'd said one of my naughty words, while Betty, blinking, began stirring her tea all over again.

"What really lovely cups you have."

"Worcester china," Aunt said. "One of my weaknesses."

"We never see them," I said, "except on birthdays, or when Mr Agate comes to tea!"

After the meal we all sat briefly on at the table, looking out at the uncluttered sunlit vista of white house garden, at the great tree on the long lawn to the left of the vegetable beds, and at the straight tidy earthen paths that looked so much like the lines on a hot cross bun.

"Conway is doing research," Aunt said, trying hard to enliven the atmosphere. "For a book. But you probably know about that."

"Your husband really understands politics, doesn't he?" Betty said politely.

Aunt looked at her with a certain reserve. "Oh yes, quite.

Conway is nothing if not dedicated."

"I don't understand politics at all," said Betty, cheerfully. "Except, of course, that we've all got to keep an eye on those dreadful Bolsheviks in Russia."

"I understand politics," I said, adding, with difficulty, "Il Ducky. Mussolini is called Il Ducky."

"Il Duce," Aunt said, but Betty only laughed. "My, serious aren't you, pet? Heigh ho, we'll have to cheer you up. Where's that piano?"

Significant, I think now, looking back, that Betty said heigh ho, for what more likely than that she'd learnt the phrase from Uncle Conway? A common enough phrase, granted, but nevertheless mightn't it have occurred, say, over a plate of tinned salmon at some quaint surreptitious tea party in a back room of the York Arms, Uncle erupting into convivial song with Auntie Alex and Betty lustily banging fish knives and tankards in accompaniment while joining in the chorus, "Heigh ho salmon o, vote for the party, o ho ho!"

Or am I going too far, imagining too much? Maybe. But I do remember thinking, at the time, that Betty had only just relaxed sufficiently to call me pet for the first time that afternoon.

The piano recital wasn't much more comfortable than the tea had been. Betty played only the latest tunes and after the first two or three frisky melodies Aunt carefully excused herself.

"Gosh," Betty said, as the door closed. "All that washing up. Your poor aunt."

"Aunt likes washing up," I insisted.

Which was true enough. The cleansing of soap and water was a constant balm to Aunt's quietly suffering spirit.

Not that I cared how hard Aunt worked, so long as I was left alone with Betty. Tunes rippled and zig-zagged under her flashing arms. Mouth open, eyes wide, I stood entranced beside her.

Until, hearing a voice outside, I darted to the window.

There, surveying the sunshine of white house garden, stood a stocky little man clutching, behind his back, a hard dark hat and some kind of book. Suddenly stooping for a closer look at a stray watering can, he presented a patch on his trousers that made me think of a brown-coloured stamp.

Still stooping, his voice travelling wearily between his knees to the open front door, "Anyone at home?" he called.

Of all the times for Mr Edgar to call, I thought, dismayed. When Betty was playing just for me!

I found Aunt Wells in the kitchen, holding a fruit glass critically to the light.

"It's Mr Edgar," I said in panic. "He's come to tune the piano again, and we can't afford it!"

"Mr Edgar? Are you sure?"

While I flew back to Betty, Aunt Wells went to the door. "Do come inside," I heard her say.

Aunt usually received her guests in the large creamy room, watched by the sailing-ship picture and big green vase, and that was where they went. Minutes passed. Betty, romping giddily away on the keys, didn't even glance across as I stood, with straining ears, by the partly open door. What were they talking about in the other room? Was Aunt trying to dissuade Mr Edgar from tuning the piano, and was Mr Edgar wailing and weeping? Or were they debating payment for the tuning of that pub piano? Whatever they were doing, or talking about, I felt like whopping Edgar on the head. Or pinching the bell off his bike. Only, this time, he hadn't come on his bike!

Presently, standing once again by Betty, watching as her arms gleamed in the chestnut tones of the piano's woodwork, I heard Aunt Wells and Mr Edgar emerging.

"Our piano!" Aunt said, looking briefly in. "You may tell your brother that it's sounding very well indeed!"

What a shock! for the little man peering in from behind Aunt Wells wasn't, I saw now, the piano tuner at all but his brother! It was the second time that summer I'd made that mistake. And, to even my surprise, at the sight of Betty a look of disagreeable astonishment seized and nipped his tired, apple-nosed face. "He was seeking orders, Gordon," Aunt Wells explained later. "Apparently he lost his previous job, and now has a post as a salesman. That was why he had an order book, and nearly empty it was too. Poor little man, he looked so ill that I hadn't the heart to say no, though what I shall do with half-a-dozen unwanted fire guards I cannot think! However, a worthy little man, though not, perhaps, as taking as his brother. There is something," Aunt mused, "about working with musical instruments that mellows the soul. That, of course, is why angels play and sing all day long, for all spirits are mellow. Except, perhaps," Aunt added, looking carefully at me, "young, new spirits. So it is as well, Gordon, to learn to play in this world. Not only will you mellow early, but save time and trouble later!"

Betty, I remember, didn't even notice the little man. She went on playing while I, leaning from the window, watched him depart.

It was, I thought, a strange departure. Left alone on the sunwashed drive he took his time, wiping with a wan edge of hand along the curly brim of his hat and vexedly along the inner band of leather. (Ah, that hat, I was to remember it later, and vividly.) It was the first time I'd seen Jack Edgar with a hat on his dark rumpled hair, and it had make him look more than ever like his brother. A new hat, unhappily at odds with his dark shabby suit.

"And her not cold in her grave," I thought I heard him mutter, looking in the direction of town. "Turtle-doves were they? Can't believe it of George, I really can't."

"Get that patch off your bum!" I shouted, forgetting Betty and leaning further out of the window. "And get off our drive!"

He put on the hat, turned, glared towards the window of the music room (I had the peculiar feeling that he wasn't glaring at me, that he hadn't even heard me) and then he was off, limping, book under arm, the long, bright, summer-arid drive.

As he vanished Sam appeared.

Up towards the white house he steamed, grit flying from every eager, hobbling stride.

"Acquaint your aunt, young Gordon. Your Uncle Conway is a-back from Rome!"

15

"A second helping, son? Course that's what you'd like, and don't I know it. Takes a boy to appreciate ice cream—least, according to my late dear Noel. Boys have bellies like boiling cauldrons, he used to say—his very words—and it's only ice cream that don't fan the flames. Well, he wasn't a scientist, more a poet as I've said before, but that was how he took the measure of it, and a dearer, cleverer man wasn't born, not on either side of the Great War."

The café, by a tree on a corner near town square, had a creamy rough-cast exterior. The large plain swelling windows were framed by paint of a pale, charming red, and the large sun awning over the pavement was a striped lilac and cherry red. Of all the awnings on that shopping parade it was the most striking, rather like skin peeled from a giant rainbow humbug, and I'd even heard rumours, via Aunt Wells, that some of the traders thought it much too jolly and lacking in dignity. How dearly, though, I loved summer and the awnings, even the pale respectable apologetic ones, and how clearly I remember our local shopkeepers pushing them back with hooked poles as the afternoon turned to late afternoon, and the long skirt of the orange evening began again to brush the sky. The awnings devoured, in a neat friendly eight-thirty-to-six manner, the heat of my boyhood; all the sunshine of those years went into their striped or plain tops, and if they faded and were rolled up and thrown away and I didn't even notice they'd gone it was because there was always a new one to bedazzle the eye and lure one into thinking that life, and summer, and awnings went on forever.

"Never used to buy me ices, dear Noel. Said they ruined every dress I ever wore. So right he was and so dear to me, my beloved Hallet."

It wasn't that I had wanted to sit in the café and be treated by Auntie Alex; it had just happened. A tug on my satchel, a blustery hallo, and there I was, tucking into a dish of pink-and-white cream while, sitting opposite, Auntie Alex stirred and stirred a cup of tea. Click went her spoon, plop an extra lump of sugar. "One of the four glad components," she said, frowning suddenly, dropping the spoon, and reaching for her handbag. "That's what Conway used to call sugar."

"Yes," I said, mouth a wedge of pink and white.

"Once, though, dropping in lumps at some little teashop— 'Marching through Georgia,' he kept saying. Almost singing he was. Well, you know his daft little songs, don't you, son? Once in a while you can giggle, but not all the time. Not in a teashop. It drove me mad, especially with all those snooty women at the other tables staring across at us. 'Marching through Georgia, Conway?' I said. 'Georgia, Alex,' he said, banging on the table. 'Georgia, land of swamps, where they grow best Virginian baccy in the mud, and have it tended by Zulus.' Then he picked up, cool as you like, a whole fistful of lumps and dropped them, one by one, in his cup. 'Hear the plops?' he said. 'Not sugar but soldiers, my girl. Soldiers falling into swamps. Drowning in the brown baccy mud. With Zulus sitting watching, just like all these hens are watching us!' And he said it loudly; they heard at all the tables. Oh, playful was Conway, I'll say that," and Auntie Alex looked very grim indeed.

With a final chilly gulp I finished off my second dish of cream.

"But there should be more to a man than that. More than playing soldiers with sugar lumps. Eh, little man?"

"May I have some more ice cream, please?"

"Ah well, what's past is past," reflected Auntie Alex, lighting a cigarette and blowing smoke pensively down inside her still open handbag. "Yes, son, you may. Don't let it ever be said that Auntie stinted a boy's belly of that which did it the most balm."

Impatiently I waited for the third dish and when it came bit lustfully into the frosty pink segment. It was good ice cream.

"It wasn't a bad holiday while it lasted, mind. Pity about the sandcastle, though."

Sandcastle? I didn't understand. But at least something filtered through.

"Blackpool! You were at Blackpool, weren't you?"

"That's right, son. You've got it."

I remembered another bit of the postcard. The one sent to Betty and used by her as a bookmark.

"Isn't there a lot of wind there?"

"Now, little man, eat up, that's good ice cream. Sick? What if you are? If a gentleman is entitled to his cups once in a while, then a boy is entitled to too much ice cream once in a while."

Although only two-thirds through, I was beginning to feel a tiny bit queasy. The remainder of the vanilla was starting to float off the dish, skirmish around under my eyeshade and then dance greenly back again to its lawful position on the plate. As for Auntie Alex, although she was being unexpectedly generous I still didn't warm to her. Why should I? And when she shut her handbag she viciously imprisoned some of her cigarette smoke while the rest, pretty and frightened, swirled away. With every ice-cream-cold minute that passed, I too began to wish that, like the smoke, I could swirl away.

"Even in his cups Noel was never rude to me. Always treated me respectfully, did dear Hallet."

There was a wandering quality about Auntie, that day in the café. Not only the way she talked, she also seemed to ramble in her person. Her comfortable body was clothed in a mauve dress that might have been made from the curtains in her bedroom, and to my eyes it wasn't clear exactly where the fussy dress began and ended. She kept smoking, changing her cigarette from hand to mouth to hand, rubbing fitfully, as her sleeves fell back, plump elbows burnt to a seaside red; and the powder on her rouge, like the coating on Turkish delight, looked much too white and sweet. As tobacco drifted under my nostrils I thought that I smelt the warmth of something stronger than tea. It reminded me of that afternoon in the cemetery when Auntie, moving rather jerkily among the tombs, had so frankly talked to me.

"Like I said, wasn't a bad holiday while it lasted. There was the tickling. That was nice."

"Tickling?"

"My tummy, son. I'd been exposing and browning it in the sun, and that amused him. He found a feather on the beach, a gull's feather, and he used it to tickle my belly button, and that I didn't mind—it was quiet decent fun. He even made a joke about it. 'I'm throwing the feather away now,' he said. 'And when some smoker picks it up to clean his pipe with, it'll set his bowl alight!' Meaning, I suppose, that I'd quite a belly button! Well, as I say, that was nice. But there was the sandcastle."

The ice cream, which despite my efforts seemed to have grown, suddenly began to resemble the mysterious sandcastle. Turrets of ice, flashing out pink gunsmoke, began dodging up and down in front of me.

"Who," I asked, burping and blinking, "tickled you with the feather?"

"Hitler," she said, "I haven't mentioned Hitler yet, have I? That was another thing. I'm interested in politics, course I am, and fact is I've always admired Hitler and why not? That moustache, and lick of hair falling smart as paint. Quite a maiden's dream, I'll say that. They do say half the aristocracy, the female half that is, are tipping their buttons his way, not that I'd know even if I didn't blame them. He can have my buttons any day, and my tummy button too! But that's Hitler and, after all, he's not Hitler, is he, son?"

Like a huge invisible heaving army laying siege to the ice-cream castle my stomach was beginning to rise and fall.

"Who—who's not Hitler?"

"Oh, he's had what Hitler would have liked, buttons and all, and what only dearest Noel in all the world ever deserved. More's the pity I ever gave it him. But I thought he was a gentleman, didn't I? There never would have been that sandcastle, not with my late dear departed one."

Foggily, "Did you build the—the sandcastle yourself?" I asked. "Did you have a bucket and fill the moat with water?"

Auntie paused to stare at me, swallowing both tea and smoke, beauty spot almost lost in the sudden puzzled creasing of her brow.

"You've got it wrong, little man. I didn't build any castle. It was just there, on the beach."

"Someone must have built it," I argued, dizzily. "It wasn't Hitler, was it?"

Scratching, with pallid thumb, her curly hair, Auntie leant deliberately across the table. "When I refer to that sandcastle I am referring to what they call an incident. An undiplomatic incident."

It was all beyond me. Clutching my writhing stomach I gazed into Auntie's bright, damp eyes.

"There it was on the beach, just built. A really posh sandcastle. And he fell on it and squashed it. In his cups in the middle of the day, mind! Sat there and looked up at me and opened up his arms, that's what he did. 'Come on, Frau Hallet,' that's what he said. 'Come on, and join me in my castle.' And they all began to laugh, the folks around. 'Come on, Frau Hallet, join me in my castle!' On his behind, arms stuck out towards me. It drove me mad. Worse than 'Marching through Georgia'." Auntie halted, turning scarlet. "Why, even wanted me to bare my tit hills he did! Told the world, there on the sandcastle, that I was to suckle a new race for him! That I was his choice, that he was the Leader! My God, if Noel only knew. No stomach for insensitivity, that good pure hubby of mine."

Despite the café, reeling pink and white around my head, I managed a last desperate question.

"Who," I burped, "sat on the sandcastle?"

"Well, son," she said, squinting down into her bosom where cigarette ash hung like trinkets of grey, "that's not for me to say. But you could ask Conway, that you could. Wouldn't have happened if your aunt had been with him. That's what I don't like. Or would it? With a bloke like that God knows!" Breathing disjointedly Auntie Alex opened her handbag, withdrew, fumblingly, a new cigarette, lit up, looked with some bewilderment at the wet tip, then, sternly, turned to rake me with her plummy gaze. "You're a proper little boy now, aren't you? Raise your cap to the daily woman, I'll bet?"

"Yes. I—I raise my cap to Mrs H."

"Then you understand how Noel must have turned in his grave! 1922, that's when poor Hallet went, and left me a real legacy. Real respect and love, more precious than money, of which he left a fair bit."

Tears, now falling steadily down Auntie's cheeks, made me glad of the eyeshade.

"Ah Conway, Conway, takes more than speeches. Takes a gent. Was Hitler ever rude? I asked him, after. Never, I said. Not in public, not mocking his lady for all the world to see. Hitler wouldn't do that, I said. Not outside of a Germanic beer cellar, anyway. Not in the fresh air, not at Blackpool. And he wouldn't ever, I said, sit down on a sandcastle. Ah well, it's over now. Not that it was ever too much anyway. Not a great lover he wasn't, for all his ticklings with that feather." She stopped, smiling bravely across through fat tears. "More ice cream, son?"

The café, in waves of nausea, seemed to be breaking about me. Up I lurched.

"No more ice cream," I begged. "Please, no more ice cream."

"Then off you go, little man. Been talking too much, haven't I? Keeping you from your tea? Oh dear, I've been keeping you from your tea."

And a new, fat tear roamed gently from her popping eye.

Suddenly, that summer, everyone's breath seemed tart with wine. Or, if not wine, beer or spirits. But not, of course, the breath of Aunt Wells. So fresh her mouth, she appeared to have spent the summer swallowing only mint. Only once, when being kissed by her, do I remember a fiercer taste, the taste, burnt and dark, of sherry. But that, later, near summer's end.

Town house, that night, was quiet, lacking even the quiet of Aunt Wells, gone to a meeting to hear Mr Agate. The arm of the Grecian lady forever holding her urn looked tired. Our clocks, bored, made no haste. Only Uncle Conway fretted, exhibiting, without the clocks' good temper, all the loudly ticking symptoms of steady unrelenting annoyance. To judge from his gestures and glares and peerings about the house, everything annoyed him; the last lukewarm rays of a day's long heat, thin as mouse squeaks, on walls which caught the evening sun; the crowded neatness of the kitchen which seemed to say 'keep out'; even the bedrooms, sanctified and lonely, as if laughter could never again touch or lighten them. Spying on him, hiding from him, clicking marbles behind a dark settee one minute, sneaking through the garden to the summerhouse the next, that was me. Does any boy ever want bed, on a summer's night?

"Gordon!" he kept calling from the landing, clutching the rail and staring down. "Gordon!"

Finally, reluctantly, I shuffled into view.

"No," I said. "Not yet, Uncle Conway. I don't want to go to bed."

"Come on up here this instant, boy. You know I promised your aunt that I'd pack you off at nine."

Uncle was in his study when I reached the landing. The

electric light was on and the blinds looked hard and green.

"Uncle," I said, halting in the doorway, "why didn't you bring us anything from Rome? Aunt Wells said that you might bring one or two presents, but you didn't, did you?"

He looked unkempt that night, pin-stripe jacket discarded, fancy waistcoat open, and a big, mole-coloured handkerchief constantly in use between stiff collar and glistening neck. A cigar lay burning in an ash tray. Less unusually, a bottle and glass stood amiably together on the desk. There was a restless air about the way Uncle rocked, in the chair behind the desk, to and fro, hands in and out of the pockets of his pin-stripe trousers as fast as a yo-yo. What, I wonder, were his thoughts as another evening of being in cups began? Dark regretful thoughts of Auntie? Or was he thinking of Aunt Wells?

"Bed, my boy," he growled. "You need it. Particularly after being sick earlier. What the devil you've been eating on the quiet I daren't think."

"Auntie Alex," I said, suddenly reminded, "said that you were in Blackpool sitting on a sandcastle. But you weren't, were you, Uncle?"

The silence was flat as the watching slats. Abruptly Uncle's eyes looked stretched and bursting.

"Auntie Alex? Blackpool? What, boy, are you talking about?"

Without quite knowing why, I felt a sense of power. I went to the blinds and trailed my fingers up and down the slats, and then tapped out a cold, impatient little tune.

"Blackpool?" Uncle emphasised. "I've been to Rome, boy, Rome!"

"Did you see Mussolini?"

Ignoring the glass, and the cigar that had now gone out, Uncle grabbed the bottle and tipped it to his mouth. It was empty. Seizing his jacket, he promptly withdrew a rippled, wine-coloured flask and, unfastening the top, took a trenchant gulp.

"That woman," he said, presently, as if from a long way off, "that singularly annoying woman."

"Mussolini," I repeated. "Did you see him?"

"Signor Mussolini?" Uncle Conway thought awhile, fingers

fat and damp about the flask except for one finger which rubbed slowly up and down. His brow was puckered as he gazed downwards, gleams of perspiration dotting between the furrows like a string of tiny silvery lights. And his voice when he spoke, like a currant in a cake, had become trapped and clogged. "Ah yes, the good signor."

At last, as though an effort must be made, and after first carefully putting down the flask beside the anxiously ticking clock with the squat golden legs, Uncle Conway scraped away his chair and stood up. "Il Duce," he said, tightening an imaginary belt and flinging out a hand in casual salute, "Il Duce!"

"I don't believe you," I cried, angrily. "You haven't seen Mussolini or been in Rome!"

Uncle Conway glared at me, really concentrating. Gradually, however, one eye wandered away, darting sideways to *Mein Kampf*, up to the light bulb in its nut-brown shade, and down again to the desk. Then, joined by the other eye, both eyes began to travel the room as if searching for inspiration and comfort. When he again looked at me it couldn't have been a reassuring sight, for, dabbing his brow, he glanced away and sat slowly down again, nearly missing, as he did so, the waiting chair. Sitting on the edge and picking up the flask, he looked at its wine-coloured sides, almost took a swig, and then, apparently deciding that now was not the time, opened, with an awkward rasping motion a drawer, and lowered the flask inside as carefully as if it held a snake. Then, about to shut the drawer, he didn't. Something in it appeared first to delay, then to rivet, his attention.

Uncle Conway's next look towards me was both sly and dignified. Excited, too, as if something had just been born inside each bright eye.

He rose, a trifle peremptorily, head cocked, a hand raised. It was immeasurably quelling, that single raised hand.

"Rome, Gordon," Uncle Conway said, sternly, "was hot. So hot a little English boy like you can't imagine. Every day the same. Hot, hot days."

Suddenly, turning from behind the desk, Uncle began twitching, then ambling, then strutting, to and fro. The old crackling feeling of being astride his, and every other, world, was clearly rushing back. At any moment, I felt, he would burst royally into song. Even his shoes, black and polished, had begun to squeak with excitement.

"My hotel in Rome, Gordon, was near a square. One of those old city squares overlooked by a balcony."

"A little balcony or a big one?" I asked, inspired. "And were there pigeons on it, making naughty messes?"

"It was a splendid balcony," Uncle rapped, frowning. "The best of all balconies! And no, of course, there weren't pigeons. Not on the balcony, anyway."

A pause while Uncle, eyes suddenly unblinking, looked up at the nut-brown shade. It might well have been a hot Italian sun at which he looked, so straight and seeing his gaze.

"One day, Gordon, there were people in the square, people everywhere. And they were all waiting, all looking up at the balcony."

Ah, the balcony.

I see it still, even dream of it still. Now, in these years of my prime, and despite other memories, it still returns to dazzle the inward eye. Not just the balcony, of course, but everything, for time has only made the Rome of that evening in the study even hotter, its skies even bluer, the white-shirted, white-frocked crowd in the square even thicker, the buildings older, more soaked by sun, more dashed by spatterings (except on the balcony) from steel-grey pigeons than buildings in any other square that ever was or wasn't. And that splendid, best-of-all-balconies balcony no less powerful, no less magnetic than in my first imaginings, and the people, oh the people, they still move in my mind like a wind-ruffled handkerchief, that white crowd, so suddenly quiet as, stepping puffily out, stepping on to the balcony ...

"Signor Mussolini, Gordon, that's who it was. Signor Mussolini ..."

Ah, then and now! Now, perhaps, it is no longer Mussolini that I see on that ancient balcony, but Uncle Conway himself! Uncle Conway on the balcony, Uncle Conway's face a pale stern blotch above the crowd, Uncle Conway's arm jerking to acclamation, Uncle Conway's voice tightening like cold silver wire across the square. But then, that warm electrifying evening as Uncle spoke, it wasn't so. As a boy I saw, as Uncle intended, only Mussolini: Benito waving to his people, and the people waving back, and there, on the edge of the throng as the jagged, powerful oration began, my Uncle Conway in his straw hat, high prim English collar and pin-stripe suit; ears, under the gentle straw, vibrating to Il Duce's every word.

But the words across the square, showering with all the colour and pride of angry rust falling from a mighty file, were obviously Uncle Conway's, for even if he had been there, and had heard Mussolini, he didn't know Italian and would not have understood. But I didn't know. To me it all sounded wonderfully real, and why not? For there, across the study, was Uncle himself acting out his day dream, one minute clapping in applause as if that Englishman on the crowd's edge, the next minute pounding and braying as if Il Duce. It was, I know now, the greatest, most creative moment of my guardian's life, and I a part of it, lifted and absorbed, perhaps forever, into that blazing Roman day of declamation, poetry and pigeons.

Poetry? Oh yes, poetry. I know. I was there!

Listen.

"We speak, we are, we act! We change the world!"

And the great roaring, and the lifting of an arm, and the quiet.

And the crowd more than quiet, vibrantly quiet, and the man on the balcony smoothing out both hands, descriptively, palms down, thumbs tucked under.

"From this place, this ancient place ... the truth, the power"—fingers straddling puffy hips, then, slowly, an arm again lifting, poised—"the glory."

"You, the people, the strong ones. Centre of the world's pool."

"Into which ... "

Something minute, almost invisible, tossed from the balcony at the crowd below, falling, tumbling through the day's hazy, gilt-edged heat.

"Our truth! A ripple, a ripple to engulf the world ... "

I remember, indelibly, how abruptly Uncle stopped, how quickly, face streaming with perspiration and eyes glazed, he sat down on the front edge of the desk.

"Caught it," he said. "Caught it in one hand! There I was, listening on the crowd's edge, and it flew to me. And, by heaven, I caught it, caught it warm from the Signor's hand!"

Uncle paused, for once in his life looking not red or purple but grey from effort, mopping his face as if in both self-

131

wonderment and self-congratulation at both the tale and his own part in it, and as if, indeed, he half believed, as I wholly believed, that such a thing had really happened.

"Always was a good cricket field, especially in the slips. Of course I caught it," he mumbled, blinking, and then, as if seeing my still face and staring eyes for the first time in minutes ('What, Uncle,' I managed to whisper, 'did you catch?') turned, reached behind him into the still-open drawer, took something out, breathed deeply and triumphantly in and out of moist, proud nostrils, slipped clumsily off the desk, grabbed my hand, opened it out, palm up, and placed, in its centre, a small polished ebony stone. The blackest, most ebony stone I'd ever seen.

I looked at it, closing my hand around it, and the stone was warm in my palm, as if, I thought, overwhelmed, as if—

"There, Gordon," Uncle Conway said, heartily, as if giving me the world, as indeed he was, "a pebble from Rome!"

16

The club, a building resembling a stack of tightly packed autumnal leaves so mellow were the colourings of its brickwork, occupied part of a quiet road near town hall. Its square windows, however, grimly half-frosted and with great crusty jutting under ledges, belied the warmth of the surrounding brick, giving the impression of an inward deadly frozen secrecy in which only ghosts and dead spiders could live, and in which even furniture withered and died to stand unburied on cold dusty carpets. Its doorstep, a splodge of mouldering stone no livelier than the windows, rarely boasted milk bottles that a boy could take a friendly kick at, although, to one side of the doorstep, there was a fancy little black iron bar worth balancing on in passing. Only at election time, when huge blue Vote-For-Agate posters had appeared cockily all over the frontage, had I ever given the place a close look, and this although famous men from Parliament had crossed its threshold, including, or so I'd heard, one man so famous that he was called prime minister! But not only ministers of the crown, and a prime minister, had crossed that old, ungainly doorstep. Aunt Wells had also been inside. It had been, on the first occasion anyway, quite the experience of a lifetime, akin to a honeymoon or the birth of one's firstborn. "One enters," she'd told a friend, voice worshipful and quivering as the wings of a moth flapping amid the goodies of a linen cupboard, "a passage of dim, unexpected luxury. Everywhere wallpaper of a rich dark chocolate, and the most beautiful little light shades on the wall as well as overhead. The gleam of brass, and old wood, and the feel of beautiful carpeting, and everywhere a splendid cosy dust-free cleanliness. One hears," she'd continued, with a touch of her own strange humour, "a creaking, but not from the floorboards, only from oneself! It is as if—as if one has suddenly become ... unworthy! One waits, in horror, for the rumbling of one's tummy!" The friend, a lady in furs with big pink ears, had rapturously clasped her hands, dropping into her coffee, like a string of tiny beads, crumbs of best digestive biscuit. "Oh, Wells, how amusing and wonderful! And did— did dear Mr Agate take you in? Was he your escort? Oh, I think that man is wonderful! A future prime minister. I don't even mind him criticising that darling Adolf, because Adolf is in Germany and darling Mr Agate is so very, very near at hand!"

It was, if I remember correctly, the last time the lady with the big pink ears enjoyed our coffee. I never saw her again, at town or country house. I never again smelt her furs, or saw the ecstatic clasp of her white beringed hands, or heard that purring voice say Adolf. But she should certainly have been with me on that fateful day when, passing the club, I saw darling wonderful Mr Agate himself turning briskly through the doorway.

Impulsively, halting, I glared down the passage after him. In the gloom his black immaculate suit seemed already lost, but his thin white neck and the outline of a top hat were clear enough.

What happened next still stirs my blood with awful pride.

Cupping hands, and liberating a blast of spearmint-laden breath, "Vote for Mussolini," I piped ferociously down the passage. "Vote for Mussolini!"

Mr Agate spun about so fast that the top hat dropped to the

carpet where it sat in a gloomy state of ebony, petrified shock.

Seeing that hat fall was almost as satisfying as if I'd kicked it from him.

"Vote for Mussolini," I repeated, even more ferociously, leaning into the passage with a grubby hand against each wall. "Vote for Musso!"

Vote for Musso! Did ministers, prime or otherwise, slumbering over brandies in great enveloping purple chairs, jolt awake and send their drinks cascading? Did tiny blue mice, invisible on rich blue carpets, rush for cover? Vote for Musso! It was a cry to wake the dead in any club, even a club as dead as the one in our pretty, dozing, tree-filled, sweltering town.

Since Mr Agate was now zooming up the passage I turned to flee. And wham! straight into a pair of broad tweedy arms that held me fast.

"Vote," I spluttered, wriggling, nose flattened in the warm itchy tracts of an unknown waistcoat, "for Mussolini!"

"Gad, sticky little devil, what?" said the tweedy man, looking hot and wide in baggy plus-fours. "Hey, Agate, take a look. Ain't he a beast?"

Mr Agate, rubbing the side of his pale neck, stood and gazed.

"Why," he said, "I know this boy!"

"Sticky little devil," the man said, coughing tweedily. "Clip his sticky ear, should we?"

Mr Agate's dinky eyebrows flew together in obvious alarm. Visions of child-beating, and the resultant distress to Aunt Wells, fluttered all too clearly through his neat and careful brain.

"Oh dear no," he said. "Though most distressing, indubitably so, we mustn't act hastily. Am I right?"

"You're sissy!" I spat out. "Not like Mussolini. Mussolini isn't. Sissy Agate!"

"Gad," roared the tweedy man, "what a sticky little beast!"

In my pocket—the rear trousers pocket with the big brown button that kept it safely fastened—lay the pebble from Rome. I couldn't feel it but I knew it was there. A black talisman, giving courage: enabling me to face the world, even face the rough noisy man who looked as fierce and bright as the flecks in his suit.

But Mr Agate was the real provocation. Just the sight of him had at once set me boiling. The rage had in fact begun much earlier, heating up inside me over a breakfast time as bitter as Aunt Wells's favourite marmalade, the sort she bought in fancy glass jars, homemade by a country lady who lived near white house and who believed in the thickest of chunks and the gayest of sour delectable shreds, and who thought of marmalade, hers at any rate, as gentle roughage designed, in the words of Sam who also bought the stuff, 'to get the bowels a-leaping'.

But it wasn't bowels that had hopped that morning, but Uncle Conway.

"That damn Agate," he'd fumed, throwing aside his newspaper. "He's just made a speech attacking Herr Hitler, if you please. And attacking Mussolini!"

"I know, I was there," Aunt Wells had said. "Such a good meeting. At least ten people."

"What," I'd erupted, with partisan fury, "did he say? About Mussolini."

"Blind as a bat, that's Agate," Uncle had ranted, banging the marmalade jar against the teapot. "And as politically redundant as pancakes in a cow field!"

"I won't have such vile, low talk, even from you, Conway?"

Aunt Wells had licked, from a trembling, furious finger, a shred of that homemade country marmalade. That marmalade had got on to her finger at all, and that she had actually licked it off instead of using a napkin, showed how mad she was. "One more word and off I go! Off to white house! Off to strawberry teas on the lawn, and magpies in the bird bath, and soft-spoken decent folk who know more of God and harvests than of politics!" She'd closed her eyes, suddenly wistful, drifting earnestly back to that gathering of the night before. "All the same, such a meeting. Mr Agate so fine, so gentlemanly. And Mrs Bradley, Mrs Mossman and I, all side by side. Three pairs of white gloves clapping. And even old Mr Wedge clapping away behind us, though he does suffer most terribly from wind and is too deaf to be fully aware of his own infirmity and its distracting effect on others, particularly at public meetings, dear old man."

"What," I'd shouted, "did Mr Agate say about Mussolini?"

"Man's a dove," Uncle had thundered. "Yet he tries to roar! No, Gordon, not Mussolini. I mean Agate!"

Flooding back, as I stood imprisoned in the club doorway, with one foot in the passage and one on the doorstep, and tweedy sleeves wrapped around my burning ears, came Uncle's words. Needing, now, something more than 'Vote for Mussolini' or 'Sissy Agate', "You're a dove trying to roar!" I yelled.

"Gad!" exploded plus-fours. "Sticky!"

"And blind as a bat," I added, scowling at Mr Agate's popping, amazed eyes. "You're like a pancake in a cow field! A—stinking one!"

So elated, so singing my blood, I couldn't stop. For, giving me responsibility as well as courage, firing me on to the utmost in daring, was the pebble in my pocket. Mussolini's pebble. The pebble from a balcony, warm, now, not from the great man's hand and the air of a great hot city but from my own warm writhing captive rump.

"I wouldn't clap you," I boasted, fierily, thinking of Mrs Bradley, Mrs Mossman and Aunt Wells, "not even if I wore white gloves I wouldn't! And I bet you're deaf, like Mr Wedge, and have a lot of wind!"

There followed a silence so terrible it seemed the club itself might slide and crash.

"Sorry, Agate old prune," said the tweedy gentleman with a huge, deep, grating breath, "but going to have to box his sticky ears. Little beast!" and, thwack! crisp and savage against my head one hairy hand, and, thwack! crisp and savage against my head the other hairy hand, and thwack! thwack! again and again, while everything about me turned red and strange and giddy! "That's enough," I thought I heard Mr Agate say, "desist!" and, "Little devil-me-ree!" I thought I heard plus-fours bark, for who, in those raw, storming shuttlecock moments could be sure of hearing anything correctly?

But I was sure when the thwacking stopped, for although the sore red song went on and on, head bursting, eyes streaming, ears stinging and wailing, at least I knew I was suddenly free to spin and topple. "Come, Agate," I dimly heard plus-fours bellow. "Let's drown our sorrows, what!" and into the club they went, Agate's arm firmly held by that tough, implacable, hateful tweed monster. And still I staggered, hands to ears, the half-frosted windows and dull old doorstep with its small black iron bar all dancing with me in a feverish flashing jig I thought would never end.

Until, miraculously, a skittering in the gutter behind, a quick scraping, and my arms were gripped, my body steadied. "It's you, lad, isn't it?" said an amiable, familiar voice. "Yes, yes, to be sure it is."

Into my hands came a large musty handkerchief. While I dabbed my eyes, Mr Edgar, tut-tutting indefatigably and merrily away, secured his bicycle more firmly on the kerb. With what little of my acumen was still functioning I decided that he looked a slightly different Mr Edgar from our last meeting, by the graveside. His lank black hair had been cut, his dark suit looked excessively brushed and clean, and he wore, in his lapel pocket, a silk handkerchief of dark blue.

"Now, young man, better are we? That's right, dab those tears away. Only tears of happiness should ever be allowed."

Somehow, even to me, it didn't sound like the kind of talk one might expect from the sad bereaved little piano tuner.

Sniffing, and muttering contemptuously under my breath, I handed back the musty handkerchief. For once, though, I could do little more than mutter, for Mr Edgar had caught me at a fine disadvantage. I was the one who was crying, while he, surely the biggest, wettest blubberer in town, stayed dry-eyed and smiling. It was enough to make me yearn to tweak his pear-shaped nose and kick him in the rear.

Fortunately Mr Edgar couldn't read my mind, for with another of those slow, placid, agreeable smiles, "Tell you what, young man," he said, "let's try to find an ice cream somewhere, shall we?"

Ice cream! Ah yes, it truly was an ice-cream summer, that summer of long ago. During its parched course everyone, not excluding Aunt Wells and Uncle Conway, must have treated me—if only to a cornet—but the occasions that I best remember are those on which ice cream was bought for me by Auntie Alex and little Mr Edgar. These were the important times, times when, one way or another, more was brewing, either in people's heads or in their hearts, than merely the cost, form or flavour of the ice cream they bought. Not that I really noticed that various things were brewing, or, if I did notice, it all floated on the surface of my mind, sinking in deeply only later.

Certainly Mr Edgar's marked cheerfulness, as he stood patiently regarding me across his bike, passed lightly enough over my head. But not his offer of sustenance.

"All right," I grumbled. "If I can have a strawberry one!"

"Ah yes, strawberry," said Mr Edgar. "My late dear wife's choice ... but then, that will be of no interest to you."

Clutching my hot buzzing ears, I tagged disagreeably along while Mr Edgar, pushing his bike, repeatedly paused, smiled, and doffed to the Saturday shoppers his hard dark hat.

Outside a large popular store, not Dapperings, for Dapperings, in those days, would have looked askance at an ice-cream counter, Mr Edgar stopped, propped his bike against the wall and took out that big homely watch from behind the new silk handkerchief. "I think," he said, " ... yes, we've just about time. Let me see, strawberry, wasn't it?"

We stood together in the hot bright store eating ice cream, Mr Edgar standing awkwardly, short legs bent apart quite as if the wafer held by both hands, and at which he took quick happy licks, were of a considerable weight.

"Well, young man," he said, presently, brushing, with a leaf-light gesture, ice cream from his pale upper lip, "I was sorry to see you in trouble."

Mr Edgar's sorrow mattered little to me. But he was being kind. And even I knew that you couldn't accept ice cream from someone, even a cry-baby piano tuner, without, in return, offering at least a crumb of politeness and sociability.

"I wonder," I said, trying very hard, "if Mussolini likes ice cream?"

Mr Edgar looked startled. "Gracious, I've no idea. But isn't that where ice cream was invented? Italy, I mean? To be sure they are good at making it and selling it."

Bored at what seemed like a lesson, I stared bleakly into the little man's deep dark eyes.

"The old Roman soldiers never ate ice cream," I stated, flatly. "That would have been too sissy. And I don't believe Mussolini does. You're telling lies!"

"Really, lad, I never said—"

There was a long silence, during which Mr Edgar, less happy now, took refuge in more quick licks.

"They built roads, the Romans did," I added, proud of my knowledge. "And Mussolini makes the trains run properly. Uncle Conway says so."

Deciding, apparently, that it would be best to change the subject, Mr Edgar finished off his wafer, wiped his fingers in the big stale handkerchief, and then looked anxiously about him at the busy shopping counters.

"Must remember to buy some candles. Perhaps, young man, you'll remind me."

"We," I said, aggressively, "have electric lights. And oil lamps at white house."

"Ah yes, your two dwellings," Mr Edgar mused. "My house, also, has electric lights, though I'm not so sure about my dream house. That, perhaps, will require oil lamps."

"Dream house?"

"My castle in Spain, young man. Always been my dream, has that, a tiny cottage in the country, with kingfisher roses, and a little garden gate, woodbine, and the little woman waiting."

"Little woman?" I said, reminded of Louisa M. Alcott. "Do you mean Beth, Jo, or Amy? Or the other one?"

"Mind, there's no telling about the kingfisher roses," Mr Edgar continued musing, quite sadly. "Blue and green, not easy colours. Though quite a treat, if possible."

"The little woman," I said. "Where's she coming from? And will she be easier than the roses?"

Mr Edgar brightened, his cheeks turning pink and smiling.

"Oh, don't you worry, lad," he said. "There'll be a little woman. Of that I do assure you."

Into my mouth, scornfully, went the last of the ice cream, pink and gushing and rather more than I could manage, and back out, immediately, came Mr Edgar's handkerchief. So gently did he dab at my grimacing lips it might have been a feather caressing me. Irate, wondering when I might decently escape (for as yet there was no offer of a second ice), I gazed out through the nearby doors at the sparkling sun-washed pavement.

"And what *do* you want candles for?" I asked, loftily.

"Ah now, there's a question. You'll be surprised, young fellow, at the answer.

"As you know," said Mr Edgar, "I tune pianos. I also have one of my own. Oh not a very good one, so old now to be sure ... But the sound, quite tolerable. So often, on Sundays especially, my late wife ... She'd put on her prettiest dress, the yellow one with white spots—a bargain, that, from a

Dapperings winter sale, for there was snow outside when she bought it, of that I do assure you—comb out her hair, lovely dark hair she had, sit down on the piano stool, and then, when dusk fell ... ''

"What?" I muttered.

"Why, I'd light the candles!"

"But you said you had electric lights?"

"To be sure. But the piano, you see, has two brass candle brackets. We had a pink candle in one, and a yellow candle in the other. My wife liked the yellow best. Yellow, she said, was sunshine and life." Briefly halting, Mr Edgar dragged a mournful finger round inside his tall white sticky collar, while, all over the pear nose, a damp began to glisten. "And that was it, you see. I loved just sitting there, in the dark, with the candles burning and my wife playing. Tunes like 'Loch Lomond'. And my wife in that pretty dress—it was the winter sale right enough, why there was snow in her hair—the light on her hair and cheek and arms ... Oh yes," and a certain energy, a spasm of virility, almost, seemed to merge quiveringly with that cloud of memory on Mr Edgar's pale brow, "oh yes, there's nothing like candlelight! And a dear one to enjoy it with."

Thoroughly uncomfortable, for this was another, embarrassingly loquacious, Mr Edgar, I gazed upwards at an air vent.

"And I still, sometimes, when I play for myself ... But not both candles. Just her favourite, the yellow one ... " Sighing, Mr Edgar tried to fold more neatly his much-used, rumpled handkerchief. "But it's not the same. Ah well, one day, and maybe not so far off," and a happier look, gaining rapidly in strength over fading wistfulness, illuminated the little man's features.

"I know a boy," I bragged, "whose mother burns candles in church!"

"Well I never," Mr Edgar said. Another spasm, compounded of memory and a suddenly revived enthusiasm, seemed to strike him. "Do you know I remember, as a lad, once lighting a candle to a pet bunny. He was dead, of course, poor little chap. But I'd heard, somewhere, that folk light a candle for the dead. As a thought, a kind of prayer ... and that's what I did for Dutch Rufus. Oh, not my choice of name I do assure you, but he was a dear little bunny rabbit. Well worth a candle!"

"Pink or yellow?" I sneered, but, obviously eager to make his purchase of new candles, and expecting, no doubt, that I would follow, Mr Edgar was already moving off.

Bet Mussolini would have bought me at least another ice cream, probably a giant double cornet, I thought, resentfully, and let my hand stray down until, with my sticky thumb, I could feel through the cloth of my trousers pocket, the hard comforting shape of the little black pebble.

Minutes later, in the sunshine outside the store, I watched the diminutive piano tuner pack his tiny bundle of candles meticulously into the worn bag on the rear of his bicycle. The whole bike, especially in the clean shimmering heat, looked shabby as ever. A pity, perhaps, that bikes weren't as easily bought and changed as candles! And then, suddenly, realisation! as something, somewhere, clicked on under my tousled thatch. Not only was this bike of Mr Edgar's the bike that had been left for quite a time leaning on the white house wall, it was, surely, also the bike I'd seen recently leaning on the wall inside the musky side passage at the York Arms! The bike that, surprisingly, had stood where that prettier bike with the bar of blue had stood. For the first time in weeks, and without quite knowing why, I remembered Betty's gentleman friend, Mr Jack Brightside, of the joke factory in Cathedral Lane. What had happened to *his* bike? Had it exploded and vanished into thin air, like one of the tricks he was supposed to sell? And what *was* Mr Edgar's bike doing in its place?

"This bike," I piped, leaping across to the kerb. "I saw it, at the public house where you tuned the piano! It *was* there, wasn't it? About," I screwed up my eyes, feeling enormously clever, "two and a half weeks ago?"

Mr Edgar, hat holding with one hand, adjusting trousers bicycle clips with the other, looked mildly astonished. After a while, with a glint of amusement in the dark eyes bright as the shine of his clips, "Well done, young man," he said, blinking benignly, "well done!"

The morning had begun well, as Sunday mornings so often did. Aunt Wells, always pleased to be off to church, from which she usually returned spiritually fortified to deal with the belchings and provocations of a differently fortified Uncle Conway, had spent longer than usual before her favourite mirror. The sun, pouring on to the glass, had brought a glittering clarity to the reflection of her person, making a wonderful summer rainbow of emerald green gloves, a soft-green drifting straw hat, and a beautiful new dress of peach colour with stray fronds of neckline, like perfectly splashed rivulets of cream milk, against the rich fruit shadings of the dress. It was, for Aunt Wells, a most daring, almost exotic, ensemble; and, fearful that it was all too bold, she had relinquished, to the unaccustomed sin of vanity, several pondering, wavering, half-pleased moments before the glass. "It does look all right, does it not, Conway? Not too startling for church? Somehow, bright colours never seem humble enough for divine worship."

Uncle Conway, not perhaps so elated, had stood nearby, watching, ready—with unusually dismal face and best bowler hat—for his Sabbath-morning walk and drink.

"What's wrong," he'd growled, "with a rattling good colour? It's only angels dress like water."

Aunt, happily troubled at her predicament, had continued to gaze at herself. Uncle, though, had suddenly crossed and, after staring into the mirror—not meeting Aunt's eyes but staring at the dress—had put a hand, clumsily, against the thin slightly freckled nape of her neck.

Aunt's skin and hair below the hat must have been damp, for, "Watercress," Uncle had mumbled, "soft brown moist watercress."

Obviously too fraught over the dress to notice the awkward, questing hand, or to hear the subdued compliment, "I always wanted, as a child, to dance like Salome," Aunt Wells had murmured. "Dance, in a peach-coloured dress, until consumed by fire!"

Abruptly Uncle Conway's hand had dropped away. "As a child," he'd retorted, looking half-embarrassed, half-shy, like a man who'd nearly made a fool of himself, "I was always being whacked. Disciplined. Fire on the burning Conway bum!"

For once, deaf to Uncle's crudity, Aunt had turned, smiling, her mind at last favourably made up towards the dress. She was, obviously, deeply content. And why not? For the sun was shining and the roots of the tall trees outside lay like old brown shoes, thick with the dust of this most wonderful of summers.

"Gordon, God's world is waiting. Are you ready for His house?"

"Yes," I'd said, dutifully clutching my slim leather bound dark red New Testament, the only unwanted gift in my last Christmas stocking, "I'm ready, Aunt Wells."

All the same, ready or not, and however impatient I was to get the wretched business over with for another week, I remember, with utter fidelity, that moment of Aunt's turning from the glass, and all the earlier moments just before. It was all sadder than sad. Sad for Uncle because, typically, he made his gesture or caress or whatever it was meant to be, at the moment when Aunt had only the dress in her thoughts, and his courage, clearly, hadn't lasted beyond that one small nervous move, and sad, too, for Aunt, who might have been willing to forgo even church for the reclamation, or repair, or exercise, of love, and a new, brave start. Oh dear, had they ever really fitted, my Aunt and Uncle? And, if they had, had they become like two neighbouring pieces of an old jig-saw, not quite the same shapes as formerly, two pieces frayed and forced about and altered by the usages and moves of time and life? Was, indeed, their interlocking ever really feasible, the girl who had wanted to dance, to swirl and float and melt in fire, the rumbustious little boy always yowling, hopping and rushing about, either from a whacking, or to escape one!

But if Sunday had begun reasonably enough, for Aunt Wells at any rate it did not continue so.

It happened on the way back from church. We had walked, Aunt and I, side by side down the long straight avenue. There wasn't a whisper of wind, only the immobile accumulated heat of the spent morning in the sparsely branched, suburban trees above us, while, below us, so scoured by sun were the paving stones one was reminded of the glistening purity of Mrs Hampton's large square hands as they dipped in and out

143

of town house washtub. Aunt, I knew as we walked, was happy. The dress scintillated, and had gone down well with fellow worshippers, or so their eyes, moving from hymn book to fellow worshipper and back as beadily and steadily as the flies crawling over the nearby stained-glass window, had proclaimed. We had passed the York Arms, on the other side of the road, and were about to turn the corner. Aunt, carrying my New Testament, for I hated being seen with a Bible and it was easy to suggest that Aunt's gloved hands were preferable against the leather to my own sticky fingers, was humming the concluding hymn of that morning's service. Her breath, peach-sweet as her appearance, barely moved the hot placid air. All the more grotesque and upsetting then, the sudden, petulant bellow of Uncle Conway's voice.

We turned. I heard Aunt gasp, saw the emerald green of her sheathed fingers tighten on the dark-blood colour of the Testament. "Oh no, dear heaven no!"

Uncle Conway was on the pavement outside the little side yard of the Arms. He was swaying, and at the same time frantically kneading, with both hands, his hapless tummy.

"Wells, help! Come and hold my hat!"

He hovered, rocking drunkenly, above the gutter. Off slipped the bowler, bouncing quickly to one side.

"His hat," I said, recovering my breath. "Oughtn't we to pick it up?"

Aunt Wells, quite shattered, looked, as if for divine guidance, up the avenue towards the distant church. A few people recognisable as fellow worshippers, dotting the road as thinly but as evocatively as the trees, were still about. Evidently deciding on a course of discretion, "No, Gordon," she said at last, in a quick steely voice, putting a hand on my shoulder and turning me about, "leave the hat. First your Uncle Conway must learn to be kind to himself. Only then will he be deserving of kindness from others. Now, let us go. I have no wish to delay."

But whatever Gods were abroad that day had suddenly turned against her, for, out through the side door of the York Arms, waving and grimacing, and curling a little finger of white, snail-shaped summons, came Auntie Alex. Down over the steps between the dustbins and a watching, slag-grey cat, across the yard beside the urinal and its inseparable

144

companion, the overlooking tree, now in high summer, its spread of leaves heaped and weary as the cat, out across the pavement—causing Uncle Conway, despite his tummy-clutching distress, to bounce quickly to one side just like his bowler — and across, with just a tinge of unsteadiness, to where Aunt and I were freshly rooted in the sun.

Cigarette in mouth, the light playing on her white dress, an obviously new affair of consummate summer finery, flashing and frothy with a large round scooped neckline, Auntie halted, with a slight careful balancing of her plump body, before us.

"In his cups, that's what, the silly monkey," she said, looking jerkily over her shoulder at the now strangely quiet, if still swaying, Uncle Conway. "Not to worry. As my late poetic Noel used to spout, When the bee stings we grin and bear it! And phrases like that don't come easy, not they. All the same it's been a carry on. With your hub, I mean. Yelling and carrying on as if he owned the place. And all in it. Saluting and making speeches and banging the bar and acting as if all the bottles was his soldiers. We're going to create a New Order, like in Europe, he kept saying. Him and the bottles, I ask you! And, when they wouldn't salute him—the bottles, not my clientele—got tearful he did. Demanded I kiss him for comfort. Yes, with my own ruby lips, the very ones once sucked by Noel! You get out, I kept telling him, you're not welcome here. You're not the respectable gentleman I thought, I told him. Next thing he began singing, arms wide-open like scissors to grab me with. Singing! Line from a hymn, or something. Other refuge have I none. That was the line. Disgusting! Thanks," she added quickly, with a last hectic rush of wobbly, excited breath, and still not looking at Aunt, "for having my daughter to tea!"

Whoosh! Across the road the tummy of my Uncle Conway was finally erupting.

"Betty," Aunt Wells said, looking as grey as the cat, "is a very pleasant young lady. And I can only apologise, most sincerely, for my husband's conduct."

"You'd think he'd have gone in the lav, wouldn't you? Creating a public spectacle seems ... oh well." Deliberately removing the cigarette from her mouth, Auntie glared at the ash at its tip, and then, as if rather too muddled to do the right

145

thing, instead of tapping it off seized her bosom and gave her breasts a lazy, reflective shake. "No more darts anyway. Our team can do without him! Not that he's been much good lately, throwing darts like air-ships in distress! Nor, definitely, I don't want him as a patron, not now or ever again." Auntie paused, becoming, suddenly, almost motherly, although still not looking directly at Aunt. "All right for cleaning women, are you? Any time you need a daily I can fix you. And hallo, son," looking for the first time at me, "eaten any good ices lately?"

Whoosh!

Trembling, damp as if from sea spray, and patently incapable, any longer, of suffering the humiliating, highly disagreeable sight of my vomiting Uncle, Aunt Wells turned away. "Come, Gordon."

A change came over Auntie. Eddying cigarette smoke seemed to twist her eyes.

"Half a mo. Your hub, isn't he? Can't have all that dreadful noise and spectacle, I can't. Not on Sunday. Oh lordy, he's moaning again. What a voice the man has."

Aunt, stopping, paler than ever as Uncle struggled slowly upright, looked desperately near to wringing her green-gloved hands.

"I have said that I am sorry."

"Being sorry won't get rid of him," said Auntie, frowning at the still tightly held Testament, though Aunt herself, by that time, must have been unaware of holding anything. "Can't you take him with you?"

"I certainly cannot. He must use his God-given legs!"

"God-given legs! Oh that's grand," Auntie Alex chortled, in the mirthful sound a strange bleak spite. "Almost poetic that. The sort of thing my late Noel deceased might have said. Not that he wasn't often in *his* cups." She paused, proudly. "And, when he was, I helped him. One good arm under his behind to keep him up, another round his waist." Sniffing, she adjusted her neckline. "That's a woman's duty, that is. In your cups it's a long long trail a-winding. That's when a hub needs his wife. Needs her strength and her legs, so to indelicately speak, more than at any other time!"

Even to me the idea of Aunt Wells staggering along the roads supporting Uncle seemed quite incredible. How it seemed to Aunt was obvious.

The Testament, clasped by both hands, moved rigidly to a position just under the circumspect flat bosom of her dress. And there, looking vulnerable, like an oblong of rich blood against the peach-frail colour of the material, it stayed.

"His legs are rubbery. Take him!"

"I must," Aunt said at last, amazed and annoyed, face tortured and drained to its thin grey limits, "say good morning."

"You're—you're not helping him?"

It seemed, for a time, as if Auntie would never recover. In fact, so comically did she gape, lips in a thick red circle, eyes as round and frothy as her neckline, that, delighted, I stuck out my tongue. And, once out, I kept it out. I never had liked Auntie anyway.

Over the road, still holding his tummy, Uncle Conway was by now staring anxiously across. The cigarette butt, in Auntie's hand, emitted, before being dropped, a last snake of shocked, angry smoke.

Suddenly, bending, she put her face close to mine. Once again I felt the warm fierce odour of her breath.

"Quite the proper little boy, aren't we, son? All in his Sunday best, fresh from morning Sunday school. Who'd have thought," she said, hands on knees, eyes, the pupils black as her beauty spot, pinched, now, with nerves and fury, "that he'd seen the glories of his Auntie Alex. That, in short, he'd seen her—to use my late Noel's immortal phrase—tit hills! Or, as your Uncle of present distress, and former playfulness, would say, mocking my Noel, 'Tit hillocks, tit hillocks, tit hillocks!'"

Sheer crucifying cold rippled down over my body. Now, at last, it was out! Now Aunt Wells would know about the purple bedroom, and my rushing under the bed, and all that I had seen!

But, when I looked, the pavement beside me was empty. Aunt must have turned and, thinking I was beside her, walked erectly away, for she was already half-way round the corner and, manifestly, had not heard a single word.

Whether it was as a result of Uncle Conway's disgraceful Sunday conduct, or merely one of Aunt's whims, I don't know. But she did, that week, scurry off to white house and hold, on the Thursday afternoon, a strawberry tea on the big lawn. All her best friends were there, Mrs Bradley, Mrs Mossman, even deaf old Mr Wedge, puffing and griping down his long blue nose, as well as along the pink wrinkled convolutions of his immoderate intestines. The strawberries were the biggest, plucked with veneration by Sam himself, and the cream that accompanied them most irresistible. It was a gathering not easily to be forgotten; it was normal and, for us, ordinary, yet curiously vivid, almost symbolic. Aunt Wells, in a new picture-hat as blue and pastel as the Thursday sky, thin arms lost in a bulky-sleeved, gushing dress of a blue even paler than pastel, seemed forever gently poking something at someone; extra helpings of splendidly iridescent cream under Mr Wedge's grumbling avaricious nose; hair-thin peelings of bread and butter for fat finicky Mrs Bradley; sober brown digestive biscuits for the quaint shy Mrs Mossman, with her habit, as she took each biscuit, of coyly exclaiming, "Oh cartwheels, I'm dropping crumbs!" even though, as each dour biscuit was tolerably firm, she wasn't dropping crumbs.

And Aunt Wells, so gracious and aware, seeming to match each guest, telling Mr Wedge, as he listened with nodding head, cupped hands, and cream-laden mouth, that a little of what one fancied did one good, and telling Mrs Bradley that bread, even with butter, was the staff of life, and telling Mrs Mossman that, even if crumbs had been dropped, by no means could a lawn be considered as vulnerable or as important as a carpet. The one big surprise, I thought, pleased, was the absence of Mr Agate from the party.

"So disappointing that he couldn't come," Aunt said. "Of course, he's busy. Dear, diligent man! All the same, I do hope that I have done nothing to offend him."

"As if you could," said Mrs Bradley. "A dear man, indeed. And so wise."

"Oh cartwheels, I'm dropping crumbs!" said Mrs Mossman, accepting a biscuit.

"Brains, that Agate chap," said Mr Wedge, grabbing and rolling his walking stick between gnarled fingers, and making, with the fingers of his other hand, a gnarled beefy shell around his large left ear. "Charm even Herr Hitler out of a tree. And that other foreigner—what's his name? That Italian chap?"

Crouching cross-legged and disgruntled (the afternoon at

148

school hadn't been a happy one) under a tree, I came suddenly alive.

"Mussolini!" I broke in, excitedly.

"That will be enough from you, Gordon," Aunt Wells said, wearily, as if back on an old, tiresome road, but aged Mr Wedge had other ideas.

His stick waved, his eyes brightened, and his right foot, encased in a high boot, just missed striking a plate of duck-egg blue languishing on the grass.

"Capital, capital! More than conkers to this youngster, what! Knows more than I do, fine little chap."

"How I agree that the horse chestnut," said Aunt Wells, quickly, blinking a trifle, "is far too beautiful for use only as a weapon of sport for boys. Plop from the trees they drop, shining in the grass. The honest brown eyes of autumn. And there they should be left. In the grass."

"Youngsters these days," old Wedge grumbled, undiverted by Aunt's desperate poesy. "No idea, most of 'em. It's the young folk of our district keep that damnable town speedway running!"

If Aunt had feared that the inflammable topic of Mussolini had been about to rear its head, then she may have thought that, with Mr Wedge's little tirade, her worries were over. But they weren't. They were just beginning. The sun drenched the last few strawberries, the pale green paper napkins, the strawberry smeared duck-egg blue plates, the pale-yellow plates with cake, the plates empty of all but crumbs, the lawn, the big tree—made hotter, too, the fury in my heart.

"I like speedway. It's good! Good! Not for sissies!"

The brim of Aunt's picture-hat seemed to tilt, the shadiness beneath vanishing in a shocked amazed twinkling of surprise. Mrs Bradley and Mrs Mossman both fell silent, their eyes a little rounder, their lips slack, while Mr Wedge, apparently not even needing to cup his hand to hear my outburst with, produced a sudden, harrowing excess of wind that flew across the party like a breeze between the tables. Nor was Sam out of it. On the edge of the lawn I could see him riveted, rump up-tilting like Aunt's hat brim. Lifting a finger he took a sudden suck, and glared across. Sam would, I knew, agree with Mr Wedge about the speedway, and abruptly, tumultuously, I hated both of them. Silly old men, what did they know, or understand? They had no pebble in their pockets, no hearts full of heroes, no speedway riders, or a Mussolini, to revere. Again, exultantly, through the shiny stuff of my trousers, I felt the pebble's thrust, its warmth from my own young body. All the way from simmering Rome it had come, to land in my pocket, in my trousers, and there wasn't a conker in the world I'd have swopped it for! Good old Mussolini! Here the world was, all bright-green and gold, and both I and Musso living in it, and that, somehow, made for joy. The Signor didn't have to mean anything, not politically anyway. It was enough that he was important, that he pumped out his black-sleeved arm, and widened his great eyes, and always had acclaim. Just as I would one day have acclaim, scorching the cinders like a Red Pope! With Betty watching and cheering me on! Lovely, jolly Betty, with her round white arms and lips of summer velvet. But how could I ride and Betty watch and Mussolini hear of my spreading fame and daring ('Dear Ben,' I would tell him, in a grown-up letter, 'I've still got your pebble. It's my lucky mascot. I never ride without it. Many thanks.') if there wasn't any speedway left to ride on? And there wouldn't be, I knew, if daft old Wedge and stupid Sam had their wretched way.

So there I was, at bay, crouching on that lawn with its genteel, gently wilting people and its remnants of strawberry tea, boiling mad all over again. Arrogant, too. As if the pebble in my pocket had turned into a glass of heady Roman wine and had found its copious way to my unaccustomed stomach.

"Ferts!" I exploded, shrilly and derisively, glaring at Mr Wedge.

The old chap's knees wobbled. "Eh? What!"

"Ferts. Up with speedway. Ferts!"

The word ferts just came. Obviously, being of my own making (I think) the word was pure enough, but to the ladies and gentleman of the tea party it must have seemed that some kind of obscenity, or blasphemy, or even accusation, was abroad. Mr Wedge, for one, looked both guilty and horrified.

"Oh terrible, terrible," crooned Mrs Bradley, rocking her fat. "What a terrible boy!"

"Well I'm blessed," said Mrs Mossman, sullenly, breaking another biscuit and forgetting all about crumbs and cartwheels.

"Ferts!" I yelled across the lawn at Sam. "Ferts!"

"Gordon! Silence, hysterical boy!" Aunt Wells, leaping up, sent her hat skipping across a table. Two thin forearms flew from the wide sleeves after it.

"Up speedway, up Mussolini, ferts!" I ranted.

"Young people and children, worship of noise and vulgarity!" Mr Wedge, fishing up Aunt's hat from the lawn with his stick, tried to contain his turmoil. "Too much cream, that's the trouble. Too much cream these days for boys."

"It is the cream," Aunt Wells said, desperately. "The boy is, I am afraid, spoilt. Gordon, you will apologise. You will apologise, and bow, to Mr Wedge. But first, as there are ladies present, you will apologise, and bow, to the ladies. Oh yes, Mrs Mossman, I insist. Oh dear, I am so very glad that Mr Agate couldn't come!"

After a long green sunlit silence during which it seemed that even the tall plain chimneys of white house held their breath, "Sorry," I mumbled, "sorry I said ferts!"

At this both Mrs Bradley and Mrs Mossman squealed a little, Mrs Bradley even dropping a plump tense hand on Mr Wedge's quivering knee, while, from the corner of my eye, I glimpsed Sam's stiffly departing rump. "I heard you a-ferting, Mister Gordon, and I wants amends," he'd be sure to say, later.

"Don't," Aunt Wells instructed, icily, faintly tremulous hands resettling her hat, "repeat that word. And bow, Gordon. Yes, properly, with one hand behind you and one across your waist!"

Ferts I said, in my mind, while twitching in a bow, ferts to everyone!

After the apologies, peremptorily dismissed from any further share in the tea party, I trailed inside, into the cool wide depths of white house, up to my bedroom over the kitchen. In my mind Signor Mussolini, Red Pope and Betty, were silent, ghostly comforters. And how I needed comfort! Fancy having to miss the last of the strawberries, a last lick of the cream on the cream dish, the last of the cakes and, maybe—if Mrs Cartwheels Mossman left any—the last of the biscuits! "Ferts!" I said, to my reflection in the ancient, well-scratched dressing-table mirror, giving, at the same time, one of my impatient Uncle Conway salutes. "Ferts!"

I was sitting on the edge of the bed, thinking of another

151

dressing-table mirror, the one in the pink bedroom at the York Arms, and how fortunate *that* glass was daily to reflect Betty's smooth arms, turning now to palest brown, and merry eyes, and feel the warm sweet mist of her breath as she leant to tidy a hair or dab her mouth, when the door opened with a sudden, lusty creak, and Aunt Wells came in. She had taken off her picture-hat and was regarding it despondently, as if it were a blue seaside pool that, reluctantly, at day's end, must be left behind. "They've gone," she said, looking also as if she ought to scold me but was too tired to begin. "Come, we've just got time to catch the early evening bus to town."

"What about the washing up, Aunt Wells?"

"All done, Gordon. In any case I'll send Mrs Hampton out here tomorrow morning to finish any tidying. Sam's clearing the lawn."

I remember the bus carrying us away, and even today I remember that bus, in a peculiar way, as the Thursday-evening bus. We sat near the back, on smelly hot brown leather, Aunt in a change of hat, a less flamboyant, more practical creation; and, peering back past it as it sat squarely on her head, I caught a last early evening glimpse of white house with failing sun across the high parsnip-coloured chimneys and a sudden dazzle in the plain upper windows. It seemed to me then, in that placid moment on the bumpy cheerful bus, that white house and strawberry teas on the big lawn would last, as would summer itself, forever.

18

At nine o'clock the following evening the front door of town house began to shake from a tempestuous, almost barbaric knocking. It was the most dreadful knocking I'd ever heard, making my thick tufty hair stand up even straighter, while Uncle Conway and Aunt Wells just sat as if turned to alabaster. In one way, perhaps, the knocking was providential, for my guardians had been brewing up their own kind of storm ever since an early supper of fried onions and slightly high sausages had failed to settle either their stomachs or tempers. Uncle Conway, smoking cigarette after cigarette to calm his indigestion, and for once not isolated in his study, had been busily arranging, so he claimed, notes for his great political treatise on modern Europe. Aunt Wells had been reading her Bible (not the Song of Solomon) attempting to instruct with her own verbal treatise on the ethics of godly and successful living. "I have often thought that lateness might well have been named as a deadly sin. You, Gordon, were late home from school. So, together, we will search for an appropriate biblical text. A text of fire and of chastisement, suitable for the modern, thoughtless boy."

"Oh, pack him off to bed, Wells," Uncle had complained. "Here am I, trying to collate my Roman notes, and all I hear is claptrap from the Sacred Golden Treasury of Jewish Etiquette! Disgusting, damn it!"

"Not as disgusting," Aunt Wells flashed, "as being a heathen!"

Uncle Conway had begun to quiver and turn colour when the pounding on the front door interrupted.

"Infamous!" Uncle roared. "Some damn Bolshevik from the sound of it! I'm off to the study."

But he didn't move. Aunt Wells, one hand on the Bible, one at her stately throat, didn't move either. The crashing at the door was frightening, as if one of the trees from the drive, like a tall strong sinister visitor, was smashing impatiently to and fro in the old tawny porch.

"Very well," Uncle Conway said at last, gulping. "I—I'll go."

Moving her Bible quickly to one side on the burnished table Aunt Wells rose, frowned at a nearby clock, and followed him out. As I followed Aunt Wells I suddenly thought how frail and faintly comical they both looked from behind: Uncle Conway with his recent haircut, short and prickly at the rear, and the rear of Aunt Wells' neck, with a big dark freckle between two loose strands of hair. And the way they walked, each differently but each in the same human fallible way, the eternal way of people ageing, their quirks and physical peculiarities growing more entrenched and theatrical every day. And Aunt Wells so close behind Uncle as he crossed the cluttered hall that, in a fashion, and despite all differences, they had a unity. I sensed, and saw, so much in those moments as the front door rattled. I saw the first vague sign of Uncle Conway's bounce becoming a hobble, of Aunt Wells' hair becoming less than lustrous, of timidity waxing and confidence ebbing. It was all there in the way they approached that clamouring door, the way Uncle Conway bent, clumsily shot back the bolts and opened up, and then the way they both moved back and stood, lost and waiting and petrified, on the thick indifferent carpet.

"It's me, Mister," said Sam, vapouring and hopping in the porch, "and I've a-brought bad news!"

Behind Sam, a policeman with a pale face and young, staring eyes appeared.

"White house!" Sam steamed, his brown teeth almost rattling. "She's a-burning! All on her on fire!"

"No!" Uncle Conway thundered. "By God, I don't believe it!"

"True, sir, I'm afraid," said the policeman.

Apparently Sam had turned up at white house to do an evening stint of gardening, and found fire. And although the fire brigade had arrived and was at work it wasn't yet in command of the flames.

Aunt Wells didn't speak for quite a while.

"The car," she said, eventually, a curious curtain, half pain, half disbelief, in her eyes. "Conway, we must go at once."

It was a quick, terrible journey. Almost unnoticed I sat at the back, wrapped in a coat—for all it was a warm evening—while Uncle Conway sat grimly, driving jerkily to his own crescendo of snorts, imprecations and mutterings. Aunt Wells, beside him, had donned a fur coat. For once she was hatless. Not once did she speak or turn her head. Her head, it seemed to me, was turned only one way. Towards white house.

As we chugged up the lane (was she, I wonder, aware of the irony that at last she was being driven to white house not by taxi or bus but by Uncle Conway in his car?) we saw the house blazing, a fire engine in the drive and people in the garden, all over the garden, on the big lawn and in the drive away from the house and even on the straight furrows and abashed dusk-dim plants of the vegetable beds.

"Oh, God," Aunt Wells said. No more. But so unlike her.

I remember the car stopping, and Aunt Wells and Uncle Conway joining the watchers. As if ashamed they made no move to draw attention to themselves, but instead just stood gazing at the fire, Uncle Conway shifting uneasily up and down inside his mac and wagging his head as if to shake off ash, Aunt Wells, numb inside her fur coat, looking so stiff she might have toppled at a touch. As for me, I stood by the car, not sure what to think or do, eyes glued to the huge greedy clawing brightness before me, aware only of a horrifying indistinct suspicion which, like the long bonnet of the car, now alive with subtle glows, curled and flickered coldly in my mind.

For, like Sam and, previously that day, Mrs Hampton, I, too, had been at white house, only earlier than Sam. Immediately after afternoon school I'd caught a bus, one of the country ones we always used and, only fifteen minutes later, was letting myself in with a gleaming key, one of several, easily obtainable white house keys that Aunt kept in case of loss. What luck! I'd thought, Sam not about, the whole place mine! Feeling guilty, yet liberated and masterful too, I'd roamed the house, stopping from time to time to listen, and then resuming, hear again with wonder my own footsteps, for they hardly seemed to belong to me so clearly and cheekily did they fall. Finally, though, as if forced to my own small territory by the long cool spaces of Aunt's favourite rooms, I'd entered my bedroom. There, Aunt Wells' kitchen clean and bleak and disapproving beneath me, I'd unfolded the big new jaggedly cutout newspaper picture. Sticking it to the scratched old mirror of the dressing table by chewing-gum blobs was easy, and so was everything else I did, for, eagerly taking from my pocket a candle, stolen, like the key, from Aunt Wells' private store, and wedging it tightly between two large books, I'd lit without difficulty the tiny wick, watching it flare to pure yellow life, the flame swaying, gently and solemnly, like an Arabian dancer, between myself and the picture of Red Pope.

19

The refreshing breezes puffed across the gentle hills, making here and there, in the mellow green and yellow grasses, a constant long-sleeved shivering. Humped on his stool outside the café the accordionist, blind face turned to the valley, played gratefully and steadily, for it was still very warm, the paint on the café shone as whitely as ever, and the blue of Bluebird above the door couldn't have been more perfect. Even Aunt Wells, clad in her own new dress of impossibly pale blue, with a straw of darker blue to accompany it rather less successfully than the picture hat had done, admitted that it wasn't at all a bad summer's day, though her voice, from the climb, was breathless and strangely tired.

"I'm glad we have come," she said, sitting this time a little away from the café, on an iron bench under a steep green bank. "Gordon, you have the trousers?"

What a question! Couldn't she see I had the trousers inside a parcel of brown paper tied with string, painstakingly assembled by herself only that morning, and that I clutched that parcel as reluctantly as she always clutched the used empty drinking glasses left around by Uncle Conway? Couldn't she see that the whole idea of giving something old and unwanted to a stranger was enough to make a small boy squirm? Or was there mud in her eye that day, the mud of a well-remembered battlefield where, hideous head wound hidden by that German helmet, her dear original sweetheart had lain amid cracks of running blood that stamped a sad red trellis on the earth? When Aunt looked at the eyes of the blind man, was that what she saw, the Great War and its victims, not excluding dear beloved? I never knew for sure, and perhaps Aunt never knew, whether that accordion player on the hills had been born unsighted or made that way by war, but whatever the truth it hardly mattered, he served symbolically to draw her most exquisite pity, if only in the form of old discarded trousers!

Not so with Uncle Conway. Only that morning, when Aunt made her request, he had made his viewpoint very plain.

"A pair of my old bags?" he'd rapped, spitting out crumbs

of toast into the coffee-aromatic air. "Really, Wells, I believe in the survival of the fittest, and not in pampering the idle bums of idle blind men! Whatever next! Why, wearing my trousers might give him the energy to populate the world with his own inferior seed."

"This blind man labours," Aunt Wells struck back, ignoring, or simply not seeing, Uncle's humour. "Those hills would not be the same without him. It is a mournful sight just to see him play so beautifully."

"A sadder sight if he played badly, surely?" Uncle Conway had leapt blithely up, a cloud of toast crumbs, scattered by his flying jacket, rolling through sunshine to the carpet. "Accordion, what an instrument! Hills demand at least a drum roll. A rum tum tum and a pom pom pom, echoing, echoing," and Uncle, standing now before a summer fireplace of unlit coal and red crinkly paper, began to thrum and rotate and jerk his stomach.

"Oh go to your study. Go and hide. That's where *you* play, isn't it? In your study?"

As if for once he didn't think he deserved such a tart response, Uncle Conway had turned a pale, surprised blue.

"All right," he'd mumbled, at last. "Take a pair. I don't care."

"I will select a pair of your older, shinier trousers," Aunt Wells said. "Thank you, Conway."

For Aunt in this at least was typical; I am sure that she never ever thought of charity as it often most unhappily is, a lesser morality. However unconsciously, her most practical thoughts and impulses well befitted her life station. She had money now, even if it didn't, as with Uncle, completely rule her.

Wriggling, on the iron bench, with the horror of it all, yet unable to contain a certain fanciful speculation, "Will the blind man play better," I said, "wearing Uncle's trousers?"

"Gordon, what a notion! Although, of course, warmer trousers might mean better circulation and a greater energy! Not to mention a greater pride in oneself and one's activities."

"But it's so hot, Aunt. It's summer. Mightn't the trousers just make him sweat?"

The accordionist, ending a tune, wiped his brow with his sleeve, after first using his fingers to wipe his nose. Then, with a new breeze stirring in the grasses, a new tune, one as blue in feeling as the café signboard. Despondently, the wretched parcel strangely heavy in my lap, I watched him play. His cap, waiting for coins, nestled beside his polished left boot. Although at times his foot moved rhythmically, it never once touched the cap.

"Oh, Gordon, how could you have been so careless? After all I have said, over the years, about the dangers of fire."

I looked at Aunt Wells. She also was watching the blind man, but not, I suddenly knew, with eyes that saw.

"I forgot," I said, not for the first time, "to put out the candle."

What had happened? Perhaps only the scratched old mirror, its anxious face reflecting the flame of the candle that I'd so wantonly lit, could have answered. Perhaps the candle itself had fallen over, or, as the flame burnt down, set fire to the books that held it. I didn't know. I knew only, as did Aunt Wells, that fire was terrible. Terrible, indeed, that a candle, and a lonely, weak flame, could be so wicked, so hungry, and that, because of that hunger, the ship with orange and tangerine sails would never again, except in memory, dip through the waters on the wall of the big creamy front room, the big green vase never again rustle to an imaginary rat, the green-black chintz on the table in the breezy kitchen reflect the morning shine of sunlight, the picture hat of pastel blue, left behind in a wardrobe, never again grace Aunt's proud head, the piano played by Betty and tuned by Mr Edgar no more brightly sound. Most terrible of all, white house itself gone. With every day that passed the bleak implacable fact of its going sank deeper in.

"Don't cry, Aunt Wells," I said, blinking as she blinked, swallowing as she swallowed.

"His only real gift," I heard Aunt whisper in the breeze, "for it was mine in all but deed. Truly, truly mine!" And then, knowing that I'd heard, and perhaps feeling disloyal, "Your poor Uncle," she added, voice soft, as if she suddenly knew, much later than she should have done, that Conway's high spirits at breakfast time were, after all, in the nature of a cheering-up gift for which she ought to have been grateful, "it shocked him too."

The blue tune finished, and a livelier song began.

"Can it be built again, Aunt Wells? Or another house?"

"Oh, Gordon, how simple your world. White house has flown, and that is that."

Half expecting to see white house in heaven, glimmering angelically, I looked towards the sky.

"Am I wicked, Aunt Wells? Will I go to heaven?"

"It will depend, Gordon, on the life you lead and the man you become. And the love you give."

"Love, Aunt Wells?" Into my mind danced a vision of Betty in her yellow dress; a foolish grin curved my lips.

"Beginning now, Gordon. You will take the parcel and place it neatly beside the blind gentleman's cap. You will say, 'My aunt thanks you for your beautiful playing and hopes that you will accept this parcel.' Is that clear, Gordon?"

As if aware of my shame the world had seemingly fallen silent, the accordion silent, no breeze across the hills, no voices or skipping of children's feet.

"Please, Aunt, you do it," I pleaded in a Sunday sitting in pew whisper.

"No, Gordon, you will do it. Though truly but a tiny act of love and contrition, it is at least a start. And who shall disparage that first small leap to paradise? Certainly, I am sure, not the watching angels on their gladsome wings of song!"

"Don't want paradise," I gritted, glaring into the silent sky. "Can't I just leave the trousers without saying anything!"

"That was my intention," Aunt Wells agreed, dabbing, first with a mauve handkerchief, then a blue, at weary slightly damp eyes. "But the time has come, Gordon, for character building. Remember when you took the ring back? That did not turn out so badly, did it? And this is such an easier thing, a mere sparrow of a gesture which, however, we may be sure will bear the ripest fruit."

Bananas! I thought, rudely.

"Proceed then, Gordon. You have nothing to be ashamed of. Conway's trousers, shine notwithstanding, are of the finest serge. Remember, 'My aunt thanks you for your beautiful playing and hopes that you will accept this parcel.'"

There was no escape. Holding the parcel as if I hoped it might disappear into myself for ever, over I crossed. Dust, as I dragged the leather soles, puffed from under my shoes, my eyes gazed at the café hoping it might vanish along with the blue of its name, along with the blind man, and along with everyone else sitting enjoying the air at that little beauty spot cut so romantically into the green hills. I saw, in the window of the café, not only my own reflection but that of another boy nearby, a grin on his monkey face, as if he guessed only too well my discomfort. And then, miraculously, I was there, within touching distance of the accordion, and the blind man's hands. Still between tunes, he was rubbing, after again rubbing his nose, a grubby finger against the shabby silvery filigree on the end of his instrument. Close to he looked strangely like that filigree, shabby with the silver traces under nostrils. There were also accordion-like folds in his cheeks, a rip in his white shirt, and red patches showed under the dowdy bristle of a cavernous chin. I didn't like him. His rough look and queer eyes scared me. And he smelt in a strange, raw way. Not even Uncle Conway had smelt quite like that.

"My aunt," I gabbled, dropping my burden, "thanks you, and hopes that you will accept this parcel!"

But it wasn't to be so easy. Before I could edge away out shot the blind man's arm, grabbing mine. The café, sky, accordion, all flashed and rocked around me.

"Fanks me fer what? What do yer aunt fank me fer?"

It was as though the ears of the blind man, big fierce swollen ears they were, had been sharp enough to hear Aunt's every word.

"Er, for—for your beautiful playing!" I tried to pull away, but was firmly locked by the unsavoury grip.

"Ain't boots, is it young charmer? Not boots. Boots is me pride. Look at 'em. Look! Newish uns, all shone up!" A great corrugated hand, scraping over my tender skin, pressed my neck down until, bent ignominiously over, I was actually breathing the gleaming leather of a warm, lifted boot. If there was, in the blind man's voice and action, an intentional humour (surely, I reflect now, he'd heard the soft bootless landing of the dropped parcel?) it quite eluded me. Instead, as he held me, I felt like pliant hapless toffee being robustly bitten into. And the smell was so terrible, stemming no doubt from a thick fetid sock that rarely saw the light of day or the soap of a washtub. Much more, I thought, gasping, and I'd faint, or die! "Wouldn't want to fank yer aunt fer boots, I wouldn't!"

"No, no, not boots, trousers!" Appalled, words rushed

160

from me. "They're—they're good. Hardly worn at all, Aunt says. Just—just a shine where Uncle Conway sits down."

"Big bum, yer uncle, eh? Big bum, big shine. That it, eh?"

Frantically, my head wagged in dissent. As did my knees, indeed my whole body.

"Uncle—Uncle Conway isn't very big! Honest!"

"Small, eh?" Down floated a fat, spiky chuckle. "No good ter me then, his bags ain't."

The boot leather, shifting, rammed my nose. The whole world, it seemed, had changed to a hard, glaring black.

"No good ter me then, eh?"

Nose running now in panic against the leather, "They're good trousers!" I reprised, desperately. A huge sick wave of hate and indignation overwhelmed me. "No patches on them either, not like that big rotten patch on yours!"

Suddenly, as if pierced by an unexpectedly cool breeze, the strong, delving fingers about my neck abated. After a moment, with a jagged, abruptly subdued, "Fank yer aunt kindly then, eh, young charmer, with many tas," the rough hand returned to the accordion and, within seconds, like a graceful lightweight broom sweeping away unpleasant cobwebs, another winsome tune blew in the air.

Freed at last, I reacted combustively. The hill, below me, fell grandly away, and, turning, arms outspread, off I whirled, chasing down over the grass, rejoicing in escape, a kind of aeroplane fleeing from the earth. Shedding in noise and flight all recent humiliation, bending to and fro, dodging roots, hurtling past trees I was, all too briefly, a happy scudding bullet of a boy. This way, the world again was mine! But soon alarm! for once started on a downward rush how to stop? my legs had taken over, pistoning furiously onward against all inclination. Stop! I told myself, knees so high they nearly met my chest. Stop! But, easier said than done, on I swept, driving, pounding, heart bursting, breath bursting, body bruised, burnt and jolted by the crazy descent. Perhaps, after all, a return to Aunt Wells on the bench, and a sufferance of the grins and sniggers of the watchers, including the smirks of the horrid monkey-faced boy, would have been preferable to this!

It ended quickly. Suddenly, the slope finished. Below me an alcove had been carved into the grassy side of an ascending path. In the alcove a bench, of iron painted green, on which two people sat. Down towards their heads, innocently close together as they surveyed the panorama, I zipped. Like a thin ping of wind shooting from a tinny old flute, like an emissary of the breeze! But the heads didn't hear, or turn, at my whistling approach. Nothing for it but to leap across ruffling, in my passage through the air, their unsuspecting hair, and crash land on the hard glinting path beyond! Up, over and down in one colossal tortured bound!

As I landed, like a dropped hen in the dust, up, in their turn, leapt the two startled people on the bench.

"Why, pet, it's you!" cried Betty, running forward. "Gosh, are you hurt? Injured?"

"Why, that young man again!" said her companion, also advancing, and I looked, stunned not by the fall but with disbelief, at Mr Edgar.

"Help him up, Georgie pet," Betty said, and I felt a familiar, gentle hand hoist my elbow.

It was, of course, *my* Mr Edgar. The piano tuner. The soft little man who liked bunny rabbits. And candles.

And not only rabbits and candles. Dazedly I watched him put a dusty, mild black arm about Betty's slender waist. "There," he said, affectionately, "the boy's all right. Quite hale, I do assure you. Boys usually are."

"Why," I asked, blankly and rudely, "are you here on the hills? Why aren't you tuning pianos?"

Mr Edgar looked alarmed, and slightly hurt. It was Betty who replied.

"Pet," she said, looking as pink and pretty as her bedroom at the York Arms, "pin back your ears. Mr Edgar, George and I, why, we've just got engaged! Engaged to be married! Isn't that simply sparkling?"

"Gordon!" I heard Aunt Wells calling from above, her voice like a stern silver trumpet through the trees. "Where are you?"

Mr Edgar took Betty's hand and, raising it, held it tightly, affably rubbing it the while against that shiny, pear-shaped nose.

"Your aunt," he said. "How nice. We must all, ah yes, take tea together at the café and listen to the music. Quite a treat, that blind accordionist, I do assure you. Afterwards, perhaps, Betty and I will give you a penny or two, or maybe sixpence, and you can take them across and drop them in his hat. You'd like that I'm sure, would you not, young man?"

20

It was at about this time that a melancholy deeper than any previous melancholy settled on town house. Aunt Wells, still awry from the loss of white house, took over more work from Mrs Hampton than Mrs Hampton liked; once, scratching angrily under her armpits in an unusual paddy, Mrs H was heard to say that if it wasn't for her impeccable sense of tradition and loyalty she would long ago have given notice. Sam, although left alone, also grew belligerently melancholic. "I ain't a-giving up on them white house weeds," he'd say, driving a bellicose spade at a hapless town house worm, "not yet I ain't." "Sam, Sam, the two garden man!" I'd chant, mockingly, freed, now, by school holidays, to be a day long pest. But perhaps the most significant melancholy of all afflicted Uncle Conway.

How the emphasis of Uncle's habits changed during that August. There was still the Sunday morning walk and drinks, though not at the York Arms. The York Arms, Uncle stridently complained, had rejected his patronage. He drank more, strutted less, and fulminated increasingly in his study. One morning, to my surprise, I even found that he had taken out that early picture of Aunt Wells and put it in a new gilt frame. It stood there on his desk, speaking, perhaps, of a secret deprivation, of a need to be worshipped or, at any rate, demonstrably admired. But if Aunt Wells saw the signal she gave no sign or comfort. She, herself, was ghost-like. She couldn't be touched. She drifted, now, in a stately deprived oblivion of her own. "A ship without a sail," she would say, over and over, moving, dusters in hand, from unnecessary chore to unnecessary chore, "a vessel becalmed, that is how I feel."

"Where," Aunt Wells asked, "is Conway?"

"Upstairs," I said, "talking to himself. I heard him say that only Herr Hitler could stem the rising tide of Bolshevism. Is Bolshevism the name of a seaside town, Aunt Wells?"

"No, Gordon, it is not. Your Uncle's phrase has nothing to do with water or the sea, more to do with the danger to money and property." Tiredly Aunt brushed a hand across her brow, squinting as if for light in the dark cool room. "Evidently, then, he is working on his book and we should not, therefore, disturb him. But I must get out, I must!" And she looked through the heavily curtained window, her eyes carefully glazing over so as to avoid a clear sunlit view of Sam's buttocks, furiously upturned as he dug.

"Bus or taxi? Taxi, I think," she said.

It was half past two, by the pendulum clock, when the taxi arrived. To my slight puzzlement Aunt Wells came downstairs holding her case.

"Just a few things, yours and mine," she told me, smiling.

But after walking along the drive under trees that by now were as warm and gracious and hospitable as ladies at a summer fete, she changed her mind.

"We will walk," she said to the scowling taxi man, glancing quickly up at Uncle's window (if he was watching he must have been as baffled as I) and then at the ribbon-silky blue sky. "It is such a lovely day. But I will pay you for your trouble."

It was the longest walk she and I had ever taken together. Each bus stop was firmly ignored. At an erect, even pace, the case rigidly held at the bottom of her flowing sleeve, Aunt Wells whisked across grassy traffic islands and over dusty kerbs, each stride part of a long tense chain. Only an occasional house or garden would slow her march; bringing forth a brief, wistful, but quite unremarkable, "That is a lovely house. A nice garden." Socks slipping perpetually over my ankles as I hurried to keep up, "Aunt Wells," I kept saying, "where are we going?" But presently, as houses fell away and lanes began, it was clear that we were in fact making for white house. Nor did this seem unreasonable, even to me. The night of the fire never had been very real, except at the time. It was one night only, one visit only, to be set against the hundreds of visits when white house was alive and well. I think that Aunt, too, at the outset of our walk anyway, had felt as I did. But if so, it didn't last. The further we walked the more I sensed in Aunt a fading optimism, her strides, faltering, began to jar on stones and trip on twigs, once she even paused to stoop and wearily press her knee. But, as she herself might have said, and indeed had said when tackling, one day, the task of picking up splinters from one of Uncle Conway's errant discarded whisky bottles, the gold of her wedding ring glinting no less than the glass, "The hand, having been set to the plough, must finish the furrow." So sad she had sounded.

The last lane before white house was excruciating. I swear, to this day, that Aunt walked it with eyes tightly shut and lips moving in prayer.

It made no difference. Ugly charcoal inside a shell, that was the new white house. The chimneys, still in position, looked like giant singed parsnips; debris had blown across the vegetable beds and even reached the lawn. It seemed incredible, one small candle causing so much havoc.

Aunt Wells put down her case, plucked a handkerchief from under her wilting sleeve, and wiped her brow. In a tiny, desperate voice, "Bother!" she said.

Turning over the case I sat miserably down on it in the middle of the lane. "Sorry, Aunt Wells," I mumbled.

"Get up, foolish boy, you will be run over. Here, let me dust the case."

She bent down and picked it up, blinking as she brushed at the hard hot leather.

A tiny spasm of impatience gripped me. Surely there was more for us to do than cry?

"Can we look round the garden? We can, can't we, Aunt Wells?"

"Of course, Gordon. I need a rest anyway. That ironwork seat on the lawn looks more tempting than it has ever looked."

But the little ironwork chair, with its uncomfortable humped seat over tall legs, was not the only object on the lawn. Under a tree, like a waiting shadow, or a piece of blackened wood from the burnt house, stood a familiar little man in bicycle clips and worn dark suit.

"Why, Mr Edgar!" Aunt Wells exclaimed.

"Oh glad to see you, very glad," Mr Edgar said, his dark deep eyes, as mournful and blinky as those of Aunt Wells had been, turning timidly beyond us towards the wrecked house. "The fact is ... I've had the most terrible shock!"

"Our piano's burnt," I snapped. "You can't play it now. Or tune it!"

Aunt, motioning me to silence, looked mildly surprised.

"But, Mr Edgar, I told you about the fire, surely, that day on the hills? I remember distinctly telling both you and Miss Hallet."

It was now Mr Edgar's turn, using that musty sprawling

handkerchief of his, to wipe his brow, leaving, however, the pear nose beneath still glistening with the peculiar dew of his troubled emotions. "Yes, to be sure you did, only ... well, I forgot. You see, I came here in a dazed condition, you might say."

"Dazed?" Aunt Wells said, adding, in a slightly deeper voice, "Condition?"

"Oh, not drunk or anything, not that I do assure you. No, it's my brother, Jack." The little man took a huge frightened breath, eyes widening to circles as big and bright as his clips. "He—he's dead!"

A curl of ash, no thicker than paper, blew across the lawn and was gone before Aunt Wells could even see let alone retrieve it.

"Dead?" Aunt said.

"Yes, this morning. Just dropped. In the road, outside Hudson's the barbers. Just paid for a haircut he had, his very last. When I heard I couldn't help thinking ... a crop for the coffin! Funny isn't it, what we think at such times? When my dear wife went it was just after a cup of tea, weak hospital tea, or so I believe, and I thought, a cup for the coffin! A ... a cup for the coffin!"

For the first time that day, and perhaps for many days, Aunt Wells came near to being her old self. Reaching briskly out, her sleeve like an unfurled banner about to go to war, she grasped Mr Edgar's trembling black elbow.

"Come!" she ordered, once again the caring hostess as she led him to the ironwork chair.

"No warning, no inkling of anything at all," Mr Edgar said, sitting helplessly on the cheerless, rusting seat. "Just ... fell."

Without replying, Aunt Wells bent and unfastened her case. Taking out, and opening, a small green bottle, she thrust it under Mr Edgar's nostrils. "Sniff!" she commanded.

Fascinated I watched the quiverings of the pear nose, now, like the eyes, watering freely.

"Lean back," Aunt said, for although the seat was virtually backless there was behind it a benign broad tree. Kneeling, she untied with great tenderness his boot laces (why she did this I never did understand, unless Mary ministering to the feet of Jesus was an unconscious biblical precedent) after first removing, with equal tenderness, the bicycle clips. "There,"

166

she said rising, and sounding as if she'd done far too little, sadly much less than she would have liked, "just rest awhile. Your brother. How terrible. How truly terrible." And, shaking her head, slid the clips on to a nearby branch where, briefly and feebly, they jangled together like tiny distressed bells.

"Not that we'd got on lately, Jack and I," Mr Edgar said, following with foggy eyes the swaying clips. "He didn't approve of my ... courting again. Not so quickly after ... my first dear lady."

"Now just lean back, just rest," Aunt Wells counselled, although how the semi-spreadeagled Mr Edgar could lean back any further was beyond me.

"I came here," Mr Edgar said, "without thinking. Just for comfort, for what other reason, you always having been so kind. Forgetting ... forgetting the fire." He paused, rummaging in his pocket as if for a second cavernous handkerchief to supplement the first. "Nowhere else to turn," he said, pulling out the pocket lining and trying, stupidly and blindly, to tug it up to his face, "not today. Betty and her mother away. Up to Blackpool, I understand. Just for the day."

"Auntie Alex loves Blackpool," I declared, haughtily, glad to have something to contribute at last. "It suits her belly button. She met Uncle Conway there, she says, but I don't believe her! She's a big fat silly thing," I added, remembering with scorn those screams of panic as I'd dived beneath her bed and clanged against her chamber pot and tried to breathe in the stuffy purple rich air between carpet and bed. And now, apparently, she had returned to Blackpool. Serve her right, I thought, if the sea breezes blew away her button, and her big white chests, and her curly hair, and the beauty spot, and the funny smell of her breath, and serve her right, too, if she fell on the sandcastle, as Uncle was supposed to have done, and cut her leg on a bucket or spade and lost a big white toe to a big pink crab in the tide!

There was a silence on the lawn just as if my thoughts had been shouted to the sky, shocking everyone. Only bees talked, humming through the lazy air, wary and, at times, hanging back, as though some miasma thrown as a barrier from the blackened house had made them cautious.

Aunt was still looking down at Mr Edgar. She wasn't moving, and I couldn't see her face. Only her hand, resting on

167

her hip, seemed suddenly a little tighter, a little paler in the saturating heat.

"Would have turned to Betty, naturally," Mr Edgar started off again. "Her mother, well, actually not my cup of tea. But Betty ... "

And he lay there, nodding pleasantly, with reflective misty eyes still slanted upwards to the sunlit clips.

"I wonder if I, too, some day ... though not, I hope, outside Mr Hudson's." Mr Edgar halted, sniffing so hard I'm sure Aunt thought, from a sudden nervous outspring of her hands, he might inhale a passing bee. "Do—do you know that, when he fell, his hat came off? A hat he'd bought to aid him in his work. Calling, as he did, from door to door, Jack felt he needed a hat to doff to the ladies. I offered him one of mine, poor fellow, to save his pennies, but no, he wouldn't ... And now, now that hat has come to me. For me to wear. As if I could. Why, I might also, in the same hat—"

"Now, Mr Edgar, please! I will not have you becoming morbid. It must have been a great great strain upon your brother, taking up new work and wondering if he could cope. And if he was already delicate to begin with—"

"Feel sick!" Mr Edgar said, suddenly struggling upright. "Very queasy, I do assure you."

"Move the case quick," I yelled at Aunt, "or he'll be sick all over it!"

Not that I really cared. With any luck the daft ferting little man *would* be sick all over Aunt's case, and that, surely, would make her furious with him?

"Dear Mr Edgar," Aunt murmured, icily ignoring me, "if only I could get you something to compose your stomach. But I have nothing at all that I can offer," and she gazed, almost desperately I thought, at a hole in the tree trunk just over Mr Edgar's head, as if wishing it were a cupboard that she might reach inside and withdraw her second-best china cups and a bottle of essence of peppermint from. "If there is anything that I *can* get you, you have only to say."

"Nothing, nothing at all," Mr Edgar said. "You've been most kind, to be sure. Most gracious. All the same," and there appeared a grey look of pain that had nothing to do with a queasy stomach and that made his cheeks shrink and the nose seem suddenly bigger. "All the same, I wish Jack and I had been ... reconciled, is that the word? I am, by nature you might say, a married man. There was no question of betraying my first dear love's memory, as he thought. I loved her, still do. There just seemed no point, to me, in not taking up again that golden thread ... or at least, preparing for it."

I saw Aunt Wells's face. Her expression was transported, a most curious mixture of pleasure and sorrow.

"Golden thread," she said, "what a beautiful phrase! What a beautiful way to regard marriage. I wish, Mr Edgar, that more men thought as you do." Looking pleased, Mr Edgar turned, dusted a slightly embarrassed hand aimlessly over the ironwork chair, shyly scratched an ear, bumped his other ear on a low branch, and sent his clips twirling merrily away across the lawn. "Quite so," he said, bounding anxiously after them, "absolutely."

Disappointment welled inside me. "Aren't you going to be sick?" I shouted.

"Gordon, really! Go inside at—" Aunt Wells stopped, hand on heart.

"Distress all round, it seems. Indeed yes," Mr Edgar said, looking quickly at the ruin behind us. "May I, for my part, say again how very deeply I feel for your ... loss. That fine house laid low, so to speak. A tragedy, a real tragedy," and, speaking, he seemed to stand a trifle taller, a trifle prouder, as though by donning the clips, rescued from under a sooty cabbage, he'd put on armour and, despite all worldly woe, was now strong enough to go on living.

"Well, must be going now," he said. "Most grateful, I really am."

"Yes," Aunt said, looking abruptly tired, sad eyes as dark as her freckles, "and so must we be going. There will be a bus shortly. I really feel unable, any longer, to look at dear white house."

Feeling as sad as Aunt, yet wanting nevertheless to bait Mr Edgar, "When your brother fell down outside the barber's," I sneered, "did he land flat on his apple nose?"

"Gordon!"

Aunt's exclamation passed me by, for, suddenly, the scene of that morning was real; the earnest little man, head newly trimmed with stray bits of dark hair round his ears, and a new dark hat just above them, falling like a log outside Mr

Hudson's nice bright shop with the pretty sunlit pole outside the door winking uncaringly, startled faces rushing to the window, customers with white capes still around their shoulders and Mr Hudson himself, pop-eyed above his carbon black moustaches! I believe that, after all, I was disturbed by Jack Edgar's death. Perhaps, strangely, more disturbed than over the death of Red Pope. Mr Edgar, however briefly, had been of my world, and to just fall down … It *was* terrible. It still is terrible, even today, and I often think that, if ever I write a book about the thirties, with all its alarming Fascist bravado and, at home, hunger marches, troubles of which I hardly knew, I shall ask for the depiction on the jacket of a hat with a hard curly brim lying neatly in a sunny road outside a barber's shop. Just the hat. No body. (It is easier, and a little more comfortable, especially as one grows older, to visualise as little as one possibly can that is unpleasant.)

The bus was nearly in town ("Well done," Mr Edgar had said, vaguely, as he saw us off, waving one hand while the other held his scratchy bike) before Aunt Wells, nursing her suitcase under sleeves that now lay wearily on the leather, spoke. "What," she said, looking not at me but through the window as if really not very interested, "was that you said about Blackpool, and your Uncle Conway?"

21

As soon as Aunt Wells heard that Mrs Mossman was unwell she left town house shortly after tea, saying she might not return before eight.

"That Mossman woman," Uncle Conway shouted through a window as Aunt, in a creamy haze of summer clothing topped by a new imperial cream hat, strode off along the drive under trees that, like jealous ladies, sighed down through their own green bonnets, "will break her neck one day! Picking up bread crumbs!"

After which, morosely, Uncle retired to his study and

drinking, while I, ambling between house and garden, tried to invent a new game for one. But the game was already fated, a game not for one but two. Two and a victim.

At half past six, bored, I went upstairs. Uncle Conway was poised alertly by the venetian blinds. From his left hand a flask drooped and dribbled.

"In luck, boy," he said, softly, without turning. "Agate. Coming up the drive."

Eagerly I joined Uncle at the blinds.

"Visiting Wells, no doubt of that," Uncle Conway said. "So when he asks to see her, say nothing. Just show him in. Remember, boy, if he knows she's out he won't enter."

"Will you give him a telling off?" I asked, excitedly.

"Telling off?" repeated Uncle, voice softer than ever, the flask swaying in his hand. "Well, let's see, young fellow, shall we?"

It had not, for Uncle Conway, been a very good day. The morning had started with the annoyance of our local paper, unread the previous evening because of a headache. As soon as Uncle had glanced at the front page the damnations had begun. It seemed that Mr Agate had chosen publicly to espouse the anti-speedway lobby, chiefly on grounds of excessive noise. And it was inevitable that as soon as Uncle began to damn and blast in pungent reaction, Aunt should counter by remarking that not only did she agree with Mr Agate but that she herself found the roar of bikes quite monstrous, and that no one, in her view, would ever ride to heaven on a motor bike. Then, trying perhaps, as Uncle's face turned royal blue, to lighten the atmosphere, Aunt had embarked on a rather tactless extollation of her own preferences. "Now cricket I think a lovely sport. Quiet, yet exciting when the bowlers and batsmen roll up their sleeves. I love sunlight on clean, hairy masculine forearms." And Aunt had looked, teasingly, at Uncle's blue serge sleeve as if it concealed a great treasure. But Uncle, crushing the evening paper, had kicked it wildly. "We'll fight, by God! I want Agate kicked, and hard. I want him rolled in cinders and trampled on!"

After that, of course, Aunt Wells and Uncle hadn't spoken all day, at least, until the outburst over Mrs Mossman and the crumbs.

Now, approaching the front door through a hush of

lukewarm evening sunbeams and frigidly aloof ornaments, I held my breath, for whatever happened Mr Agate must not be allowed to turn and walk away. My ears, whenever I remembered, still ached to the thumping reprimands of Mr Agate's friend, the tweedy man outside the club. Then there was the MP's disrespectful disgraceful attitude towards Mussolini, as well as towards the speedway. That Mr Agate needed a lesson and that Uncle Conway was the man to administer it, of that, as the blood stomped indignantly through my veins, I was in no doubt. And, as Uncle had made clear, I had my modest part to play. Not a hint that Aunt was out, not by a flicker of hair or eye.

Opening the door I again held my breath, but Mr Agate only nodded at me, quite cheerfully, as though determined to be agreeable.

"Is your good aunt available?" he asked, mildly, holding what looked like a brand new umbrella of silky black obliquely across black, tartly creased trousers, the umbrella's tip resting precisely upon a pale grey spat.

Silently I stood to one side. The instant Mr Agate had passed me and was safely in the hall I slammed the door.

The slam was considerable. The Grecian lady held on to her urn, but only just, while Mr Agate's neat eyebrows flew upwards in abandon.

"Really, young man. Have regard for property! Why, one of the most effective speeches I have yet made in the House was almost whispered. Not, of course, that a speech in the Commons is an apt simile for the closing of a door. But, depend upon it, that which is whispered is a thousand times more riveting than the loudest hosanna. Am I not right, sir?"

A terrible calm befell me. His umbrella, I thought. It could be used as a weapon!

Looking, as a sunbeam fell into one eye, probably rather sinister, I held out my hands.

"No need for that. Shan't be staying. Merely a flying visit to make one or two preliminary arrangements with your aunt. Besides, think better with a brolly between my knees. Always have."

Stonily I marched ahead into the room with the old brass lamp standard. Aunt Wells' Bible, the only companion of a vase of dahlias, lay starkly on the table.

"Ah, the good book," Mr Agate said, picking it up and opening it according to the attached pale blue ribbon. "The Song of Solomon! Rich fare indeed. No, don't touch my umbrella! I have told you that I require it!"

"What are you afraid of?" I complained. "There aren't any holes in the ceiling! It won't rain in here."

Somewhat loudly, for an advocate of quiet, Mr Agate replaced the Bible on the table.

"Will you kindly fetch your aunt? I've no time for nonsense."

Without moving my feet I widened my knees, put my fists on my hips, and, keeping an eye on the umbrella, glared up at the man from Westminster.

"Why don't you like speedway racing, you sissy dirty rat?"

Even if he'd remembered in that moment that he had an umbrella Mr Agate couldn't have used it, so amazed was he. In fact he appeared to be slowly turning into a dahlia as blues and reds, the colours of the flowers behind him, seeped into his cheeks and made a patchwork of his refined, clenched hands.

After a while his mouth opened, but for once no words, whispered or otherwise, came out.

During that long silence probably only the Bible moved. To a new, apprehensive position a little further away from the vase.

"I asked you to fetch your aunt," Mr Agate said at last, dabbing his brow. "I shan't ask again."

Behind me at the door I heard Uncle Conway cough. A deliberate, showy, inebriated cough that we rarely heard except during the high noon of his cups.

"Evening, Agate! Evening my dear old cherry fruit cake! Evening my dear old charmer from the back benches!"

It said much for Mr Agate that he did not immediately take a dive through the window and escape to sanity. Instead, umbrella clasped to waistcoat like a starved pet crow, he made an obvious and determined effort to ignore Uncle's rather indigestible jocosity.

"Good evening, sir. Is you wife available? A matter of some urgency involving our ladies' committee."

"Of course, of course," said Uncle Conway, advancing with a certain nasty merriment. "Always is a matter of some urgency, and always does involve our ladies' committee, doesn't it? Be honest, man! You fuss Wells for one reason only. You think we've got money, and that's why you really come calling. Why damn it, Agate, you're nothing but a Bolshevik!" And, with the satisfied air of someone who'd had the last possible word, Uncle Conway reached in a pocket, threshed studiously about, and then drew out what looked like a new unopened flask.

"Sir, you are as impossible as your nephew! I am here to see your dear lady only. Please remember," glancing under a brilliant white cuff, moved delicately back by the tip of a finger, at a wrist watch, "that my time is important."

"Bravo! Bravo! Clap the man," roared Uncle and, without knowing why, I began to clap my hands.

"Each clap," Uncle said, with an artful leer, plus a definite drunken pride, "represents a second. Save you looking at your watch, eh, Agate? Tick off time by listening to the boy."

Mr Agate, moving angrily forward, his eyes on the door, found Uncle's chubby outflung arm blocking the way.

"Oh no, Agate. Not yet. I want," Uncle paused, struggling for the right word, "explanations."

"Explanations! Of what, pray?"

Inspired, perhaps by the word pray, Uncle tightly shut his eyes.

"Why," he said, keeping them shut and rocking slightly as he talked, "of your foreign policy, of your ... knavish views on our speedway, of why you so ... frequently, and surreptitiously, visit my wife. Isn't just the money, is it? Damn it, Agate, you're a man. Got your eye on her, haven't you? Got her all lined up for a spot of Parliamentary misconduct, what?"

Mouth clamping shut as the top of his umbrella, leaping upward in surprise, jabbed his chin, Mr Agate stepped back. His right hand, groping for support, touched the Bible.

"You may well," Uncle grated, "fall back on your Jewish joke book!"

At this even the dahlias seemed to shrink inside their stems, and turn their heads uneasily downwards.

"Sir, you are offensive. Impossible and offensive!"

Thrusting out a forefinger Uncle Conway wagged it tauntingly under the MP's recoiling nose. "That European

174

jaunt of yours," he accused, in a hoarse rolling voice. "Saw it all with closed eyes and mind, eh, Agate? Met all the wrong people, heard all the wrong views. Did you see Herr Hitler, for example? Did you even try?"

"If you remember I went to Rome," snapped Agate. "Hitler wasn't there! And no, Mussolini didn't impress me! I have already given your good wife my opinion of Mussolini. And will you instruct that wretched boy to stop clapping? I already have a headache!"

Tired of clapping anyway, I put my hands together and shook them in the air like a boxer in the moment of victory. Then, to make the headache worse, "Uncle Conway likes Mussolini," I jibed. "Signor Mussolini stood on a balcony and threw him a stone! So there!"

"This boy," Agate faltered. "I begin to wonder if he, also, has been ... imbibing."

"It's in my bedroom, a lovely black pebble!" I insisted, furiously. "I can fetch it and show it to you, you sissy rat!"

Back skidded the Bible, propelled by Mr Agate's trembling hand, striking, and upsetting, the vase of dahlias. Flowers and water swirled across the table, especially water. Mr Agate, grabbing the seat of his suddenly dampened trousers, sprang forward with a wrathful squeal, dropping, in the process, his umbrella. As he lunged for it so did I, our heads cracked together and mine, luckily, survived the better. While Mr Agate floundered dazedly on creased trouser knees I leapt to my feet triumphantly brandishing the brolly. Uncle Conway, unable to resist temptation, sneaked to Mr Agate's far side, took a bumpy breath, and let loose a mild inaccurate kick in the direction of Mr Agate's rear. It was now Uncle's turn to hit the carpet while Mr Agate rose.

Somehow, arms jerking like a black painted windmill, he snatched back the umbrella and pushed by me to the door. Queerly, in that moment of ignominious flight, his spats were suddenly the most noticeable thing about him, perhaps because his face, now grey, was itself spat-like, so that, as he scurried out into the hall, he was almost a person with three faces, one over each foot and one below his hair, and all three scared!

"Think about politics, man, think!" Uncle yelled after him. "That's what politics mean, thinking. And while you're about

175

it, don't knock the speedway! If you do, we'll come marching!"

"A-marching!" I yelled, as an encore. "A-marching through Georgia!"

Puffing extravagantly for a thin man, Mr Agate wrestled with town house door as if chased by Lucifer himself, while the lady with the urn, arm gracefully perfect, watched him coldly.

"And stop pestering my wife, milksop! If you must know, she's agin veal. Thinks it wicked. But, by heaven, I'll bleed you and serve you on her plate!"

"A-bugger and ferts! A-bugger and ferts! Mussolini! Mussolini! Mussolini!" I chanted, wildly, as Agate, ashen, squeezed through the door.

The instant he'd gone Uncle Conway began to sober.

"That," he said, opening wide the door and gazing down the drive, "was very naughty of us, Gordon."

"Why?"

Without speaking he sat down in the porch, clasped his hands over the unopened flask, and continued gazing along the drive. So dolorous his mien, so furry and vague his eyes, that I sensed a sudden, real unhappiness. Why that should be I didn't understand. Mr Agate was routed, Mr Agate had been told off, Mr Agate had been mocked and upset beyond all our hopes. Wasn't that what Uncle had wanted from the moment he'd spied the dapper little man striding so unsuspectingly up our drive? To upset and make him lose his temper? To put him to rights and send him packing as quivering and depleted as yesterday's left-over jelly? For the day was still a long way off, several years indeed, before, in wartime cups, his nation at odds with once beloved Adolf, Uncle was to write, despairingly and abjectly, in his diary, 'Damned Agate was right!'

Or was he, those moments in the porch, thinking not of himself but of Aunt Wells and the grievous social deprivation he had just caused her, as he said at last, in a voice as dolorous as he looked, "Because, Gordon, that man will never again darken our door. He will never again visit us, and be a feather in your good Aunt's cap!"

22

All three of them were in the park. At first I hadn't noticed. In the afternoon sun the lake was a smooth glittering distracting whisper that swept me back to that other sunny afternoon when, after my visiting the York Arms to return the ring, Aunt Wells had rewarded me by taking me out in a boat. I still remembered, below tucked up sleeves, her slender freckled forearms, tense from holding the oars, and the way the sun filled her eyes and forced shut her lids. In the middle of that water we were strangely and deliciously alone, and I'd dropped my hand contentedly in the blue water, to be surprised by the sudden chill. "Life's little surprise, Gordon," Aunt had explained, talking suddenly with a freedom and candour that only the novelty of our isolation could have justified. "Blue and inviting, but also cold. Like life. It is only by continual immersion—which takes courage—that one finds warmth and comfort. When, for example, I married your Uncle and discovered that he already drank, for a young man, quite heavily ... At first I was shocked. Then, to an extent, one recovers, and continues living and loving. One can even learn to ignore. It is matter of the will. It is, at times, as if the battle itself warms one's love."

"But why, Aunt Wells," I'd asked, "does Uncle drink quite heavily?"

The oars had risen in the sun, lazy, like shrunken brown paddle-steamer wheels about to brave the river.

"That, Gordon, I cannot answer. Except, perhaps, to say that your Uncle was born to be impatient. With himself, the world, and everything around him. Impatience," Aunt had added, "is the bane of life. There is little that does not require patience. Life should always be tasted slowly and fully, not grabbed at and gulped. Especially love, which is life."

"You mean," I said, with prideful sagacity, "that Uncle is greedy for his second glass before the first is empty?"

Aunt had smiled, moving first one oar, then the other, leaning back with hat slightly over one eyebrow, and with a slight hot odour of physical endeavour.

"It is indeed true, Gordon, that the impatient man, quick in his movements, drinks faster than the calm slower man, and therefore often drinks more."

I turned from the lake, eyes full of sun, glitter, and memories of that afternoon with Aunt, and saw, on the grassy bank sloping to the water, all three of them, Auntie Alex, Betty, and Mr Edgar.

Mr Edgar was lying flat out, the soles of his boots clumsy and dark against the grass. Although there was no sign of the old bicycle he still wore clips, enabling an extended view of socks of quietish brown-and-yellow diamond pattern. His jacket was lighter than usual, more dark grey than black. Betty, leaning beside and over him, was fastening and unfastening the jacket buttons, fastening and unfastening the buttons of the darker waistcoat beneath, and then, with a breathless giggling, hovering threateningly with her left hand over Mr Edgar's trousers. Something, as I watched that silly game, caught at heart and throat. Without fully knowing why, I burnt inside.

On the other side of Betty, a little way removed from the scene of prankish buttoning, was Auntie Alex smoking a cigarette. She was sitting upright, and there seemed an awful lot of plump bare chest above the neckline of her frothy dress. "Why," she howled, pointing at me and looking, I thought, more friendly than at our last encounter, "the young ice-cream merchant himself. Hallo, son!"

"Good afternoon," I said stiffly, watching Betty.

Betty looked round. "Hallo, Gordon," she said, smiling.

"Terrible, that fire at your white house," Auntie Alex said, eyes screwed against smoke, cigarette trundling to a corner of ripe, down-turned lips. "As if your poor aunt hadn't enough to cope with. Betty was saying what a lovely house it was, weren't you, love?"

"Lovely," said Betty, coiling into Mr Edgar like a snake and kissing his chin.

"My poor Noel always wanted a country house to retreat into. Mind you, they're for gentlemen only. Or should be!"

"Now, mother."

"Gentlemen and great men," said Auntie Alex stubbornly, "they're such as need retreats. Whew," she wiped her brow, mopping carefully all around the beauty spot, "lovely day isn't it, son?"

178

Mr Edgar, coming to life, jerked up, grabbed at Betty's bare arm, kissed it frantically, and as suddenly capsized. Betty, highly pleased and giggling strangely, began immediately undoing Mr Edgar's shirt. I stared, aghast, as the plume-shaped top of a nest of black chest-hair appeared, unfolding itself gradually upright into the sunshine like recently trodden turf. Into this springy nest roamed Betty's white fingers. Mr Edgar became transformed. Yelping he grabbed Betty, pulled her down, and began pecking madly all over her neck. Then, suddenly, the kisses were quieter, slower, and Betty pressed down harder. As she did so Mr Edgar's hands grew gentler, lightly stroking, pliant as daffodils in a wind.

"There's your butterfly touch for you, son," Auntie Alex said, pouting out smoke and nodding approvingly. "Just like my Noel, bless him, the poor deceased lamb. Rare is the butterfly touch, but Noel had it, the lamb."

"I like mutton chops best," I said, mind still on Betty and Mr Edgar and all the terrible kissing and stroking.

"Children, aren't they?" Auntie went cheerfully on, leaning sideways and slapping playfully at Betty's wriggling bottom, "but that's what sweethearts are, kids. Can't blame them, either. Why, many's the game I played with Noel. Once, I remember, we sat in a cemetery. Oven hot it was, like today. With our backs against a big posh tombstone. Everytime he kissed me I told him it wasn't proper. What about the deceased? I said. You poking your tongue in my mouth and them below having to suffer it all with no tongues to complain to us with. That's tragic, I said. Dear Noel, he answered me though. By poking his tongue back in, half-way down my blessed throat! Ah, what a tongue! Like ice cream in summer, hot tea in winter!"

"Mother!" Betty exploded, lifting herself up from Mr Edgar's chest and looking reprovingly round. "Can't you talk nicely? I warned you about all that sherry after dinner."

Sniffing, Auntie threw her cigarette towards the park lake, rubbed a chubby arm, and, as though fired by some romantic idealism, looked, even to me, suddenly very pretty.

"Sometimes wish he'd been cremated. Could have talked to his ashes. Taken him about. Taken his urn to Blackpool. Mind, a good strong urn. Steel maybe, with a little glass window. Have to be strong, specially for travel. Not that I'm a sentimentalist. Optimistically, I'm always looking for a new gentleman, a new Noel. It's lovely to have a gentleman. Noel would understand. Alex, he'd say, it's the flesh! You've good honest flesh, and monumental tit hills, to consider. Well," Auntie ended, "I'm always bearing that in mind. And, if I was with another, in Blackpool say, I'd be delicate and put a cloth over the urn at bedtime just like it was a bird-cage. But then, he's not cremated, is he? So I can't take him anywhere at all."

"Mother, if you don't stop!" Looking thoroughly annoyed, Betty sat properly up at last. "Gordon, when do you start school again?"

"In two and a half weeks," I mumbled. Why, oh, why was her one hand still resting on Mr Edgar's horrid black chest?

"You must come to our wedding," said Mr Edgar, idly, from low in the grass. "Yes, to be sure, our wedding. We owe you. Brought us together, young man, that you did. Absolutely."

"Yes, pet, you must come to our wedding," Betty smiled.

"We've got a lovely darts team now, at the Arms," Auntie Alex butted in, talking seemingly at random. "No trembling hands amongst 'em, like some I could mention in the past. And if your aunt should want a cleaning woman ... "

The Arms! In my young life only Betty's arms had ever seemed to matter. At the top of the bank I looked back and saw them in the clear hot sunlight, barer, lovelier, than they had ever been.

Back home, the front door was wide open. An attempt, perhaps, to relive white house breeziness? Pausing in the hall I stroked the Grecian lady, her arms beautiful as Betty's but icier. No, I thought, I didn't want to see the wedding! Suddenly everything to do with Betty hurt. Suddenly it was all gone, all the sweet strange feeling, lost somewhere between the cosy body and fretful wistful voice of Auntie Alex and the nauseous black and curling hair of Mr Edgar.

"Gordon, go and wash!" Aunt Wells said, emerging briskly from the kitchen where she had been preparing a tea. "Cleanliness, remember, is the soap of angels. And the silver wing of health."

She looked rather strained, as so often lately, and her breath was sharp with the tasting of the sherry used in her delicious home made trifles.

"Aunt Wells, I've just met Auntie Alex in the park!"

"That woman," Aunt Wells said, "is not your aunt. Off you go upstairs! And put some clean socks on."

But I didn't change my socks. Or wash. In my room I opened a drawer and took out the Roman pebble. It felt cool and comforting in my palm, extraordinarily light too, as if I held no more than a black feather. Surely, I thought, it was the darkest, most wonderful stone there had ever been. It never altered or caused distress. It would always be a black and marvellous pebble. The most significant and precious of all my treasures.

I was on my bed, still clutching the stone and enjoying daydreams of tremendous lustre and beguilement—Mussolini tossing pebble after pebble to a thousand cheering people in sunlight bright as bayonets—when Aunt burst in.

"Gordon, didn't you hear me calling for tea? Haven't you washed?"

"Look!" Eyes glowing I held out my palm. "Uncle gave it me!"

Aunt Wells looked, her eyes totally without sparkle or understanding.

"It's the pebble that Signor Mussolini threw," I told her, proudly.

"Gordon, I'm tired. Too tired to be bothered with nonsense."

"Mussolini did throw it, Aunt Wells. When Uncle Conway was in Rome."

Without a word Aunt Wells took the stone and turned it over. After a moment, her face clearing, she gave it peremptorily back. "This did not come from Rome, Gordon. Or from anywhere except an English beach. I distinctly remember Conway playing with it. Tossing it from hand to hand as he sat beside me on the shingle. Clearly he thought it a most striking pebble. It was on the day when we left you at home, remember? On our wedding anniversary outing, earlier this summer."

Was Aunt mad? Had making sherry trifle all afternoon affected her reason?

181

"It came from Rome!" I shrilled, outraged.

"I do not know what extraordinary tale your Uncle has been telling," Aunt Wells said, "but, clearly, it is one that should be forgotten. Change your socks and go downstairs to tea."

Leaping from the bed I pranced before her like a small berserk matador.

"Signor Mussolini was on a balcony. He threw the pebble and Uncle caught it!"

"That, Gordon, will be enough. And I am sick," Aunt Wells added, moving to the window, hand to throat, "of hearing of these awful men. Hitler, Mussolini! Unprincipled men without background or breeding. Germany, for one, I would not trust an inch, even without Hitler. She is, I think, quite capable of causing another terrible World War. Oh I know your Uncle thinks otherwise—he has, I believe, a great delusion," and Aunt sighed, fingers rigidly to throat before, anger lapsing, she said quite mildly, "Oh Gordon child, it was that day out—I remember so well. Our anniversary. And the sun like today, hot and wonderful, the whole shore glittering. The beach a million gleaming points."

"It *was* Mussolini's! Uncle Conway said it was. He was there, in Rome!"

"Rome *and* Blackpool?" Even in front of me Aunt Wells could not restrain her bitterness.

"Ask Uncle! He'll tell you!"

"For the last time, Gordon, that pebble was picked up off the beach on our outing, earlier this summer. Conway played with it, and then, like a little boy, put it in his pocket. And that, I suggest, is where you put it now. In your pocket." And with a last great frown Aunt sailed to the door.

"It was Mussolini's!" I shouted. "You're a liar, Aunt Wells!"

Aunt turned. Her face looked suddenly deathly tired.

"On second thoughts, Gordon, you may stay in your room. Your Uncle and I will take tea without you. There are things that we must, and will, discuss. And the matter of this pebble, unimportant as it may seem, is one."

"Rome!" I cried, kicking (with unchanged socks) the sternly closing door, "the pebble came from Rome!"

23

This morning I woke sweating, the spilt earth dark blood of Ypres running through my brain. In my waking mind were suddenly three soldiers. A German and two British. One of the British Uncle Conway, the other Aunt's dear beloved. In the submerging scarlet-lit dusk the German rose to threaten dear beloved. And Uncle Conway not far off, a younger thinner Uncle Conway, stupidly, wildly, hurling a grenade and killing not only the Hun but also dear beloved! Blowing off half his face so that like a bloody dented spinning top he twisted and fell, and after that, as the dusk and the scarlet flickering continued, Uncle crawling to dear beloved and covering his face with the helmet blown from the Hun.

Was that it? I wondered, sitting, shaking on my bed. A little bit of battle that no one knew about? Was that how dear beloved fell at Ypres? By the panicky hand of Uncle Conway?

In a turmoil, the vivid scene still shackling in a vice my uneasy, dream-dazed mind, I threw on clothes, It was still hardly more than dawn as I reached the place where Uncle Conway lay.

Under the unheated trees of early morning I gazed down, gripped by visions.

There was, from the unheated early morning grave, no clue and, standing there, some of my excitement died. But not altogether. I wondered still.

Was Uncle Conway, that enigma among men, not simply, as my own left-wing prejudice had always insisted, a Fascist sympathiser, defending his own wealth, but more a guilty man, hiding the truth even from himself? "Woman, woman, can I help it if you lost your beloved at Ypres?" Oh Uncle, was self-delusion the key to your confused and ranting soul? You must have served, you were fit and of fighting age, but you never talked of it and that was strange. Strange, for you were a talkative man. Why, Uncle Conway? Why was your army service ignored even in your diaries? And your drinking? What of that? And how did you first meet Aunt Wells? Did you seek her out, a soldier from the same battalion as her late dear beloved, and then, despite your secret, fall in love with her? Hounded, even as you gave her daffodils and proposed marriage, by guilt? Oh it was all accidental, that thing at Ypres, true, but you never told Aunt (which was a mistake because it meant you didn't trust her love) and in not telling you became the man you were, a poor lover, and a lover of all things German, for guilt made you the one, and guilt made you the other, for if anyone had to kill dear beloved it should, by rights, have been a German, shouldn't it? Uncle Conway, and, at times, weren't you almost that, more German than the Germans?

Oh Uncle, it would clarify so much. I stare at your grave and almost kneel to question imploringly through the clay. The trees above are dripping with the early morning, the light grows stronger if not yet absolutely daylight clear. So much time has passed since boyhood's everlasting sunshine, there are things I cannot check or ask, nor, perhaps, do I really wish to. For, as excitement dies and the waking dream becomes much less than real, the only thing that matters is that your life, now gone, is laid forever peaceably to rest.

But you have to feel and think something a little more dramatic than a piety like that, standing so early at a graveside beneath the trees, and what I thought was, well, it could have happened.

"For heaven's sake, woman! I want my tea, not a soul to soul natter about damn all!"

"With all your bombast, Conway, you are a coward. Evading the issue!"

"Issue, what issue? Here, give me the bread and butter, I want my tea"

There was a crash. In my mind, as I left my bedroom and crept downstairs towards the flying angry voices, I saw bread and butter, together with little pyramids of pale-blue plate (and crumbs enough to send Mrs Mossman insane!) all across the kitchen floor.

"You dropped that plate deliberately. This is damnable, Wells, damnable!"

"As damnable as Blackpool? As damnable as sneaking off on holiday with that public-house woman?"

Around me as I crouched the dark pictures, the sword of Cromwell, the lovely china lady, all hushed as if part of the avid listening air.

"Wells, really!"

"I do not know you, Conway, I never have. Only of Blackpool am I certain. At one time I thought ... fraülein, yes, fraülein almost certainly; now I wonder if you have ever been abroad on research, so called. And perhaps I do not care. Perhaps I just want one thing. That you keep your evils to yourself. That you wreathe your mouth in silence."

"Cut me up a plump white fraülein! Butter her with bread! Bite her, bite her, on the knee! And spread, spread, spread!"

At Uncle's defiant merriment a shiver, like a change of light, ran through town house air. It was as though the lady were shifting her Grecian urn to a safer position atop her head, and the pictures uneasily adjusting themselves on their cords, and the big sword twitching with a sudden ill humour.

"There is one thing," Aunt Wells said, "that must be made plain. I will not have Gordon exposed to your drunken fantasies. I will not, any longer, have him afloat on a sea of lies. Giving him a stone and telling him it came from Rome! From that bully, Mussolini!"

"Signor! Signor Mussolini! And yes, dear, I remember the pebble. Black as a swastika, that's why I kept it!"

"Gordon is becoming only a little less impossible than you are, Conway. As for my friends ... I do not know how I exist in this town. How I go on living. Why, Mr Agate scarcely speaks to me these days! It is as if I have offended him."

"Oh, fine. Fine, fine! We've upset Agate, have we? Oh praise be, oh glory. Oh glory glory glory!"

"One day Mr Agate will be prime minister!"

"Why? Is he circumcised? What other qualifications he may possess I cannot think."

"You have ruined my life, Conway. I will not stay here another instant. This time I will leave and not ..."

A pause, one so dark and burning that even I, with a door between, felt scorched.

"But it's destroyed, isn't it, Wells? Just a ruin. No escaping to it this time. No flying off to white house to live with the boy. No respite from your lawful wedded husband. Too bad, old girl. Queen of the invisible croquet hoops, that was you at white house! All tea guzzling, rose clipping and good works, with best brown bread crumbs for the peacocks. Only there weren't any peacocks except for you!"

The kitchen door flung wide. Out, gasping, came Aunt Wells.

"No escape!" Uncle raged behind her. "No damnable escape!"

Obviously blind to my presence Aunt passed me and ran up the stairs.

"Invite Herr Hitler!" Uncle screamed up after her. "Invite a real man to tea!"

The door of Aunt's bedroom slammed.

Presently, as I sat trembling on my bed, the door opened and in she came, hat on head and case in hand. She was clearly trembling more than I and her eyes, light and fluttery, only briefly focused. Bending, she gave a slight quick kiss against my brow, and again, though fainter now, I smelt the sherry of that afternoon.

"Goodbye, Gordon. Be as good as you can. And do not forget to say your prayers."

After a while, going to the window, I saw her walking quickly down the drive. Above her, without budging from their pride, yet seeming to move in a tiny graceful ripple of farewell, the line of tall trees. (Years later, in a dream repetition of that same nightmare scene I saw them differently, as ladies in a courthouse gallery, watching a trial, stirred as one by some sensational revelation.)

Uncle Conway, hands clenched, blue ill pockets below his eyes, was in the hall, sitting on a crabbed little antique chair. There was about him a dawning realisation of what had happened, and his own culpable role.

As I came slowly down the stairs he turned to greet me, looking suddenly even older than Sam.

"She's gone, boy," he said, in a voice small as the chair on which he sat. "Wells has left us!"

24

All that night I slept not on a bed but on a couch of probing thorny clock chimes, or so it seemed. As each hour struck, Where, I wondered, twisting fretfully, was Aunt Wells now? Incredible that she wasn't in her room, listening, nightdress ruffled about her thin throat, to those same chimes. I tried thinking of Aunt at white house but it wasn't easy picturing her, case in hand, among charred ruin and night-cold ash. What Uncle Conway thought as he paced the night away drinking in his study (how many times, I wonder, did he flick at the venetian blinds, adding their restless clack to his own loud heartbeats?) I never knew, but in the dawn, stooping over me with tell-tale breath and weary bluish face he seemed, by the certainty in his voice, to know the answer.

"Had a bad night, boy," he told me, rummaging vaguely inside his half-open waistcoat. "Thought I might be calling the police, well, better to be on the safe side, Wells being so upset. Walking out like that ..."

And Uncle continued to stand, blinking with each shake of his head while tenderly rubbing his chest.

"Where is Aunt Wells then?" I asked, tossing back rumpled bed-clothes.

With a sudden brash grin Uncle caught my wrist. His grip, iron hard and confident, make me yelp.

"You'll find out, young prince of darkness, you'll find out. Just get washed and dressed. We'll breakfast on the way."

Shaven, and in his best suit and best hard hat, Uncle looked passable enough as even Mrs Hampton, hovering threateningly clothes brush in hand, reluctantly acknowledged. Mrs Hampton, and Sam, saw us off. They fidgeted near the car while Uncle, as usual, drew down his hat to an inch above the eyebrows.

"Keep things going, will you both?" he ordered, bright and grinding as the gears. "Wells went yesterday. Joining her with the boy."

"Went where?" asked Mrs Hampton, bristly as her clothes brush.

Uncle didn't answer and Sam, muttering and glaring, looked as if about to spit with fury.

"Goodbye, Mr Gordon," and, "You drive a-proper, mind," I thought he said, but Uncle Conway, still cheerful and, apparently, with no hangover, waved—more a salute, really, stiff and fat and full of morning hope—and was off.

At the corner of the road I glanced back. Beneath the big trees Sam and Mrs Hampton looked lost and unhappy, their arms drooping and forlorn. For once not even the trees waved.

For a time Uncle Conway and I sat side by side in silence, each of us self-locked in thought as we breezed, with only an occasional gawkish snatch of gears, along the quiet unwinding roads. I did notice, though, that as the minutes passed Uncle changed. That first early morning surge of pomposity, in itself strangely reassuring, had vanished; his driving, and smoking, became jerkier. As clouds of Craven A billowed pungently between us, "Where are we going, Uncle Conway?" I kept asking, between coughs, but, as if the telling might make the journey less practicable, Uncle kept his counsel. "We'll stop at a café for refreshment," was all he said.

But the café drink, muddy lukewarm coffee in a pale-brown beaker, wasn't enough for Uncle. Back in the car he drew out from between two sections of the green leather upholstery a tall cold bottle, and drank richly from its long green neck. Then, as though trying to look suddenly like a priest, Uncle put down the bottle and swished the palms of his damp puffy hands gravely together. "Not to worry, Gordon," he said finally, smacking, with fresh confidence, his wet cosy lips, "we'll find your aunt. We'll find Wells."

We kept on driving, and now I pulled my cap lower against the brilliant morning sun. The world, that morning, was truly as brilliant and warm as any day that summer. And, as the miles juggled away under us, I thought of all the summer's happenings, its fleet half-sweet half-sour moments, of Betty and her pale beautiful arms, of the fledgeling and still mysterious desires she'd made me feel. Would I ever again, I wondered, stand in that dusty little room at the York Arms and watch her play that old piano, or stand in the pink glowing bedroom and watch her pink-toothed comb raping lightly through her hair? And then I thought of Mr Edgar, not, for once, with distaste, but simply of his perpetual, "Well done, well done!" Wasn't that, for me, the most important thing about him? That and the ice cream he'd once bought me? I thought of Mr Agate, that other little man who distrusted Mussolini and hated speedway. What a time we'd given him, Uncle and I! If only Red Pope could have seen us rout him, how he would have clapped us! And there was Auntie Alex to remember. She, too, had bought me ice cream. And talked to me in the cemetery. Queer how agreeable that little talk now seemed. And as our car blew past another car, trading rude jolly honks, it suddenly appeared to me that being alone with someone, anyone, was always better than company of three or four. Just like now. Being alone with Uncle Conway was at least man to man, with all the feeling of a common purpose, finding Aunt. Last night in the dark I'd worried, but not now, under a hot cheerful sun with Uncle smoking blithely beside me. If there was, as we travelled, a cloud, it could only have been the abiding sorrow of white house. And, for me at any rate, the falling dead of that other little Edgar (with time the chill has only deepened).

The heat, building up, was making us sweat. After attempting a swig with one hand on the wheel and splashing his black tie Uncle pulled in to the side of a grassy-banked drowsy road.

"It's hot," he growled, rubbing stiff podgy knees. "Find me some matches. Want another smoke."

Again his mood had changed; once more it resembled his movements, jerky, uncertain.

"Uncle Conway, where are we going?"

"All in good time, Gordon, all in good time. The thing is we're on our way. Another hour and we should be there."

Even at the side of the road there wasn't much shade. After a while, elaborately, eyebrows nodding tiredly, cheeks and brow shiny, Uncle took off his jacket and rolled up his sleeves. His hat, heavy and woeful and black as mourning at a graveside, dipped lower than ever.

Above us, with orange-coloured ease, the sun climbed and shone. No cars appeared, and no breeze touched the few wilting nearby trees.

Glaring at the dusty dark-green hedgerow, "Should never have married your Aunt," Uncle said abruptly.

"Why, Uncle Conway?"

Without answering Uncle tipped the bottle to an even

greater height above his upturned gurgling mouth. Then, after a pause, using the black tie, now wetter than ever, to dab his lips, "Matches, Gordon. Where are they? Strike a light, boy!"

But there weren't any matches and the minutes dragged by, smokeless and silent except for the suck of Uncle's lips assailing the bottle, and the quiet plash of diminishing liquid inside the thick secretive green glass. If it was a respite it was one that Uncle must have vastly cherished for, even with his bottle emptied, he still delayed, frowning from its damp cloudy neck to the glinting cloudless stretch of road ahead. Doubt and torment chased across his eyes, he climbed in and out of the car and even tried, still grasping the bottle, vigorously to turn the crank-handle. At last, with an extra deep breath as if he could bear delay no longer, he lifted the bottle, took aim at the hedgerow, and suddenly tossed. It was a clumsy throw for, shaving my watching head, the bottle vanished over the top into the field.

"Damn hedge!" Uncle grumbled. "Only thing I could ever throw properly was a dart. And that hedge ain't a dartboard!"

Whether it was Uncle's use of the word hedge I do not know, but suddenly there popped into my mind another memory of that summer.

"Uncle," I said brightly, "has Mr Quedgely written any more letters?"

Uncle turned, staring, his eyes quite blank.

"Quedgely? Who the devil's that?"

"He wrote a letter to the newspaper that you didn't like. About Herr Hitler and Germany," I said, but Uncle, eyes still blank, only mopped his face with the tie.

"Must find your Aunt, Gordon," he muttered, feverishly. "Must find your Aunt!"

In an intense silence off we drove along the endless sun-teased road. Uncle, morose, made no further effort to speak. On the wheel his hands hugged palely together, making a skull. I remember, as the chalky road dipped down and down, feeling suddenly, inexplicably cold. I thought again of death, and of how Aunt Wells had replied to my question, "What happens when you die?"

"Ah, Gordon, if only the angels, so close to us, could answer that. What magic, what lovely reassuring music. Silver tongues and trumpets, hosannas to our king."

"Yes, Aunt, but what *happens*?"

"Happens, Gordon, is just a word. An everyday word. As your Uncle might say, a word beyond computation. Ordinary words, I think, always are. But I know what you mean, and really, the answer is that there is no time for *anything* to happen. That is the lovely thing. One minute one thing, the next something else. Something wonderful!"

"Like lightning?" I'd said.

"Oh yes, Gordon, exactly that."

I remember, as the chalky road dipped down and down, watching with fascination Uncle's tie drying in the heat. I remember, as the chalky road dipped down and down, sudden knollish woods. Then, as trees vanished altogether, I glimpsed, in the distance, a view of silver. Minutes passed until, almost startling to the eye, the silver returned, flickered, fields disappeared, and suddenly we were moving under a great fervid blue, with, to the right, a haze of friendly sea.

"Look!" Uncle said, halting the car and stumbling excitedly out. "This is it! Where we came, Wells and I, on our outing together earlier this year. On our wedding anniversary trip, the day we left you behind!"

Jumping eagerly out I joined Uncle on the cliff. Below us, to one side, a long glittering beach, and, round the corner, in a bay, a little town with a long esplanade and a front row of white, comfortably basking hotels behind which, the colour of chopped up carrot and turnip, rose all sorts of little houses. "This," said Uncle Conway, peering forward and lifting a suddenly nervous arm, "is where we also spent our honeymoon, many years ago. And where, I hope, we can find your Aunt Wells now!"

Uncle drove straight along the sea front to one of the hotels, stopping with a jolt that made me topple.

"And here," he said, "is where we stayed those years ago. Our honeymoon hotel."

It was one of the smaller hotels, tall but very narrow, with its name, 'Sea Cliffs', in grubby pale-blue lettering. It had seven hot white steps and a single black railing leading to a porch and a pebbly glass outer door. On a portico, under an orange-and-blue awning, were three empty cane chairs, and, seen between the balustrade, a fat unkempt grey cat curled by a saucer of even greyer milk. A couple of off-white tea-cloths

191

had been hung out at the end of the portico to dry; from somewhere inside I caught the wistful eddying float of a wireless playing dance music.

"Not my idea, this place. Wanted to splash out even though we'd not much money then." Obviously apprehensive, Uncle kept wiping his face and glancing at the windows. "We managed, though. Not bad, as honeymoons go!"

"Is Aunt Wells inside, Uncle Conway?"

Uncle turned and glared. Just before leaving the cliffs there had been a touch of the old bravado, a bracing of the shoulders and perking out of the double chin as, before starting up the car, he'd said, "Well, off we go. Shoulder arms, my boy, and off again to war. The only way!" But that bravado, as if pricked by the salty tang of promenade air, had now deflated, leaving only worry, resentment and, eventually, a kind of fearful courage.

"Wait here, Gordon, while I see."

Left alone I, too, pulled out my tie and mopped my face. I, too, was sweating. And not just from blistering noonday heat. Where *was* Aunt Wells? Faith in Uncle wasn't strong. How could it be, for wasn't our whole trip a gamble? Why *should* Aunt Wells return to the scene of that rare and fleeting early happiness, that place of, as Uncle had suggested, a reasonable beginning to married life, or was Uncle wise enough to know that she would? And was that beginning quite so reasonable, or merely a time when Aunt had made allowances? Oh I didn't think quite that way, with quite such depth, not then, but I did sense the gamble and Uncle's own mounting doubt. Was Aunt inside? Was she?

I see myself now, a small cap-twisting boy waiting in a car. With a sudden breeze from the sea lifting the hair about my ears. And eyes fixed on a door, waiting tautly for that cloudy glass to open.

Wait, Uncle had said. I waited.

The door opened and out came Uncle Conway, still brow-mopping but smiling palely as he hopped down the steps.

"Was right, boy," he said, climbing in. "Your Aunt arrived here directly from the station, late yesterday. She took a room for the night."

"May I go in and see her?" I exulted.

"Not that simple, Gordon. She rose late, missing breakfast, and went out. No one has seen her since."

192

I looked at Uncle. The smile hadn't lasted. He was biting his lip, and rubbing his chest again.

"Tired," he said, suddenly. "Too damn hot. And too much to drink."

"Can we go on the beach, Uncle Conway? She might be paddling."

But Uncle, staring blindly at the bright and busy esplanade, wasn't listening.

"A good woman, Wells," was all he said. "And I do love her, Gordon, that I do."

Of course you loved her, Uncle Conway. Well I understand that now. But, at the time, I scarcely heard you.

"Can I go on the beach, Uncle Conway. Buy an ice cream? Find Aunt Wells? Look, there's a Punch and Judy!"

Slowly Uncle groped for a bottle. There wasn't one. Only hot green upholstery.

Frowning, he looked at the beach, thinning a little in the luncheon hour, and as the warm steely sea hissed closer.

"Very well, Gordon. She might be there. But careful, careful how you cross."

"Are you coming, Uncle Conway?"

Uncle Conway hesitated, then shook his head. "I'll sit here a bit. Want to think."

"Can I have some ice-cream money, Uncle Conway?"

While Uncle Conway, scowling, fished in his pocket I gazed impatiently at the beach.

"Those people," I said. "What are they looking at? Those people over there, by the water."

Uncle looked. "Dunno," he said, and then he looked again, very hard.

"Perhaps they've got a bottle from the sea," I said. "With a message inside! Or a big fish!"

"A fish, do you think?" Uncle's eyes were fiercely screwed.

"I'll look!" I cried. "You wait here, Uncle Conway."

"Gordon, damn you boy, wait—"

The beach was shifting and flinty and resistant under my excited feet. Over I scudded, joining the little knot of people as, from varying heights of adult command, they peered down.

Poking between two of the white-shirted, grey-trousered men, I, too, peered down. But what they were looking at I cannot now remember (probably some curious fish, or flotsam) for, beyond that little knot of people, walking along beside the tide, I saw the thin, dutiful figure of Aunt Wells. Aunt Wells wan and tired under her straw of blue, Aunt Wells looking exactly as one might expect her to look after a journey, a troubled night, and a long morning walk without benefit of breakfast.

Turning I waved, frantically, towards Uncle Conway, now crossing the esplanade. Then off, off over the shingle to meet her. Oh how I remember, as she saw me, that sudden wonderful astonished smile—like a lantern, unlit, catching the moon—and the thin arms opening, and the magic of eau-de-Cologne, warm skin, and safety.

It was later that day, before the afternoon Punch and Judy, and before we all returned home in the car that, almost without thinking, I took the pebble from my pocket and tossed it cheerfully away. Black as it was it vanished immediately, lost to me forever among all the other pebbles on that white and shining shore.